MALICE

MALICE

HUGH FRASER

URBANE
Publications

urbanepublications.com

First published in Great Britain in 2017 by Urbane Publications Ltd
Suite 3, Brown Europe House, 33/34 Gleaming Wood Drive,
Chatham, Kent ME5 8RZ
Copyright © Hugh Fraser, 2017

A CIP catalogue record for this book is available from the British Library.

ISBN 978-1-911583-06-6

Design and Typeset by Julie Martin
Cover by Julie Martin

Printed and bound by CPI Group (UK) Ltd, Croydon, CR0 4YY

urbanepublications.com

MIX
Paper from
responsible sources
FSC® C013604

The publisher supports the Forest Stewardship Council® (FSC®), the leading international forest-certification
organisation. This book is made from acid-free paper from an FSC®-certified provider. FSC is the only
forest-certification scheme supported by the leading environmental organisations, including Greenpeace.

1

London 1964

The phone's ringing. I turn over and put my head under the pillow. It rings and rings and finally I get out of bed, go into the hall and answer it. Tony Viner's voice is low and mean.

'Get over here now.'

'In a while,' I say.

'Now.'

The line goes dead. I go back into the bedroom and put on a dressing gown. My watch says it's half past eleven. The bed looks so inviting but Viner sounded well chafed and he can be an evil bastard so I know I've got to get going.

I go into the kitchen and put the kettle on. I stand by the window and look up at the blue sky and the fluffy white clouds racing each other towards the rooftops of Hamilton Terrace. For a moment, I wonder what it might be like to wake up in the morning, have a quiet breakfast and toddle off to work in a bank or an office, all safe and sound, and no nasty villains shouting at you down the phone. The kettle whistles and I make myself a cup of Nescafé and a piece of bread and marmalade and take them through to the bedroom. As I open the wardrobe and think about what to wear, the phone rings again and I go into the hall and answer it. It's Bert Davis.

'Don't go to Viner's.'

'What are you on about?' I say.

'Be outside yours in five minutes.'

The line goes dead. Bert Davis is one of George Preston's minders. George and my dad built up a strong firm out of protection and extortion after the war, until they ruled Notting Hill and most of Shepherd's Bush. When my dad got shot by a mob from Bermondsey, George became the governor and now he's well into Soho and the West End. He's got muscle and he makes Tony Viner look like Mickey Mouse, so I know where I'm going. I go into the bedroom and put on silk underwear, stockings and shoes. I slide a blade into my suspender belt and wonder how the fuck Bert can know about Viner's phone call. I slip into my black Jaeger dress, apply a light make-up, finish my coffee, put on a grey suede jacket and drop my Smith & Wesson into my shoulder bag.

I take the lift to the ground floor. Dennis is behind the porter's desk, reading a paper under the counter. I open the lift gate and walk across the foyer.

'Morning Miss,' he says.

'Morning Dennis. Been on all night?'

'Ten hours straight.'

'You should be in bed.'

'Is that an offer?'

'You cheeky old bugger.'

I walk past the desk, give him a pretend cuff round the

ear and he laughs as he goes to the glass door and opens it for me. I slip a ten bob note in his pocket as I pass him. I've kept him well oiled ever since he took a good slap from a couple of ferrets who tried to get the key to my flat off him.

Bert's Jaguar is parked outside in the service road. I get in beside him. The engine's already running and he doesn't look at me as he pulls out onto Maida Vale and turns left into Elgin Avenue.

'Where are we going?' I ask.

'The governor wants a word.'

We drive to the end of Elgin, cross over Harrow Road, turn right beyond Westbourne Park Station and he parks the car in front of George's house in Lancaster Road.

The front door's opened by an old bloke with a walking stick and a shaky hand who I recognise as Jacky Parr, one of my dad's old firm. He was a feared man in his day and I know he taught my dad a few tricks, but he's well past it now. He looks me up and down.

'Blimey girl, if old Harry could see you now he'd be right proud. Eh Bert?'

'Easy now Jacko,' says Bert as he walks past him. I smile at the old fellow and follow Bert along the hallway to a room at the back. He knocks on the door and a voice tells us to come in.

George is sitting in an armchair with a glass in his hand. He's wearing his usual handmade suit and crocodile shoes. He was a boxer for many years and although he's getting on a bit now he's still in good shape. He points at a chair opposite him without looking at me and I sit down. Bert goes to the sideboard, picks up a whisky bottle and holds it poised above George's glass. He gets a nod and pours, then he shows me the bottle. 'Drink Rina?'

'Yeah, go on.'

He pours one and hands it to me, turns and looks at George, who's still staring at the fireplace, and goes out of the room. The silence continues and I'm beginning to wonder if George has had a stroke when he gives me a long look.

'What the fuck are you playing at?'

'Eh?' I say.

'You're supposed to be on my fucking firm and I turn round and you're sniping for Tony Viner and fuck knows who else.'

'I never said I was yours.'

'I could have you down for life.'

'But you won't.'

He stares at me like he could smash his glass in my face because he knows I'm right. I killed his son while he was raping my sister Georgie when she was a child but he can't grass me for it without it becoming known that his boy was a nonce and his other son was too chicken to get revenge for it.

'You've got some fucking neck,' he mumbles.

'What do you want George?'

I wait while he drains his glass.

'Viner's making moves on my clubs.'

'So what else is new?'

'Danny Teale fronted up to a couple of his mob last night at the Nucleus and they pulled his teeth out, broke his fingers and had his girl away. I want you to do Viner and find the girl.'

'You want to start a war?'

'Viner's a fucking headcase. He's taken too many liberties and caused enough aggravation. He's got to go.'

If it became known that I'd killed a man like Viner I could have half of North London after me.

'Get someone else,' I say.

'What?'

'I'm not doing it.'

'You will when I tell you what's coming your way.'

'What are you on about?'

'Your old man pulled off a big winner before he copped it. No one ever knew where he hid the cabbage, until now. Do this bit of work and it's yours.'

'How much are we talking about?'

'Two hundred large.'

'You're kidding.'

'In used notes.'

'You'd give that to me?'

'Harry was your dad. It's only right.'

George is a ruthless bastard but he does have respect for the code. While I'm thinking about how I could change my life with that kind of money, Bert comes back in and tops up my glass. I take a drink, look at George and wonder how far I can trust him.

'Who's the missing girl?' I ask.

He takes a photo out of his pocket and passes it to me. Danny Teale and his brother Jack are sitting at a table in some club with a couple of other heavies, smiling and toasting the camera. Danny's got his arm round a pretty blonde girl, who can't be more than eighteen.

'A bit young, isn't she?'

'That's how he likes them. They're getting married.'

'What's her name?'

'Dawn.'

'The ones who crunched him?'

'One's called Brindle, he's one of Viner's. That's all we've got.'

'How did you know Viner phoned me this morning?'

'I've got a man in there. If you're game for this, he's waiting at the Royal Oak to fill you in.'

I killed a man for Tony Viner a couple of weeks ago, and from the sound of him when he phoned me, he's got some beef about it, so it might be good if he goes out anyway. The money's too good to refuse and I want to know what's happened to Dawn. I drain my whisky glass.

'All right.' I say.

'Good girl.'

'I'll need expenses.'

George stands and looks at himself in the mirror above the mantelpiece. He's well over six feet tall and broad with it. He tweaks his tie, smooths his hair down and takes a fold of notes out of his back pocket. He counts off two hundred quid and passes it to me, then he walks to the door and opens it. Bert is standing in the hallway. I walk past George and follow Bert out of the front door to the car. He drives down Great Western Road, turns left into Westbourne Park Road and pulls up outside the Royal Oak.

'Your Georgie still at that boarding school?' he asks.

'She's finishing there soon.'

'Gone all right for her with all the posh girls, has it?'

'Not bad.'

He doesn't need to know that she put a girl in hospital for calling her a guttersnipe when she first arrived.

'You're looking good Rina.'

'Cheers Bert.'

The pub's quite crowded for a lunchtime but I find a space at the bar and order a whisky. A bald bloke next to me turns round, looks at my tits and breathes beer fumes at me.

'I'll get that for you love,' he says.

'I'm all right thanks,' I reply.

'Only buying you a drink.'

'I said I'm all right.'

'Suit yourself, you stuck-up cunt.'

The barman, who I know from the street we grew up in, puts my drink down and winks at me.

'I'd leave it out Derek, unless you want to get hurt,' he says.

'You and whose army?' says Baldy.

I walk away from the bar and sit down at a table by the window. I glance back and see the barman lean towards the bald bloke and speak into his ear. As he listens, a look of fear spreads across his face. When the barman moves away he comes to the table and loiters for a bit, looking embarrassed.

'Er, sorry for what I said there, love,' he says. 'I was out of order. Bit pissed, you know?'

I give him a quick nod and he walks out of the pub. A tall bloke, in a grey overcoat, gets off a stool at the other end of the bar, comes to the table and sits opposite me. He puts his pint on the table, takes a packet of Players out of his pocket and offers me a cigarette. I shake my head.

'Where do I find Viner?' I ask.

'He'll be in the Royal Vauxhall tonight.'

'You're kidding, aren't you?'

'Straight up.'

The Royal Vauxhall Tavern is a pub where drag artists perform and the last place I'd expect to see Tony Viner.

'Does he still live out Essex way?'

'Big place outside Chigwell.'

'Family?'

'Just him and his Pit Bulls.'

'Who's Brindle?' I ask.

He lights a cigarette and takes a long drag on it.

'Hard case from up north who's not long on Viner's firm, trying to make his mark.'

'He certainly made one on Danny Teale.'

'Him and Brindle robbed a big house together a while back. Brindle set it up, did the work, all Danny really done was the alarms. Brindle just found out Danny pocketed a diamond necklace from the job and didn't tell him, so he had to settle up.'

'What's he done with the girl?'

'No idea.'

'How will I know him?'

'He's young, about twenty-five, short, muscly, blond hair, leather jacket.'

'Where does he live?'

'I don't know.'

'Can you find out?'

'It'll cost you a score.'

I take two tenners out of my purse and hand them to him under the table. He takes out a pen, writes a number on a beer mat and passes it to me.

'Give me a day,' he says.

I put the beer mat in my bag.

'What's your name?' I ask.

'Ray.'

'What's Viner's beef with me?'

'You just done a bit of work for him.'

'So?'

'He's got it in his head that George Preston gave you the same job and you got paid twice for it.'

'That's bollocks.'

'It's what he thinks.'

'How do you know?'

'I was there when he phoned you.'

'And you told George?'

'Yeah.'

The man I killed for Viner was a well-known grass who

offered up one of Viner's boys for murder and I reckon maybe George has tried to take the credit for it, to up his reputation and to put one over on Viner. Ray downs the rest of his pint.

'Another drink?' he says.

'I've got to go, thanks.'

If this geezer's working for George, nosing around in other firms and playing both ends against the middle, I reckon the less time I spend with him the better. I pick up my bag and head for the door. Bert's Jag is now parked across the road and I go over and get in.

'Where's Danny Teale?' I ask.

'Powis Square licking his wounds, I reckon.'

'What number?'

'I don't know.'

'Can you show me?'

Bert moves the car off, turns into Chepstow Road, then into Talbot and when we get to Powis Square he points at a house near the end of the terrace.

'Ground floor flat,' he says.

The curtains are drawn over the bay window and a couple of raggedy boys with dirty faces and knees are sitting on the steps, looking at a Beano comic. One of them looks up as the Jag passes and nudges the other one to have a look. A streetwalker comes towards the car and then backs off when she sees me.

'She's out early,' says Bert.

'Drop me round the corner.'

Bert turns the car into Colville Terrace and parks.

I walk back into Powis Square and the tom we just saw looks at me as if I might be trouble. I give her a smile as I walk between the two boys and up the steps to Danny's house. She smiles back and moves on along the pavement. I ring the ground floor bell. After a while the curtain of the bay window is pulled aside and an old woman has a quick look at me and disappears. I hear shuffling steps behind the door and then the woman opens it. She's tiny, like a little shrew, in her apron and cap, with a pointy nose and sharp eyes that narrow as she looks at me.

'Is Danny in?' I ask.

'Who wants him?'

'Rina Walker.'

She turns and scurries along the hall and into a door on the left. Moments later she pops her head out, beckons me to come in and disappears again. I step into the hall, close the front door behind me, walk into the flat and follow the old lady into the front room.

Danny Teale is sitting on the sofa, facing a television that's showing some kids' programme with puppets. His hands are bandaged, his face is cut and bruised and his lips are swollen and sunken at the same time. He nods weakly to me and raises a bandaged hand towards an armchair. Danny mumbles something to the old lady which includes the word 'mum' and she goes to the television and switches it off.

'Cup of tea?' she asks, in a high chirrupy voice.

'I'm all right, thanks,' I say.

She looks to Danny, who shakes his head and says,

'Hag.'

While I'm wondering what his mum has done to deserve the abuse, she takes a packet of Park Drive off the mantelpiece, lights one, puts it in Danny's mouth and he takes a long drag. His mum sits close beside him on the sofa holding the fag for him.

'Sorry you got hurt Danny,' I say.

'I'll fucking kill him.'

His words are slurred and unclear and without his teeth he sounds like he's about a hundred years old but there's no mistaking his fury at what's been done to him.

'Brindle. Right?' I say.

'Yeah.'

'Who's the other one?'

'Never seen him before.'

'Do you know where Dawn is?'

'He's got her somewhere. He wants two large by the end of the week, or he'll do her.'

'When did he say that?'

'What time did he phone Mum?'

'Just gone nine o'clock this morning. Fucking bastard! I'll have his eyes out for what he done to you, and if he touches your Dawn I'll string him up by his bollocks and cut his fucking head off!'

'All right Mum.'

Danny nods to the cigarette and she puts it to his mouth with a shaking hand. He takes a drag and waits while she settles.

'You're going after?' he asks.

'I'll do what I can,' I say.

'What, her?' says Mum, looking at me with disbelief.

'She's good,' Danny replies.

His mother gives a harrumph and takes a drag of the cigarette herself. I smile at Danny.

'Any idea where he might be keeping her?' I ask.

Danny shakes his head. 'Could be anywhere.'

'Do you know where he lives?'

'Most of Viner's lot are Finsbury Park way, but I don't know where.'

'Where does he go of a night?'

'I'd check Viner's clubs. He's so far up his arse to get the earners.'

It seems like I'm not going to get any more and I'm reaching for my bag and about to get up when Mum says,

'You'd better tell her about Dawn, son.'

I sit down again. Danny looks at me, then lowers his eyes.

'She's pregnant.'

2

Bert drives me home and I get out of the lift at my floor and walk past Lizzie's door. She's been in Dubai for the last week, doing strange things to some bankers over there, and I wish she'd come home. She's stopped having clients at her flat, since she found one of them hanging by the neck on the back of a door. She's got a job as a hostess at the Kazuko club in Rupert Street now, which gets a lot of foreign businessmen, so she does the odd bit of mistress work abroad when the money's right.

I let myself into the flat and there's a letter on the floor with the Leavenden School crest on it. I pick it up and see Georgie's neat handwriting. I go into the kitchen, sit at the table and read that she's doing fine and has just been picked for the school lacrosse team. She goes on to say that her form mistress has suggested that she takes the Cambridge University entrance exam. When I think that she might be going to Cambridge, I feel so proud I nearly start crying. She's been through so much in her young life, growing up in a foul slum with rats and mice, her mother lying around drunk all day, being raped by a monster when she was only nine and her little brother dying, who she loved so much. Through it all she kept trying so hard with her school work, always studying and reading. I was so glad to be able get her into Leavenden School a couple of years ago, well away from all the rough stuff I'm mixed up with.

She's done so well there and if she can go to Cambridge, I'll be over the moon.

She tells me that she'll have to stay on for an extra term after her A-levels to do the exam and asks me if that would be all right, as it would mean paying extra fees. I go into her bedroom, find a bit of notepaper and sit at her desk while I write back to her that I'm really pleased she's taking the entrance exam, the fees are no problem and well done to her for getting in the lacrosse team.

As I'm putting my letter in an envelope I notice there's a second page to Georgie's where she tells me they've got an exeat coming up and she wants to go and stay with her friend Annabelle at her big country house and ride ponies and such. Annabelle lives at Ringwood Hall in Berkshire. I was there a couple of years ago, when I put a stop to her grandfather's nasty little sex games with dead girls. His crimes were covered up and the part of the house where he did foul things was burnt down. Annabelle will never be told what the old pervert got up to and neither she nor Georgie will ever know I was there.

I add a couple of lines to my letter saying it's fine that she's going and I hope she has a good time. As I fold the notepaper I notice how spidery and bad my writing is compared with Georgie's. I put the letter in an envelope, seal it and find a stamp in one of the drawers. I'm really glad she's made a close friend at the school. She's never really had friends before, always staying in her room reading or working, or going to galleries or concerts on her own.

I get up from the desk and have a look at Georgie's bookshelves. I've just finished *Northanger Abbey*, which I loved, and I look along the row of Jane Austen's books that she's got and see that I've read them all now. Daphne du Maurier is the next author along the shelf and I take out *Rebecca*. I open it and read the first page where she's dreaming about going to Manderley and it makes me want to go there too, so I put the book under my arm, go into the hall and put my letter to Georgie on the telephone table. I haven't got time for a good read now, if I'm going to get to the Vauxhall Tavern and find Viner, so I put the book in my bedroom, go into the living room, open up the radiogram and put on the Rolling Stones album that came out the other day. I pour myself a whisky while Mick tells me to get my kicks on Route 66. I saw their first gig at the Marquee a couple of years ago. Me and Lizzie had gone to see Alexis Korner's Blues Incorporated, who Jagger was fronting at the time, but Alexis Korner got a BBC gig or something so the manager let the Stones fill in at the last minute and they gave us a great night playing all rocking bluesy stuff. We used to go and see them in the clubs after that, when they got the regular line-up together.

I turn the volume up, go into the bedroom and have a look in the wardrobe for a suitable outfit for a drag night in Vauxhall. I reckon it's either the Ossie Clark trouser suit, in a tonic mohair, or the Dorothy Perkins polyester one. I try them both on and decide that the Ossie Clark, with the box jacket and the tighter trousers, looks more butch. I find a white blouse with button down collar to go with it and a pair of black Chelsea boots. I sit at the dressing table, put my hair up and add a bit more make-up round my eyes. I don't want to take a bag so I take a hundred from what George gave me, put it in my pocket, along with a pencil torch, and drop the rest in my underwear drawer. I take my Smith & Wesson out of the wardrobe, slide it into the back of my waistband and check in the mirror that the jacket is long enough to hide it.

It's dark and raining when I leave the building and walk round the corner to where my Mini Cooper's parked in Hall Road. As I'm driving towards Marble Arch I realise I'm starving and it could be a long night, so I decide to stop at the Wimpy Bar on Edgware Road. It's crowded and all the seats are taken. I stand in the queue and listen to a couple of girls in front of me slagging off some boy who's been two-timing them and mucking them about something terrible, although they go on to agree that they'll still use him for a night out and a bunk-up now and again. I get to the front of the queue and order a burger to take away. When I see the meat sizzling on the hotplate an idea strikes me about how I might be able to get to Viner.

I pay for the burger, go outside and look round for a phone box. There's one on the corner a few hundred yards away and I bite into the burger as I approach it. I go into the phone box, dial a number, push a coin in the slot and after a few rings the man I want answers. I tell him what I need, he says he can do it and I say I'll be round in twenty minutes. I walk to the car, finish the burger, drop the wrapper in a litter bin and drive down Park Lane, round

Hyde Park Corner and over Vauxhall Bridge to Elephant and Castle. I park outside a chemist's shop at the top of Walworth Road and ring the bell. A light goes on in the back, and Ben Griffin lifts up the flap of the counter, lets me in and hands me a small package. I take the wad out of my pocket, peel off thirty quid and give it to him.

'Cheers Ben.'

'See you Rina.'

I drive on to Kennington Lane, park beside the Royal Vauxhall and wait until I see a group of Mods approaching. As they walk past me I get out of the car and follow them into the pub. It's big and almost full, with a horseshoe shaped bar that curves out into the room from the back wall. The crowd is mostly men in suits or jackets and all quite discreet, except for the odd bit of make-up here and there. There are a few butch-looking women and a group of leather queens over in one corner. The Mods I tagged along with get drinks and stand near the back of the room. I make my way through a fug of cigarette smoke to the end of the bar, order a large whisky and find a place near the back wall, next to a pillar. I look around and notice that there's another bar, off to the side, which you can see into through windows that have the names of different whiskies and gins on them in gold lettering. When I move forward to get a better view through the window, I see Tony Viner at the bar talking to a young bloke with blond hair in a black leather jacket, who I reckon is Brindle.

As I move back behind the pillar to stay out of sight, music starts up and one of the barmen calls to everyone to take their glasses off the bar. A slinky figure, in a short silk dress, very high heels and a tall black wig, steps up onto the bar and sashays back and forth along it, swinging his hips and miming to Shirley Bassey singing 'I've Got You Under My Skin'. There are claps and whoops as he points and pouts at different men in the crowd and flicks up his dress to give us a glimpse of his frilly knickers. I look round and see Tony Viner clocking the action through the glass. Brindle takes a quick look over his shoulder and turns back to his pint. The song finishes, The Supremes take over with 'Stop! In the name of Love' and our man goes into a high kicking routine which has the crowd braying and me thinking he's going to fall off the bar any minute. The act winds up with him passing his silk scarf between his legs and sliding it back and forth over his crotch as he slowly lowers himself into the splits. He gets a good round of applause as he stands up and takes a bow, then he leaps off the bar into the arms of a big bloke in a black suit who gives him a kiss and carries him off to a table in the corner.

People crowd round the bar and order drinks. Viner's still talking to Brindle as the music starts up again and the barman calls for glasses to be cleared off the bar. He picks up a hand mic and clears his throat.

'Ladies and gentlemen – Mrs Shufflebottom!'

The applause gets louder as a blousy middle-aged blonde, in a sequinned evening gown and a fur coat, is helped up the steps onto the bar. He takes the mic and goes into a routine about his fur coat being very expensive and very rare and known in the fur trade as "untouched pussy" and how it can't be found anywhere in London at the moment. The crowd give a big laugh and he goes on to say how he was kissed on both cheeks by a Frenchman the other night, when he was bending down to tie his shoelaces and how the Frenchman had told him he reminded him of Liz Taylor because his figure had gone for a burton. While he goes on in the same vein and the crowd gets louder, I turn round and see Viner looking through the glass at a teenage boy near the bar, in jeans and a blue shirt, who looks to be on his own. Viner says something to Brindle who has a quick look at the boy and goes out of the door into the street. Moments later I see him come into the main bar and I back off behind my pillar while he makes his way towards the boy in the jeans and starts talking to him. The boy turns and looks into the other bar and after they've talked a bit more, he follows Brindle towards the door. Viner leaves the other bar and I go after them.

When I get through the crowd and out of the door, Brindle is hailing a cab on Kennington Lane and Viner and the boy are walking round the side of the building. I get round the opposite side of the pub in time to see Viner following the boy onto the waste ground at the back. They pick their way over the rough stuff towards Vauxhall Gardens and disappear in among some bushes. I've no desire to get any closer to what's about to happen so I walk away and stand behind a tree.

Ten minutes later Viner emerges from the bushes, straightens his jacket, walks towards the road that runs between the pub and the railway line and gets into a black

Mercedes. I hurry to where my car's parked near the front of the pub and move off just in time to get on his tail as he pulls out onto Kennington Lane. I glance in the mirror and catch sight of the boy walking back into the bar. I follow the Mercedes over the river, up through the City, into Hackney and onto the A12.

An hour later, as we get near Chigwell, Viner turns off the main road and I switch off my lights and follow him along a two lane road with big detached houses on either side. I keep well back and after a mile or so he turns into a driveway and stops. A pair of electric gates open slowly, the Mercedes passes through and the gates close behind it.

I get out of the car, climb over the stone wall and drop down onto the grass. The house is set back behind trees at the end of a gravel drive. It's big and ugly, like the man who owns it. The Mercedes is parked at the head of the drive. There are dogs barking and Viner's walking towards a squat brick building at the side of the house. I move to where I can see him, as he looks through a barred window and says something I can't make out. The dogs stop barking and Viner goes to the front door, unlocks it and walks in.

Lights go on in the house and I sit down, lean back against the stone wall and wait. When the lights go off, I stand up, take the gun out of my belt, release the chamber, give it a spin and snap it shut. I look up at the sky, see the moon sliding behind a cloud and walk slowly towards the house. I circle round to the side and creep towards the kennel. I crouch below the barred window, until I'm sure

I haven't woken anyone, then I straighten up slowly, take the pencil torch out of my pocket and shine it through the bars. Two Pit Bulls are lying asleep, one in each corner. They're wearing collars with evil-looking spikes on them and they're some of the ugliest dogs I've ever seen. I go to a woodpile nearby, select a solid piece of oak about four feet long, go back to the window and bash it against the iron bars. The dogs wake instantly and bark up a storm. When I hit the metal again they leap up at the window, snarling and yelping and slavering as they try to push their heads through the bars. Lights go on above. I back off and stand beside the door of the house. An outside light goes on, the door opens and Viner, wearing a purple silk dressing gown, walks towards the kennel. 'What the fuck's wrong with you two bleedin' idiots?'

I step forward, smash the oak beam against the back of his head and he falls flat on the ground. The dogs are going berserk. I take the packet that Johnny gave me out of my pocket, pull out two pieces of raw meat, hold them up to the window bars to give the dogs a good sniff and chuck them inside. The dogs go after the meat, wolf it down, return to the window and carry on jumping up and down and barking. I go to the body on the ground and turn him over. I pocket some keys that he dropped when he went down, kneel on his chest, put my hands round his throat, press both thumbs into his windpipe and hold on until he snuffs it.

The dogs are quietening down now as the anaesthetic in the meat gets to them and by the time I've unlocked the kennel door they're lying unconscious on the floor beneath the window. I drag Viner inside, close the door and turn on the light. I get hold of one of the dogs, drag it over to the body, open its jaws, sink its teeth into Viner's neck and pierce his carotid artery. Blood spurts and I drop the dog and stand back so I don't get any on me. When the bleeding stops, I pick the dog up, open its mouth and rip open Viner's face, neck and hands with its teeth. When I've made him look as though he's been well mauled, I take out my gun and shoot the other dog in the head. I wipe my prints off the gun, wrap Viner's hand round it and drop it beside him. The dog I've torn Viner up with is starting to come round and I take a quick look in his mouth to make sure he's got plenty of Viner's flesh in there. I smear some blood round the other dog's mouth as well, then I go out of the door and close it behind me. When I look through the window, I see the surviving dog get up slowly and sniff round Viner's body for a bit, then he goes over to the other dog and nudges him with his nose. When he gets no response, he wobbles over to a metal bowl in the corner, laps up some water, lies down, puts his head on his paws and goes to sleep.

3

The moon's shining bright and I'm feeling good as I drive into London through Stratford, then Stepney and into Whitechapel. When I get into the City I find a quiet street and park behind a Triumph Herald. I wipe the inside of the Mini clean of prints, take the blade out of my suspenders, get out and look in the window of the Herald to check no one's in there. I pick up a sharp stone from the gutter, smack it hard against the window and the glass shatters. I reach inside, open the door, sit in the driving seat and use the blade to prise off the panel under the steering wheel. I cut the wires at the back of the ignition barrel, connect the red ones, touch the brown ones together and the engine starts. I look back at my old Mini as I pull the Herald away and I feel sad for a moment. It's got me out of a few tight spots over the last few years but I'm saying goodbye to it now, just in case some midnight dog walker saw it outside Viner's.

I drive west, dump the Herald on Abbey Road, wipe it clean and walk to the flat. Dennis is behind the desk when I go in and he calls the lift for me and tells me that Lizzie got back from the airport an hour ago. I feel a thrill of excitement as the lift climbs to our floor. I open the gate and almost run to her door. I knock and wait until I hear her ask who's there.

'The Sheik of Araby,' I say.

She laughs and opens the door, looking tanned and beautiful.

'Come into my tent girl,' she says, as she pulls me inside, gives me a long kiss and leads me along the hall.

'Bed or bath?'

'Both,' I reply.

She turns into the bathroom and I hear water running as I go into her living room and make for the whisky bottle on the dresser. I pour two large ones, take them into the bathroom and give one to Lizzie. We take a drink and set the glasses down on the shelf beside the bath. Lizzie holds me for a moment, purrs in my ear, then she slips my jacket off my shoulders and undoes the buttons of my shirt and then my trousers, like she's undressing a child. When she finds the knife in my suspender belt she waves a finger at me, tells me I'm a naughty girl and puts it on the floor next to my clothes. I get into the bath, she slips off her nightie and joins me in the warm bubbly water.

'So how was Dubai?' I ask.

'Great. Money for nothing.'

'How come?'

'I was a beard.'

'Come again?'

'He's a woofter, but he can't let on to his banking friends and his family, and Arab society and that, so he's got me out there as his girlfriend from London. A bit of hand holding and a few pecks on the cheek in public and that was it.'

'Nice one.'

MALICE

'I had to go to bed with him, for the look of it, and then move to the sofa when he called for his boot boy and shagged the arse off him.'

'Charming.'

'I spent the days by the pool soaking up some rays.'

'I can see.'

I slide my foot along the inside of Lizzie's thigh and she smiles and half closes her eyes. A few moments pass before she asks,

'Where have you been tonight?'

'Just a bit of work,' I reply.

'Go all right?'

'I reckon.'

'Good girl.'

She's well aware of what I do and I know she worries about the danger I'm in sometimes, but we're agreed that the less detail she knows, the safer she is.

Lizzie finishes her whisky, pulls out the plug and we get out of the bath, wrap ourselves in big fluffy towels and go into the bedroom. We slowly dry each other off and then slide between the sheets.

• • •

We wake early in the afternoon and go and have coffee and croissants at the French café in Clifton Road. I leave Lizzie for a minute while I go to the phone box on the corner, phone Tommy Gaynor at the breakers yard, tell him to get my Mini from the City and put it in the crusher. He says he'll send his truck over there now and I tell him

I'll go by the yard in the morning and see him right.

It's a nice sunny day so we take a cab to the Kings Road. We walk along past the Markham Arms to Bazaar and have a look at Mary Quant's latest. I find a dark red mini dress with off-white collar and cuffs, take it into the fitting room and put it on. I come out and find Lizzie fastening the belt of a shiny black PVC trench coat with matching hat and boots.

'I thought you'd packed in the mistressing?' I say.

'Good look though, eh?'

'If you want to join the SS.'

'I was always too tall.'

I take a white trouser suit off the rail, that looks about her size. 'Do me a favour and try this on.'

'Spoilsport,' she says, as she takes off the coat and hat and goes into a fitting room.

I try on a couple of wide brim hats, decide they're not quite me and settle for a John Lennon style cap. Lizzie floats out of the fitting room and gives me a twirl in her wide trousers and short jacket. She looks lovely and she knows it.

'What would I do without you?' she says.

She slips her arm round me and we look at ourselves in the mirror. I reach for a white hat off the stand beside us and put it on her head.

'Perfect,' she says.

We tell the assistant that we want to wear the clothes we're buying, and she comes out from behind the till, snips off the labels and then puts our other stuff in bags for us. I pay out of George's money and we leave the shop and hail a cab. When we get to Maida Vale, Lizzie says she needs to get ready for work and tells me to drop by the club later, if I feel like it. We kiss goodbye, she gets out of the cab and I tell the driver to take me to Lancaster Road.

George Preston's in the back room with his barbells and weights when I get there, so Bert gives me a cup of tea and tells me about a blag that happened in the week, at a bank in the City, and how the blaggers wore Batman and Robin masks and got away with a prize of half a million. George comes in wearing a tracksuit.

'Fucking good job Rina,' he says.

'Cheers.'

'Your dad would have liked that one.'

He lights a cigarette and sits in an armchair.

'You done a fucking blinder.'

'Who found him?' I ask.

'Cleaning woman. Called the Old Bill and they swallowed the dog fight, had the bodies away, snuffed the Pit Bull and the inquest's in the bag. You not only done him double quick, you made him look a cunt as well. Killed by his own dogs? What a fucking Mary. Give the lady a drink Bert.'

Bert pours whiskies, gives one to me and the other to George, who's sitting back in his chair, looking smug because he knows he can claim the job as his own and get the respect.

'How's it going with Dawn?' he asks.

'Give us a chance,' I say.

'Fair enough, only his mum's giving me such an earache about it you'd think Princess Margaret had gone missing.'

'She's a busy old bird.'

'Pain in the fucking arse.'

'Brindle's in a game tonight,' says Bert.

'Where?' I ask.

'I can find out.'

'Give us a call.'

I finish my drink and stand up. George is looking at my legs.

'Are you sure that dress is short enough?' he says.

'Go and lift your weights.'

'I'd rather lift you.'

'Get stuffed.'

He laughs. 'Give her a monkey expenses,' he says, as Bert moves to the door.

'Cheers George. If you weren't such an old lech, I'd call you a gentleman.'

Bert goes out of the room, comes back a moment later and hands me a wad of notes. I put them in my pocket and remind myself that I need to pay Georgie's school fees for the extra term she's doing, to take the Cambridge exam.

'Do you want a lift?' asks Bert.

'You could drop me in Harlesden,' I reply.

I say goodbye to George and follow Bert to the car.

When we get to Harlesden I get out of the car just past the Mitre Bridge and walk up Scrubs Lane to a second hand car lot on the left, past where my lock-up is. I'm looking along the front row of cars when a leery looking bloke in a brown suit and a trilby hat comes out of a shed at the back of the lot.

'Lovely day for a new motor, eh Miss?' he says, as he approaches me.

I ignore him and walk among the cars until I spot a dark blue Cortina, with a £150 ticket that looks as if it might do me. Trilby sidles up beside me.

'Now how did you know to go for the best car I've got, eh? This one's a beaut. One year old, belonged to a dear old lady, drove it like a kitten, serviced from new. You won't go wrong with this one, love.'

'Give us a drive then,' I say.

He takes a chain out of his pocket, with about fifty keys on it, searches through it until he finds one with a Ford tag and takes it off the chain. He opens the door for me and puts the key in the ignition. I get in and start it up while he walks round the car and slides into the passenger seat.

I drive up Scrubs Lane and turn on to the North Circular, where I can get up a bit of speed while Trilby blathers on about how the Cortina's the best car Ford have made since the Model T and the rest of it. The car seems good and fast and once I've tried the brakes and nearly tipped him through the windscreen, I motor back to the forecourt, park it and offer him a ton. He says it's not enough, so I get out of the car and walk away. He follows me and after a bit of haggling he settles for £120. We go into his office and he gives me the log book and a receipt. When I open the log book I notice that the dear old lady's name was Graham Smith.

On the way to Maida Vale, I drive down Abbey Road and see that the Triumph Herald's gone from where I left it and I hope it's made its way back to the owner. I park the Cortina in Hall Road and dump the log book in a bin on the way to the flat.

I let myself in, go into the kitchen and put the kettle on. I open the cabinet and find a tin of spaghetti hoops and a bit of Cheddar cheese that's not quite mouldy. I open the tin, put the contents in a pan, light the gas under it and grate some cheese. The kettle boils and while I'm filling the teapot the phone rings. I turn the gas down under the spaghetti, go into the hall and answer it. It's Bert with the address of a spieler off Caledonian Road where Brindle's going to be playing cards later. He reckons it's an all-nighter with some big money involved.

I go back into the kitchen, pour myself a cup of tea, dish up the spaghetti, add the grated cheese and take it through to the lounge on a tray. I turn on the TV, sit on the sofa and watch 'Dixon of Dock Green' while I eat my tea. It's all about a bent copper called PC Carr that Jack Warner suspects and when Jack finds some snide gear at the copper's house, he's so outraged that he makes him take off the police uniform that he's disgraced before he escorts him to the nick to be charged. Jack does his nice little chat at the end and when he says that Carr was the only bent one he's ever come across, I laugh out loud and nearly spill my tea. He'd be spoilt for choice at Paddington Green nick these days, that's for sure.

I wash up the dishes, go into the hall and dial the

number on the beer mat that I left by the phone. A woman answers and I ask for Ray. He comes on the phone and gives me an address for Brindle in Holloway. I go into the bathroom, use my blade to unscrew the panel at the end of the bath and take out my spare gun. I release the cylinder and see that it's full, then I go into the bedroom and change into jeans, ankle boots and a leather jacket. I put the gun in my belt and the leather wallet with my lock picks in my jacket pocket, along with a knuckle duster and a pencil torch. I pick up *Rebecca* off the bedside table and head for the door.

I drive along Marylebone Road, past King's Cross, turn into York Way then do a right and turn south on to Caledonian Road. The door to the spieler is in an alleyway off the Cally just before it meets Pentonville Road. I park where I can see the door and wait. The clock on the dashboard is showing just gone nine-thirty. After a while a group of four heavy-looking blokes walk past the car, go into the alley and knock on the door. It's opened by a Ted in a drape suit and a bootlace tie. As they go inside, I can see that Brindle's not among them.

I sit back and open *Rebecca*. I put the book up on the steering wheel so I can keep an eye on the spieler while I read on through her dream, as she wafts like a ghost through the grounds of Manderley, which are now neglected and overgrown by sinister and vicious plants that are strangling the trees. Just as she's catching sight of the great house, where she's lived herself at some time, I see Brindle walk past the car. I close the book and lower my head as he turns into the alley. He knocks on the door of the spieler and the Ted lets him in. I put the book on the seat beside me, wait for a bit until I'm sure he's not coming out again, then I start the car and head for Holloway.

4

Brindle's place is a terraced house in a street off Parkhurst Road with an entry between it and the house next door. There are no lights on so I knock on the door, duck into the entry and wait. When there's no response I go round to the back, climb over the garden wall, pick my way over a pile of rubbish and get to the back door. I kneel down in front of it, turn on the torch and have a look at the lock. It's an old mortice, so I hold the torch in my mouth and take out my lock picks. I put the cut down key in the lock and slide a wire pick in above it. I feel for the levers with the pick, lift them one by one and then turn the key.

I creep through the kitchen and into the front room. I shine the torch over a sofa and two armchairs, a low table and a TV in the corner with a record player and a pile of LPs and 45s next to it. I go into the hall and up the stairs. The two bedrooms are empty and there's no sign of a woman's presence, either there or in the bathroom. The front bedroom has a double bed and a wardrobe that's full of men's clothes and shoes. The back bedroom's empty apart from a desk and chair. I open the desk drawers and find a pile of papers in one, and a Walther 9mm pistol, a butcher's knife and a cut throat razor in the other. I pick up the Walther and it feels good in my hand. I release the clip, see that it's missing two bullets and wonder who copped them. The razor is sharp as fuck and may well have striped a few unlucky ones. I close the weapons drawer, open the other one and have a look through the sheaf of papers. It's mostly bills for the house, car insurance and the like, and I'm about to close the drawer when I notice a letter from Bedford Borough Council addressed to J. R. Brindle. It's a demand for the rates on a house called Keepers Cottage in Leighton Buzzard and it's dated a couple of weeks ago. I memorise the address, close the drawer and go downstairs. I lock the back door behind me, hop over the wall and go back along the alleyway to where I've left the car.

I know I've heard of Leighton Buzzard but I can't think why. I've a vague idea that it's north or west of London somewhere. The clock on the dash says it's midnight and I really want to go to the Kazuko and have a few drinks and a laugh with Lizzie and the girls, but I decide that the sooner I sort this business with Dawn the better. It's not going to go away and Brindle's taken a dire liberty. I head for the North Circular, stop at a garage, fill the Cortina up with petrol and buy a road map. Leighton Buzzard is about forty odd miles away and off the A5.

An hour later I'm driving through the town centre and when I pass the station I remember why I've heard of the place. Ronnie Biggs and the boys lifted two and a half million quid off the Glasgow Mail Train a couple of miles down the track from here. They might have got away with it as well, if Mike Field had torched the farmhouse that they used as a flop, like he was paid to, instead of doing a runner, although I heard they were grassed up by some weasel as well.

The address I'm looking for is on the far side of the town. I find the road and follow it as it goes into the country. It's difficult to see any houses in the dark but I catch sight of a sign on a five bar gate and when I stop and reverse back to have a look, it says Keepers Cottage. On the other side of the gate is a small stone house at the end of a short track.

I drive on for some way until I get to a sharp bend in the road. I go on round it and leave the car with two wheels on the grass bank. I walk the distance back to the cottage, climb over the gate, go sideways along the hedge for a bit and then curve round towards the back of the house. As I'm creeping along the wall towards the back door and feeling for my lock picks, I trip over something, stagger forward and send a rake clattering across some flagstones. I hear a woman's voice.

'Johnny?'

A light goes on above me and I flatten myself against the wall. Moments later a window opens.

'Johnny, is that you?'

I stop breathing and wait until the window shuts. After a moment, I hear what sounds like someone coming down some stairs and I slip round to the side of the house as an outside light goes on and the back door opens. I peer round the corner and see the slight figure of Dawn looking out into the night. She sees the rake on the floor and picks it up. As she goes to lean it against the wall I take a step forward.

'Hello Dawn,' I say.

She goes rigid with fright and holds the rake in front of her.

'Who the fuck are you?'

'I'm a friend of Danny's. I've come to take you home.'

'Fuck off. Now!'

She swings the rake at me. I step forward, grab the shaft, rip it out of her hand and slap her across the face. She staggers sideways and I drop the rake, take her by the shoulders, turn her round and push her through the back door. She twists towards me and swings a fist at my head. I duck the punch, grab her round the throat, force her onto a chair and back off. As she gets up again, I take the gun out of my belt and point it at her head.

'Sit down Dawn.'

The fight goes out of her and she sinks onto the chair. I wait for a moment then I sit opposite her at the kitchen table.

'I've not come here to hurt you,' I say.

'Then why the fuck are you pointing a shooter at me?'

'In case you try to deck me again.'

I smile and lay the gun on the table. She looks at me for a moment.

'Who are you?' she asks.

'Like I said, I'm a friend of Danny's.'

'Well you can fuck off out of it and tell that evil bastard I'm never coming back. I've had enough of his beating and slagging and his nasty little witch of a mother.'

I'm not sure why I'd got Dawn pegged as a timid little thing but I certainly wasn't expecting this mouthy bit of work I'm looking at. She takes a cigarette out of a packet on the table and lights it. After a couple of drags she seems to relax.

'I know you from somewhere, don't I?' she asks.

'Maybe.'

'Why are you here?'

'Danny said you'd been captured by Brindle.'

'He would, wouldn't he?'

'So what did happen?'

She looks as if she's trying to decide about something, then she says, 'We only made it look like that.'

'Why?'

'I've been seeing Johnny for a while. He's shown me what a mug I've been, taking Danny's dogshit for two years, and I love him for it. Danny knocked me about something terrible and when I wasn't locked in a cupboard, or cooking his meals, his mother had me out hoisting from shops.'

'Why did you stay?' I ask.

'They had me crushed and scared of my own shadow. I felt like nothing, until I met Johnny. He saw me getting caught in Selfridges, doing the bag switch with a girl who legged it, and he stepped in, showed the shop walker his piece and made him let me go. He took me home and he was kind to me and made me feel like a person. I went back to Danny but I started seeing Johnny when I was supposed to be out hoisting and he gave me clothes and that to take back to the old cow to keep her happy and now I'm having his baby, although Danny thinks it's his.'

'Why didn't you just leave Danny?'

'We knew that if I did, I'd be marked for going with someone from a rival firm and Danny's such a mad fucker he'd probably try to kill me, so Johnny made it look like he'd captured me.'

'He's asked for two large to give you back.'

'I know. If we get it, we're off together.'

'And if you don't?'

'We're off anyway.'

'Where to?'

She stubs out her cigarette.

'I've said enough. You'd better go.'

I'm thinking she's probably right. I believe what she's told me and it's getting late. As long as Dawn's where she wants to be I'm off the case. George'll have to sort this for himself and make it look like he's got satisfaction for Danny's beating so as to preserve his precious reputation. I put the gun in my waistband and move to the back door.

'What will you tell Danny?' she asks.

'That I couldn't find you.'

She stands, comes towards me and we share a smile.

'Thanks,' she says.

I let myself appreciate her beauty for a moment and the look of pride in her own strength that is in her eyes. I take her hand.

'Have a good trip,' I say, as I walk out of the door.

I go along the drive to the gate. As I'm opening it, I hear a car coming. I close it again, move along the hedge and hide myself behind a tree. An Austin Princess stops on the road and I see Brindle get out, open the gate, drive the car through and close it. He parks in front of the cottage and goes in through the front door. I walk back to the gate, climb over it and head off along the road. By the time I get to the Cortina I'm knackered and looking forward to my bed. I get into the car, turn it round and drive back towards Leighton Buzzard. As I'm about to pass the cottage, the Princess backs fast out of the gate and blocks the road in front of me. I stamp on the brakes, lock the wheels and skid to a stop, inches away from it. Brindle gets out, jumps over the bonnet, rips my door open and pulls me out by the arm. I go for his bollocks with my knee but he pulls back in time and laughs. I grab his jacket, pull him towards me and nut him. He stops laughing, staggers back and pulls a gun out of his jacket before I can get to mine. I step sideways and try to kick it out of his hand, but he whips it out of the way, puts a leg behind my ankles and pushes me over. I land on my back on the grass verge and he stands astride me, points the gun at my face and pulls back the hammer. I close my eyes and wait for it.

'Had a nice little chat with Dawn, did you?' he says.

I open my eyes and a drop of blood lands on my forehead. As he wipes his bloody nose on his sleeve, I swing my foot up and crack him in the bollocks. He lets out a shriek, drops his gun and lands on the road clutching his groin. I grab his gun, get to my feet and cover him as he lies on the ground whimpering. After a bit, he looks up at me.

'I just want to talk,' he says.

'Come round for tea sometime.'

He gets painfully to his feet and leans against the Cortina.

'You and me could do each other some good,' he says.

'Like you and Danny Teale?'

'He well deserved it.'

'Maybe.'

'He nearly killed that girl.'

I look at him nursing his manhood and decide to take a chance. 'All right, what do you want to talk about?'

'Come and have a drink.'

'And get killed with a rake?'

'She's gone to bed.'

'Get your limousine off the road before the farmer wakes up and get in my car if you've got something to say.'

He gets into the Princess, drives it along the track and parks it in front of the cottage. I back the Cortina in between the gate posts and watch Brindle in the mirror as he limps towards the car with one hand round his balls. I put his gun on my lap where he can see it, move mine to the front of my waistband and keep a firm grip on it as he opens the door and slowly lowers himself onto the seat. He breathes out slowly, shuts the door and looks straight ahead.

'I know you done Viner,' he says.

This takes me by surprise and I consider whether to deny it, but decide it's best to try and find out who else knows. I can always kill him if he's the only one.

'How come?' I ask.

'I clocked you at the Vox and followed you to Viner's.'

'You got in a cab at the Vox.'

'Only as far as my car. I knew you'd seen me.'

'So what are you going to do about it?'

'Nothing. You saved me the trouble.'

'How come?'

'I'm taking over his firm.'

'Oh yeah?'

'And I want you to come in with me.'

I have to admire the gall of this kid, but he's got about as much chance of getting control of Viner's interests and the people who work for him as I have of becoming Pope. George's heavies will already have moved in on his clubs and pubs for the protection and they'll knock him out of the way soon as look at him.

'I've got commitments elsewhere,' I say.

'Unless you do your governor as well.'

I take a look at the twenty-five year old boy sitting next to me who's either off his head or got more neck than a giraffe. Either way he's dangerous. If I refuse his offer, I'll be a threat to him because I know his plans and he'll try to kill me. I'd do him now if it wasn't for Dawn and the danger of Danny getting hold of her. I decide it's best to string him along.

'I'll think about it.'

'You won't regret it. It's all going to be about drugs any minute. Those old crumblers know nothing about it. I've got the supply lined up. I just need to get the selling together and I'm going to be made.'

A tractor chugs past on the road. The sky's getting light.

'I need to go,' I say.

'Meet me at the Nite Spot tomorrow night, about ten.'

He opens the car door, puts his hand out for his gun and I tighten my grip on mine as I hand him the Walther.

5

I'm stuck in traffic on my way to the breakers yard in Kensal Green. I twiddle the knob on the radio, around the two hundred mark, until I find Radio Caroline and get the Beatles singing 'A Hard Day's Night.' When it finishes, Simon Dee says he's falling off his chair because it's blowing a gale out on the North Sea. The Supremes take it away with 'Baby Love' as I go up Scrubs Lane and turn left into Hythe Road. When I pull up outside the yard, I see Tommy Gaynor walking into the café opposite. He gets a cup of tea at the counter and sits at a table. I cross the road, go into the café and join him.

'You're a nice sight to see first thing,' he says.

'I always dress for you Tommy.'

'I'd rather you'd undress.'

I laugh and the old woman behind the counter looks up.

'You want me to bring out the rolling pin, love?' she says.

'Maybe you should, but I'll have a cup of tea first.'

'Coming up, love.'

She pours the tea, finishes buttering toast, puts it on a plate and comes out from behind the counter. Tommy raises his hands in surrender as she gives him a dirty look and puts the toast in front of him. She winks at me, puts my tea on the table and goes back behind the counter.

'Is my Mini gone?' I ask.

'You could put it in your handbag.'

'What do I owe you?'

'Just give me a pony.'

'That all?'

'We got some parts off it before it went in the squeezer.'

'Cheers Tommy.'

I take the wad out of my pocket and give him twenty-five quid.

He looks over at the counter, sees that the old woman has gone into the back kitchen and leans forward.

'You interested in a bit of work?' he asks.

'Depends what it is?'

'Jewellers in Mayfair.'

'No thanks.'

'You haven't heard it yet.'

'Let me guess. I put on a mink coat and a posh voice, go in the shop, ask to see some top form stuff and they open up the safe to get it. You and your mates run in with masks and guns, clear the safe, sweep the shelves and leg it.'

'You've got it.'

'And I get questioned by the filth and go on the books as a witness.'

'Not if you leg it with us.'

'And be in the frame with a description?'

'They'd never find you.'

'Leave it out, Tom.'

'It's all right. I can find someone easy enough.'

'There's one born every minute.'

He chuckles. 'There's no flies on you, eh?'

I finish my tea, thank him for crushing the car, wish him luck with the blag and leave. There's a traffic warden walking towards the Cortina but I jump in and drive off before he can get his book out. I don't know how they find people who'll do the job considering how many have got dotted since they brought them in a few years ago. I drive along Harrow Road, turn into Elgin Avenue and park in Hall Road.

Keith, the daytime porter, is behind the desk and he wishes me good morning as I walk across the foyer to the lift. When it gets to my floor I get out, go along the corridor and linger outside Lizzie's door for a moment, wondering if I should knock. My watch says eight o'clock and I reckon she won't have been long back from the club and probably needs her sleep. I decide to be good and let myself into the flat. I go to the lounge, lie on the sofa and open *Rebecca*. Half a page later I'm asleep.

I'm walking along the top of an enormous five bar gate when I slip and fall down and down under the earth and then Dawn catches me in her arms and carries me up again into the air and she's running across the fields away from the cottage and I look back and see the Austin Princess bucking up and down as it comes after us. Dawn runs faster and faster but the Princess is gaining on us and then it's on top of us and Dawn drops me and the car runs over me and then over Dawn and the car takes off into the air and Dawn catches hold of the back bumper and she's hanging from the car as it flies higher and higher and then she falls off and she's floating back down above me and I run and catch her in my arms and we lie on the grass together and hold each other and she's crying and I'm kissing her and stroking her cheek and then a big bird is standing over us and it's got Johnny Brindle's face and blond hair and a long beak and it bends towards us and starts pecking at Dawn's shoulder and I can't move to stop it and the pecking is getting louder and louder...

Someone's knocking at the door as if they're trying to break it down. I get out of bed, put on a dressing gown, pocket my keys, go into the hall, look through the spyhole and see no one.

'Who is it?' I snap.

The knocking stops.

'Marlene.'

I don't know a Marlene but that shrill, squeaky voice sounds familiar. I unlock the door and Danny Teale's mother is in front of me, her red face screwed up in anger. I could tell her to sling it but I wouldn't mind knowing a bit more about her and her nasty son.

'What do you need Marlene?' I say.

'Where is she?'

'Where's who?'

'Dawn, you stupid fucking bitch!'

'I don't know.'

'Yes you fucking do!'

Just as I'm about to slam the door in her face, Lizzie comes out of her flat.

'Is that you Marlene?' she asks.

Marlene turns, looks at Lizzie and seems to calm down for a moment.

'Hello Liz,' she says.

Lizzie comes over, stands next to me and looks down at the old woman.

'What brings you over this way then?' she asks.

Marlene takes a moment to notice how close Lizzie is to me.

'I got a bit of business with this one,' she says, giving me a look.

'If you're trying to get her on your team, I wouldn't bother love. She'll have all the dresses she nicks for herself, you won't see a penny.'

'Like I said, I need to talk to her.'

Lizzie looks at my dressing gown. 'Why aren't you ready?'

'Ready for what?' I ask.

'You've forgotten, haven't you?'

'Forgotten what?'

'Lunch with his Lordship!'

'Oh my God!' I say, putting my hand to my forehead.

'Get your glad rags on then.'

I go into the flat, wait behind the door and listen to Lizzie telling Marlene that we're meeting Lord Carstairs at The Athenaeum and now we'll be late and what a dizzy blonde I am for forgetting. Marlene asks what time we'll be back and Lizzie says we might go on somewhere afterwards and that she'll tell me to phone her if she'll give her the number. Marlene tells it to her, Lizzie says goodbye and comes into my flat. I wait until I hear the lift door open and close before I speak.

'You're a mind reader.'

'I thought I'd step in.'

'I'm glad you did.'

'She's an evil old cow.'

'How do you know Dawn?'

'From when she was a stripper, before she moved in with Danny and the old bitch got her on her thieving team.'

'Team?'

'She's been at it for years. She's got a load of girls kitted out with the big bloomers and the coats with the long inside pockets to stuff hoisted gear into. She dresses them up really smart, so they don't look like they'd ever nick anything and then teaches them all the tricks – the bag switch, how to roll up a mink cape and put it down their baggy trousers, stuffing dresses in their big knickers and all that. They walk in the shop thin and come out fat. She threatens to hurt them if they don't bring in enough gear.'

'Dawn's done a runner from Danny. He's been knocking her about.'

'That doesn't surprise me.'

'She's with a face called Johnny Brindle.'

'Who's he?'

'Come and have a coffee and I'll tell you.'

We go into the kitchen, I make us a cup of Nescafé, we sit at the kitchen table and I tell Lizzie how badly Danny's treated Dawn and how she met Brindle.

'I once saw Danny Teale tie two cats together by their tails, sling them over a washing line and laugh his head off while they clawed each other to death,' says Lizzie.

'Sick cunt.'

'I heard that Marlene stuck a hat pin in a bloke's eye once.'

'They make a right pair.'

'So how come you're involved?' she asks.

'Brindle beat up Danny and captured Dawn so it wouldn't look like she was leaving him for a face from a rival firm. George got the news and put me on getting her back.'

'And Marlene can't afford for Dawn to be on the loose in case she grasses her up, so she wants a result?'

'And she's not going to get it.'

'Good.'

Lizzie sips her coffee and looks out of the window. In a way, I want to tell her about Brindle's offer to me and get her advice, because her instincts are always good and I know she loves me but I also want to keep her away from the heat in case she gets hurt. I look at her fine profile and think how lucky I am to have her. She finishes her coffee and looks at her watch.

'I should go,' she says.

'Working?'

'A little Japanese bloke at The Savoy.'

'Straight?'

'I hope so, but with my luck he'll probably want to eat

curtain rings while I shove the pole up his arse.'

'Just make sure he doesn't eat you.'

I follow Lizzie into the hall, where we hold each other and share a long kiss.

'You be careful of nasty old women now,' she whispers.

'Mmm...'

We part and I open the door for her.

'Graham Bond's playing at Chelsea Art College tonight, if you fancy,' she says.

'Lovely.'

'Leave about eight?'

'See you then.'

I close the door, pick up the phone and dial the front desk. When Keith answers I tell him that if ever the old woman who was here earlier comes asking for me again, he's to say I'm out. He agrees and I remind myself to tell Dennis the same thing.

I make myself another cup of coffee and take it into the lounge. As I'm on my way to the bedroom to get my book, the phone rings and I pick it up.

'Sorry to trouble you Miss,' says Keith.

'What's up?'

'That old woman's come in and got into the lift before I could stop her and she's on her way up.'

'OK,' I say.

There's a knock at the door. I put the phone down, go into the bedroom, take my spare Smith & Wesson out of the wardrobe, go to the front door and open it. Marlene's there with a twisted smile on her face.

'Not going out after all, eh?' she says.

I grab the lapels of her coat, lift her up with one hand, pull her inside, hold her up against the wall and press the barrel of the gun into her forehead. She's like a quivering bird in my hand.

'You come near me again and I'll blow your fucking head off.'

She stares into my eyes as I angle the gun so that it's pointing at her mouth. She slowly nods her head and I lower her to the floor and let go of her. She pulls her coat around her, folds her arms and looks up at me.

'We just want her back,' she says.

'I know what you and that sick bastard have done to her.'

'We've looked after her.'

'Locking her up, beating her half to death and sending her out robbing and risking bird?'

'You want to mind your own business, you fucking slag!'

I point the gun at her head and pull back the hammer.

'Get out. Now!'

I pull the door open. She looks at me as if I'm dirt on her shoe, walks along the corridor and calls the lift. When it's clanked up from below she pulls back the gate, steps inside, wrenches it shut and turns her back on me.

6

The cab drops us outside Chelsea Town Hall and we walk along Kings Road to the Art College on the corner of Manresa Road. It's a warm night, the skirts are short and the trousers are flared. The smoke of a joint wafts past me from a group of long-haired boys and hippy chicks who are laughing about something as they pass us. I'm noticing how many new clothes shops there are and we do a bit of window shopping as we go. At the corner of Manresa Road, we go into the Art College and make for the student bar. Lizzie sees a bloke she knows who's one of Graham Bond's road crew and she starts talking to him while I go and buy a couple of large whiskies. When I get back with the drinks Lizzie tries to introduce me but he's talking so fast she can't get a word in. He's rabbiting on about the band being at the end of a tour of France and Germany and how there's been a lot of rucking on the road, particularly between the drummer and bass player, who hate each other, and how much drugging and drinking went on and how the drummer got busted with smack in Frankfurt and the manager had to bung the German filth to get him out of the nick. He goes on about the groupies and the wild nights for a bit longer and then he downs his pint, looks at his watch, says he's got to go and asks us if we want to come backstage for a line of something. Lizzie looks at me and I shake my head.

She tells him no thanks and he nips off.

'Where do you know him from?' I ask.

'His mother kept a nunnery for the gentry in Shoreditch. He used to mind it with his brother until his mum caught them putting the black on punters and chucked them both out.'

We hear a band starting up and we follow a line of people paying their two bob at the door and go into the hall as the band finish a bluesy instrumental and get a bit of clapping from the kids near the stage. The keyboard player says something to the drummer, then he counts the band into a driving rhythm and a black girl in a tight white dress comes on, grabs the mic off the stand and powers into 'Let the Good Times Roll'. Lizzie whirls me round and we shake it up while the black girl rocks on with some soul and rhythm and blues numbers. When she slows it down with 'Stormy Weather' we get close and a bit too clingy, judging by a few of the looks we're getting. The set finishes and the keyboard player asks for a big hand for Doris Troy. She accepts the whoops and the applause with a bow and goes off with the band.

The roadies come onstage and start moving the gear. The one who was talking to us before is leaping about and picking up speakers and cables like he's swallowed a ton of speed. We go back into the bar and Lizzie buys drinks. As I turn round to look for a table, I see a tall figure looking at me from the far end of the room and I recognise Ray in his grey overcoat. He nods towards the door and heads for it. I turn to Lizzie and tell her I've seen someone I need to speak to and that I'll be back in a minute. She says she'll find a table and I go through the door to the entrance hall. Ray's standing in a corner with a snidey look on his face and I go over to him.

'That your missus?' he asks.

'Either tell me something or fuck off.'

'Stay calm.'

'What is it?'

'I've got the news on Brindle, if you want it.'

'I do.'

'It'll cost you a bullseye.'

This slimy piece of work ought to be put down, but if Brindle really is warming up for a war I could get hurt and I need to know what he's got.

'All right,' I say.

'Be at the Nucleus. Midnight.'

I walk back to the bar and see Lizzie at a table with an older man in a suit and tie. I sit between them.

'Rina. This is Gerald,' she says.

'Hello there,' says Gerald, as he shakes my hand.

'Gerald teaches textile design,' says Lizzie.

The wink she gives me, unseen by Gerald, tells me she's met a punter.

'Doris Troy's awfully good, isn't she?' he says.

'Awfully good,' I reply.

After an awkward silence, Lizzie says, 'Gerald has a collection of early Danish wall hangings.'

'Oh, that's nice,' I say.

'You'd both be welcome to come and see them. I'm

only round the corner in Oakley Street.'

'I'd like that,' says Lizzie.

'What about you Rina?'

'I'll give it a miss thanks Gerald.'

'Not your cup of tea?'

'Not really.'

'Fair enough.'

He stands and puts on a grey fedora.

'Shall we go Margery?'

I try not to laugh as Lizzie squeezes my knee under the table.

'I want to powder my nose so I'll see you outside in a minute,' she says.

'Right ho.'

Gerald smiles and leaves us.

'You don't mind if I go and nick a fiver?' asks Lizzie.

'Of course not.'

'Only the Japanese at the Savoy bumped me off, the little fucker.'

'How come?'

'Soon as I'd done the business he disappeared while I was getting dressed.'

'Didn't you get paid first?'

'I did but when I looked in my bag it had gone. I went downstairs and the doorman told me he'd got in a cab.'

'Cheeky sod.'

'I shouldn't be long.'

'If I'm not here I'll be at the Nucleus later.'

'I'll catch up with you there.'

She gives me a peck on the cheek and I watch her walk away through the tables and hope she's going to be all right. I've told her she should carry a tool when she's working but she says it could give a punter ideas if he saw it and I suppose she's right.

I hear Graham Bond kicking off with 'Wade in the Water' so I go back into the hall and push through the crowd to the front. I look up at the saxophone player, who's blowing up a storm, and let the music take me.

• • •

I get out of the cab at Seven Dials and walk up Monmouth Street to the Nucleus. I know one of the two bouncers on the door as it happens so I get in without any trouble and go down the stairs into the club. There's a bar along one wall with men standing two or three deep and a bandstand in the corner where a pianist is plunking out some Frank Sinatra song. There are card games being played at tables towards the back of the club and hostesses with men in suits and bottles of champagne sitting at the tables in the middle. A couple of blokes are playing the fruit machines that line the wall opposite the bar. One of them thumps his machine, curses, strides to the bar and slumps onto a stool. I walk past him to the end of the bar near the bandstand and ask the barman for a large whisky.

'Are you working?' he asks, as he puts it on the bar.

'No,' I say.

'That'll be three and six then.'

I take a ten bob note out of my purse and give it to him.

He goes to the till, gets change and hands it to me. I take a drink and look round at the girls at the tables and the men they're sitting with, who are stupid enough to feel good just because a pretty girl is pretending to fancy them for a few quid. Half of them will be married and lying to their wives. I'd like to chuck them in the sea and watch them drown. When one gets up and walks past me to the gents, I see that he's an ugly little fucker who probably can't get his oats unless he pays for it, so I suppose I might throw him a lifebelt.

As I drain my glass and signal for another, Ray gets onto the stool next to me.

'Looking good tonight,' he says.

I ignore the remark and while he gets himself a drink I notice that without his overcoat he's broad as well as tall and looks as if he might be able to take care of himself.

'So what have you got?' I ask.

'Depends what you've got,' he says. I open my bag and take out a fold of ten fivers that I sorted in the taxi on the way and give them to him.

'Brindle's old man is Dan Garner,' he says.

Garner is a Birmingham boss with a big firm and a long reach. A South London mob had a beef with him a while back, sent a team up there to sort him and they ended up in a lay-by on the A5, cut into pieces and laid out on the bonnet of their car, with their heads stuck on the front bumper.

'So what's Brindle doing in London?' I ask.

'As soon as he was born his dad fucked off and moved

in with a bit of young skirt. Brindle's mum went on the game to feed her kid. When she got strangled by a trick Garner dumped Brindle on the steps of an orphanage. When he was fourteen Brindle got out and started running messages for one of Garner's boys, proved himself handy with a tool, did a bit of villainy and got on the firm himself a couple of years later.'

'Why's he left then?'

'He met a woman a while back who turned out to be his auntie and she told him who his dad is and how he treated him when he was a kid. Brindle confronted Garner, expecting him to be made up to meet his long lost son but Garner, who'd just taken up with another young bit of crumpet and got her up the duff, denied all knowledge of him and threatened to kill him if he didn't shut up and disappear.'

'Sounds like a nice fella.'

'Brindle's a chip off the old block.'

'Yeah?'

'He's trying to build an army to wipe his old man off the map for denying him his inheritance.'

'He's got some bottle.'

'Now Tony Viner's gone, he's got a good few of his firm on a weekly wedge already and he's looking for more.'

'That can't be cheap.'

'He done the Batman blag, up Cornhill.'

'Half a mill?'

'They reckon.'

There's more to Johnny Brindle than I thought. The

Cornhill blag was top drawer and with that kind of money he can buy a lot of muscle in this town. Loyalty tends to take a walk when there's a good earner in view. I reckon his attack on Danny Teale was more likely done to provoke George Preston to take revenge on Viner than to get Dawn away from Danny, and he's certainly not looking like a man who's planning to elope with her any time soon. I'm wondering how safe Dawn is and if I should try and see if she's all right when I see Lizzie come into the club. I give her a wave and she makes her way towards us, stopping at a table to talk to one of the girls who's sitting by herself.

'That it?' I ask Ray.

'If I get anything else I'll be in touch.'

I get paper and a pencil from the barman, write my number down and give it to him. 'Are you going to tell George?'

He ignores my question, moves along the bar and joins a hard-looking team at the far end. I reckon the slimy creep is going to hang back and see which way it goes, so he can get on the winning side when the dust settles. Lizzie slips onto the stool he's just vacated.

'How was it with Gerald?' I ask.

'It was going fine till his wife walked in.'

'Caught you at it?'

'Why do posh women always throw things?'

'How do you mean?'

'It's so wasteful. She's flung a fortune's worth of china at him, which has bounced off his bonce and smashed on the floor, when she's wearing a cracking pair of high heels which she could have done him a serious injury with and popped them back on again after.'

'I hope you told her.'

'I tried, but she wasn't in the mood for a conversation.'

'Did you get paid this time?'

'Too right. Do you want another?'

'Cheers.'

Lizzie gets the barman's attention after a couple of attempts and he refills my glass and pours another whisky.

'How did Gerald know you were in business?'

'He asked me what I did, so I told him.'

I'm laughing at my girl's chutzpah when I hear a commotion and shouting from above. I look up as the two bouncers crash through the door, roll down the stairs and hit the floor. Four men in masks carrying iron bars and hammers come down the stairs, followed by a man in a crash helmet holding a shotgun. He stops half way down and raises the gun. 'No cunt moves or I start blasting!'

The whole place falls silent as he sweeps the barrels round the club.

'Everyone into the back! Now!' he shouts.

I grab Lizzie's arm and we follow the crowd as they move into the back of the club. Tables are knocked over and cards and money go on the floor as people try to get as far away from the advancing gunman as they can. While everyone's pushing and shoving, I get the blade out of my suspenders and when the crowd settles I end up at the front, standing between Lizzie and Ray.

The man with the shotgun covers us while a runty little bloke goes behind the bar and empties the till. The others head for the fruit machines and tear into them with hammers and iron bars. They're laughing and smashing away at them until the bandits are a pile of twisted metal on the floor. The little fellow who's done the till comes out from behind the bar and starts smashing the gilt framed mirrors hanging round the walls. When he crosses in front of us, he sees some notes on the floor and bends down to pick them up. At the same moment, the man with the shotgun turns and shouts something to the fruit machine boys. Ray grabs the bloke who's picking up money, lifts him above his head, throws him at the shotgun man and knocks him flat. I leap forward, grab the shotgun, fire both barrels at the ceiling and all hell breaks loose. The heavy mob, who were at the end of the bar with Ray, rush at the invaders and there's kicking and punching and iron bars swinging and heads being hammered and girls screaming and God knows what mayhem. Ray grabs the shotgun off me by the barrels and swings the stock at someone's head. I put my arm round Lizzie and we get low and force our way through the mass of bodies. I stripe a couple with the blade on the way, and after catching a few flying fists and swinging boots, we make it up the stairs and out.

We hurry along Monmouth Street to Shaftesbury Avenue and hail a cab. Police sirens start wailing in the distance as we get in. I tell the driver to take us to Maida Vale. We sit back and I hold Lizzie's hand. As we drive up Tottenham Court Road her breathing slows and I feel her relaxing. I look at her face and check for bruising but she's clear.

'Are you all right?' I ask.

'I got a kick in the leg, but I got him back.'

'Yeah?'

'Scratched his face.'

'Good girl.'

'You OK?'

'I'm fine.'

'Who's your man who nobbled the shotgun merchant?' she asks.

'His name's Ray.'

'You made a good team in there.'

'He was fast.'

'So were you.'

I smile and kiss her on the cheek.

'You were with him at the bar when I came in, weren't you?' she says.

'Just talking.'

'What do you reckon the bundle was about?'

'Probably the fruit machines from the way they were smashing them up.'

'Which mob is supplying them, you mean?'

'That and the protection.'

'George has hold of that place, doesn't he?'

'Last time I looked.'

'There's been a lot of aggro in the clubs lately, with different firms going after Tony Viner's spread.'

I wonder what I've started by killing Viner, but then

I remind myself that if I hadn't done him George would have given the work to someone else and I wouldn't be in the way of picking up two hundred large.

The cab pulls up in front of the flats. I pay the driver and we go into the foyer and tiptoe past Dennis, trying not to wake him. He's still snoring with his head on the desk when we get into the lift but the sound of the closing gate makes him jerk upright and we have a giggle at him looking around in confusion as the lift rises. We go into Lizzie's, have a quick nightcap and go to bed.

7

A few hours later I'm in my kitchen making coffee. I couldn't get to sleep for worrying about this Brindle business and I've slipped out of bed and come home, rather than disturb Lizzie with my tossing and turning. I need to try and contact Ray to find out if he got away last night and see if he knows who the raiders were. I take my coffee into the hall, find the beer mat that's got his number on and I'm just about to lift the receiver and dial when the phone rings. I answer it and it's Georgie, sounding out of breath.

'I've got to be quick because I'm not supposed to be on the phone,' she says.

'Is something wrong?' I ask.

'I told you we're going to Annabelle's today.'

'Yes.'

'I've got nothing to wear so I want to pick up some clothes from home on the way.'

'How are you getting there?'

'They're sending a car. Annabelle says she'll tell the chauffeur to stop at the flat.'

'Do you know what time you'll be here?'

'About one o'clock.'

'I'll make some lunch.'

'OK. I've got to go.'

The line goes dead and I put the phone down. I'm glad

I'm going to see them both as I've only met Annabelle briefly before. I remind myself to go shopping later for something nice for lunch.

I pick up the beer mat again and dial Ray's number. It rings and rings and I finally give up, replace the receiver and go back into the kitchen. I sit at the table and watch the leaves rustling outside and the birds flitting about between the trees. I open the window so I can hear the birdsong and make another cup of coffee. The argument about whether or not I should tell George what Johnny Brindle's up to starts raging in my head again. If I don't tell George and he wins the war with Brindle and then finds out I knew what Brindle was planning and didn't tell him, he could have me killed. On the other hand, if I do tell him and he goes after Brindle and doesn't get him, Brindle will know I marked George's card and have me killed himself. Either way, it feels like I'm fucked.

I take the coffee and sit back down at the table. I'm wishing my dad was still alive so I could ask him what I should do, but then again, he spent half his life inside and got himself shot, so maybe he wouldn't be the best person to advise me. I sip coffee and look at the sky. Thinking about my dad reminds me of our Jack and how he died so young and how sad it was to see him in the hospital trying to breathe with the mask on and the tubes and everything and the posh grumpy doctor who said he'd caught the whooping cough because he was growing up in "slum conditions" and how that made me feel it was my fault. I dig my thumbnail into the inside of my wrist until the pain pushes the memory away. As my wrist starts to bleed, the phone rings. I wrap a dish cloth round the cut, go into the hall and pick up the phone.

'Governor wants to see you,' says Bert Davis.

I curse myself for answering the phone without thinking. I need time to decide what I'm going to do and at least I need to find out if Ray knows who was holding the shotgun last night. If it was Brindle, it means he's got a fair mob behind him already. I decide I'd better see George.

'Where?' I ask.

'Walmer Castle, half an hour.'

I put the phone down, pick it up again and dial Ray's number. Just as I'm about to give up, he answers.

'Pick anyone up last night?' I ask.

I hear him give a bit of a chuckle.

'Nice one with the boomstick,' he says.

'Thought I'd fire the starting pistol.'

'You didn't hang about,' he says.

'I had to get my friend away.'

'We don't want the crumpet damaged, do we?'

I'm looking forward to the day I hurt this smug twat.

'How did it go?' I ask.

'We smashed the fuck out of them.'

'Did you get the masks off?'

'The Old Bill did.'

'Who had the shooter?'

'Guess.'

'Brindle?'

'Got it.'

'Did the Bill make any collars?'

'They just swept up the card money, called an ambulance and fucked off.'

'You reckon Brindle's got them squared?'

'Likely.'

I hear a woman's voice calling him and the line goes dead.

I feel like a long soak in the bath, but if I'm going to see George there isn't time. I have a quick wash, go into my bedroom and put on clean underwear and stockings. I look along the rail in the wardrobe and select the brown pinstriped dress that I got from Biba in Abingdon Road when it opened last week. I put on make-up, slip into a pair of court shoes and pick up my handbag. As I'm approaching the lift, I remember Marlene's ratty little face snarling at me through the gate and I go back and get my Smith & Wesson.

I park the car in Artesian Road and walk round the corner to the Walmer Castle. It's only just past opening time and Bert is standing alone at the bar. The landlord is by the till, writing something in a notebook. George is sitting in the far corner talking to a couple of men in dark suits who I don't recognise. I join Bert at the bar.

'Usual?' he says.

'Go on then.'

'Whisky for the lady, Ken,' says Bert. The landlord turns and looks at me.

'Coming up,' he says. He pours a whisky and puts it on

the bar. 'That's on the house if you promise to come back tonight.'

'Busy I'm afraid,' I say.

'How about a barrel?'

'Make it a distillery and I'll think about it.'

While he's thinking up his next line, the men George has been talking to get up and leave. George nods to me and I go and join him. He's looking like he's ready to kill half of London.

'You were at the party last night.'

'I left early.'

'I want that blond-headed cunt hurt so he never walks again.'

'You need to know something.'

'Go on.'

'He's told me to off you and share the proceeds.'

'And what have you told him?'

'That I'm thinking about it.'

'Who's he got?'

'A few of Viner's mob but I don't know who.'

'Fucking little cunt.'

'You want me to do him?'

'I need to know who'll be coming up behind him when he's gone.'

'That's what I thought.'

'Tell him you're on for it but it'll take a bit of time. Find out who he's got and I'll put the frighteners on.'

'Why not use Ray?'

'This one's yours.'

His answer tells me that he doesn't trust Ray any more than I do and I'm beginning to think I've made the right decision going with George.

'Did you find Dawn?' he asks.

If I tell him what Danny's been doing to a young girl he's likely to lose his legs as well as his teeth. George is a violent man and he'd never stand by while a woman's being hurt. I decide to keep it simple, for now.

'Not yet,' I say.

'Keep looking.'

'When do I get my dad's money?'

'When you find Dawn and we sort out Brindle.'

George gets up and walks towards the door of the pub, stopping to say something to Bert on the way. As he reaches the door, a group of young blokes in leather jackets come in, laughing about something. When they see George, they go quiet and stand back to let him pass.

Bert comes over to the table and sits with his back to the room.

'You want to be careful on this one Reen.'

'I know.'

'There's a lot of loose change about since Viner's gone.'

'What do you reckon to Ray?'

'He'd sell his mother.'

'How's Danny?'

'Out of the game for a while yet. You want another?'

'I ought to get back,' I say, feeling the landlord's eyes on me as I walk to the door.

On the way home I stop at the butchers in Portobello

Road. There isn't time to do a roast for the girls, if they're coming at one o'clock, so I buy some lamb chops and get an extra one in case Lizzie's around and wants to join us. Although it's not market day there's a couple of fruit and veg stalls open and I have a chat with one of the stallholders, who I've known since I was a kid. I notice that his wrist is bandaged and he's got a cut on his neck. When I ask him what happened, he says he was in the ruck down in Brighton at the weekend between the Mods and Rockers that's been in the papers. I've seen him riding his Norton Dominator, so I know which side he was on. I don't ask him any more about it as I know the Rockers were outnumbered and got a good kicking from the Mods for once.

An old woman asks for a pound of potatoes and while he's weighing them out a kerfuffle starts outside the Duke of Wellington over the road. A black man is being hustled out of the door by a couple of blokes in dirty overalls. The black man takes a swing at one of them and they both jump on him, push him down onto the pavement and start pummelling him with fists until he lies still. They roll him into the gutter and go back inside the pub. A couple of people walking past take a quick look at him and move on. I leave my carrier bag on the stall and go across the road. As I reach him he starts to come round, tries to get up and falls back down. I take his arm and help him to his feet.

'You all right?' I ask.

He mumbles something that I can't make out and leans against me. I put my arm round his waist and help him round the corner and away from the pub in case the cavemen come out again. As he recovers and straightens up I notice how tall he is. He leans against a wall, sways a bit and I can see they've given him a right shiner. He rubs his other eye and takes a look at me.

'Good woman,' he says.

'You OK?' I ask.

'Yeah, me fine.'

He reaches into his pocket, takes out a lump of hash about the size of my fist and a pen knife and starts cutting off a slice.

'Me make you little present,' he says.

'No thanks.'

'You don't want?'

I tried it once with Lizzie. It made me feel slow and woozy and I didn't like it. I shake my head and he shrugs, cuts off a small piece of hash, swallows it and puts the lump back in his pocket. He probably got thrown out of the pub for selling.

'I'd better go,' I say.

'Which way you walk?' he asks.

'I've got a car. Take care.'

He says something that I don't catch as I walk off round the corner. I cross the road to the stall, pick up my carrier bag, buy some potatoes and carrots and walk up to Blenheim Crescent where I've left the car. I stop at the bakery on Great Western Road and get one of their apple tarts for pudding, then I drive along Elgin Avenue to Maida Vale.

I let myself into the flat, phone Lizzie to tell her the girls are coming to lunch and ask her if she wants to join us. She says she'd love to and she'll be over as soon as she's finished a client. I go into the kitchen, turn on the radio, unpack the shopping and start peeling the potatoes and carrots while Emperor Rosko gives it a bit of lip until Roy Orbison chimes in with 'Pretty Woman'. When Roy's done warbling, Rosko blathers on about life onboard ship for a bit and then Cilla rides the airwaves with 'Anyone Who Had a Heart'. Just as she's finishing moaning about her old man cheating on her, Lizzie knocks on the door and I go and let her in.

We have a cuddle in the hall and go into the kitchen. She sits at the table while I open a bottle of cider, pour two glasses and put one beside her.

'How lovely to see Georgie. How long is she here for?' she asks.

'She's on her way to the country with her friend Annabelle and she needs to pick up some clothes.'

'Oh. Well at least we'll set eyes on her.'

I put the carrots and potatoes on to simmer, so they'll be ready when the girls arrive, and melt the fat in the frying pan for the chops. Lizzie washes her hands in the sink.

'I thought you weren't doing business at home any more,' I say.

'That was only Gerald. He's no trouble.'

'That bloke from Chelsea?'

'His wife's chucked him out.'

'Where's he living?'

'Staying with his brother in Mayfair.'

'All right for some.'

'He's asked me to start an escort agency with him.'

'Come again?'

'The wife's divorcing him. He reckons she'll get the house and stick him for maintenance for her and the three kids. He's the second son, so his brother got all the money when their mum and dad died, and his job's only part-time, so he needs to find an earner.'

'Do you want to do it?'

'I wouldn't mind. He reckons he knows a good few men who want a bit on the side but need it discreet and he says he can talk to the porter at his club in St James's. I know enough girls to make it work and there's a few hotel doormen I can cut in.'

'You could have an office.'

'I know. Brass plate, all legit!'

'Get you.'

'I just need to see if I can afford to get it going with photos of the girls and a brochure and all that business.'

'I suppose you need to do all that?'

'They've got to see what they're getting.'

'Sounds great.'

'There's that many punters getting rolled up the West End these days, I reckon it might be the coming thing.'

She means the habit some toms have of telling a punter they need money to book a room, arranging to meet them and then disappearing with the cash. If the punter finds the girl later, when she's back on the street, and kicks off at her, a minder will come up to him, tell him he's plain clothes Vice Squad, say he's arresting the girl for soliciting and ask the punter to go to the station and make a statement, which gets rid of him in one.

I hear a key turn and the front door opening. We go into the hall and there are the girls looking smart in their school uniforms. Lizzie gives Georgie a big hug and a kiss and I say hello to Annabelle and take her into the kitchen.

'Would you like a glass of lemonade?' I ask.

'That would be nice, thank you,' she replies, standing rather hesitantly by the door. I put the chops in the frying pan, pour a glass of lemonade and put it on the table. I pull a chair out for her and she sits down. Lizzie and Georgie are still chatting away in the hall.

'We met on the train on Georgie's first day, didn't we?' I say.

'Yes, we did.'

'You took her under your wing and showed her the ropes.'

'I suppose I did rather.'

'It was kind of you to do that. It was all a bit strange to her at the time.'

'We were all new girls once.'

Lizzie and Georgie come in.

'I may as well get some clothes sorted out while you're cooking,' says Georgie.

'OK.'

'Come and give me a hand will you Bella?'

'Of course,' says Annabelle, following Georgie into her room.

Lizzie sits at the table and picks up her cider. 'She's looking so good.'

'I know. The school really suits her.'

'I swear she's grown.'

'She's all sporty these days.'

I join Lizzie at the table. 'Have you noticed how she talks?'

'I know.'

'She's had elocution lessons.'

'At school?'

'Yeah. Deportment as well.'

'What's deportment when it's at home?'

'How to move gracefully,' I say, gliding over to the stove and picking up the potato pan.

'Get you, Margot Fonteyn!' says Lizzie, coming up behind me and holding my hips. As she's kissing my neck, the door opens and the girls come in. I move quickly to the sink and drain the potatoes. Lizzie picks up the carrots and follows me. What she's just seen will be no surprise to Georgie, but I'm not sure about Annabelle.

'Did you find some clothes?' I ask.

'Yes,' says Georgie, as she and Annabelle sit at the table.

I add a bit of butter to the potatoes and carrots, take four plates off the draining board and dish up. Lizzie gets some knives and forks from the drawer and we sit down to lunch.

'This is very nice,' says Annabelle, after a couple of mouthfuls.

'Better than school grub,' says Georgie.

'Don't they feed you well?' asks Lizzie.

'Some days are better than others,' Annabelle replies.

'Thank goodness for the tuck shop,' says Georgie.

They go on talking about the school and having a giggle about some of the teachers. Annabelle does an impression of one who's got a Welsh accent and we all laugh. As I see how lovely Georgie's looking and how much confidence she's got in herself, it makes me want to get away from London and all the squalid stuff I'm tied up in and this flat with dirty dishes in the sink and villains on the phone and start again. So that she's got a proper clean house to come home to, with a good big garden, where Annabelle can come and stay with her and ride ponies and such. As soon as I get my hands on Dad's money I know what I'm going to do.

8

After I've cleared the plates and the girls have made short work of the apple tart, they leave us and go on to Annabelle's, saying they hope we can come to Sports Day which is next Saturday. Lizzie and I have coffee and then she has to get back to Gerald because he wants to talk about the agency. I do the washing up and then take *Rebecca* into the lounge and lie on the sofa.

The young girl who's telling the story doesn't seem to have a name but she's got a wonderful way with words. Her description of Manderley in her dream really makes me see it and feel the flowers and the foliage as she walks along the path towards the house. I've got to where she's met the mysterious Maxim in the hotel in Monte Carlo. Mrs Van Hopper, who she works for as her companion and who's a right bitch, has got the flu and Maxim's taking the girl out in his car and she's getting all hot and excited. I read on to the part where Maxim proposes to her and asks her to go to Manderley with him and she accepts and she's overjoyed and feels she's starting a new life, then Mrs Van Hopper tries to spoil it all by telling her that Maxim's not in love with her and he just needs someone to look after his great house. I really want to read on and go to Manderley with her but it's getting late and I've got to meet Brindle at the Nite Spot.

I make the bed, take a black Cardin number that's sheer

and tight-fitting out of the wardrobe and lay it on the chair at the dressing table, while I put on fresh underwear and fishnet stockings. The blade goes in the suspender belt and I slip on the dress and a pair of black heels. I go into the hall, dial the porters' desk and ask Dennis to call me a cab, then I tidy up my make-up, brush my hair and put my gun and my knuckle duster into my handbag.

While I'm waiting for Dennis to ring, I pick up my book again and read about them arriving at Manderley and how she feels nervous and badly dressed in a stockinette frock and a stone marten round her neck. I put the book down, go into Georgie's room and look up stone marten in her encyclopaedia. When I find what it is, I realise she's wearing an animal fur, probably with a face.

Oxford Street's quiet and so is the cab driver, once he's given up trying to find out why I'm going to the Nite Spot and if I'm on the game or not. He turns right into Regent Street and we go round Piccadilly Circus, where there's plenty of action and people out for the night and Eros on one leg with his little bow and arrow. I get him to drop me at the corner of Charing Cross Road, give him half a crown and walk along until I can see the entrance to the club. I stand in a doorway nearby where I can watch the bouncers outside, in their black suits, talking and smoking fags. After a while a cab draws up and a couple of men get out. One of them staggers a bit and his mate has to hold him up while he pays the driver. The cab moves off and the drunk bloke waves his fist and shouts something at the driver. The bouncers move forward and one of them holds his arm out, like he's barring them from the club. While the bloke who's less pissed tries to reason with them, the drunk one lurches past the bouncers and heads for the door of the club. One of the bouncers grabs his collar and the drunk turns and throws a punch at his head. The bouncer gets him in a headlock, throws him onto the pavement and puts his boot on his neck. The second bloke starts roughing it with the other bouncer and I move forward while they're exchanging punches and slip into the club behind them.

I go down the stairs into the usual fug of cigarette smoke and booze. There's a mirror ball hanging from the ceiling that's wafting ripples of coloured light round the room, and a trio on a small stage at the far end of the club playing some cool modern jazz. All the tables except for a couple are occupied by hostesses and punters and there's a good crowd at the bar. Brindle's sitting on a bar stool, deep in conversation with an older man with long hair, in a worn tweed jacket and polo neck pullover, who looks a bit frumpy and out of place among the shiny suits around him. I walk past and catch Brindle's eye. He says something to the older man, who looks over at me. Brindle gets off his stool and makes his way through the crowd.

'I can't talk now,' he says.

'Thanks for wasting my night,' I reply.

'I've got to settle something with this bloke first.'

I can see the man looking at me from the bar and smiling. I might as well try and find out who he is, in case he's involved in Brindle's plans.

'I can wait,' I say.

The older man comes towards us, looks me up and down and holds out his hand to me. He's got an intense look on his face and his eyes are shining.

'I'm Mike,' he says.

'Rina,' I reply.

'I don't know whether Johnny's told you but he's acting in a film I'm making.' He turns to Brindle. 'Shall we find a table?'

Brindle looks confused.

'Won't you join us Rina?' says Mike.

'Why not?' I reply.

Mike leads the way to a table in the corner. Brindle shrugs his shoulders and we follow him and sit down. Mike calls a waitress and when we've ordered drinks he turns and looks into my eyes.

'May I tell you about the film I'm making?'

'Sure,' I reply.

'It's the story of a woman.'

'Oh yeah?'

'A woman who won't be beaten. She's a London girl from the wrong side of the tracks who's abused by men as she struggles to care for her sister's baby after she's been committed to a mental hospital.'

'Sounds interesting.'

'We've been shooting for a couple of weeks and I've not been happy with one of the leading actors. I didn't feel he quite had the right touch. I asked the casting director to find someone who's background is rooted in the world in which the film is set and she introduced me to Johnny. He did an excellent screen test and he's just finished his first few days' filming and done a very fine job.'

'That's nice,' I say.

He claps Johnny on the shoulder and they clink glasses. Mike turns back to me. 'Are you from London Rina?'

'Yes.'

'May I ask what you do?'

'Not a lot.'

'A lady of leisure,' says Brindle.

'Have you ever acted Rina?' asks Mike.

'Like in a play?'

'Yes, or another medium.'

'No.'

'I ask because I'm concerned to make the film authentic. I want the characters and their situation to reflect the appalling state of the disadvantaged and underprivileged in this country, particularly single women with children, and the ignorance and selfishness of those who are in control of the wealth that could be used to help and support them.'

'Sounds good,' I say.

'Would you be interested in testing for a part?'

'I don't think…'

'There is a role in which I think you might be perfect.'

'It's not really my…'

'The heroine's younger sister is a lingerie model, in her early twenties, and while on a photographic shoot, she is assaulted by…'

'It sounds interesting Mike but it's not something I'd want to do. Why don't you ask one of these girls who work here? They're acting all the time with the punters.'

'I could yes, but I feel that you have the perfect look for the role, self possessed and strong, yet somehow vulnerable. I knew it as soon as I saw you come into the club and as a friend of Johnny's you'd be company for each other on the set and so forth. We're filming in Hoxton so you won't have far to come.'

A bloke gets up from a table near us and leaves. The girl he's left behind is blond and about my age.

'How about her, over there?' I say.

Mike looks over at the girl and then leans close to me. 'She's nowhere near as beautiful as you my dear.'

I catch a whiff of an unpleasant odour that I only ever smell on men. I smile and sit back a little.

'I've got to go and meet someone I'm afraid.'

'That's a pity,' says Mike.

'I hope your film goes well,' I say, as I get up from the table.

'I'll see you out,' says Brindle.

Mike stands and shakes my hand. 'Do come and visit the set sometime, if you'd care to.'

'Thanks. I'd like that,' I reply.

Brindle walks with me to the stairs.

'Are you in or not?' he says.

'Are you, now you're a movie star?'

'That's just a bit of a laugh.'

'I need to know what you've got.'

'Give me your number.'

'I don't talk about work on the phone.'

He takes some keys out of his pocket and offers them to me.

'Blue Merc round the corner in Bear Street. I'll be there as soon as I get rid of Alfred Hitchcock.'

I take the keys from him and go up the stairs. When I get into the street I take a couple of deep breaths of night air, turn into Bear Street and see a blue Mercedes sports car parked on the right hand side. The key fits and I slide into the passenger seat and wish I'd brought *Rebecca*.

The car's facing Charing Cross Road and after a bit I see Brindle and Mike come to the corner with a girl between them. Brindle walks to the car alone and opens the driver's door.

'I've got to go,' he says.

'What?'

'He's testing that girl for your part and he wants me to do a scene with her at his hotel.'

'In her underwear.'

'Could be.'

'Have fun.'

'Can you come to the set lunchtime tomorrow so we can talk?'

'Maybe.'

'Hoxton Square. You'll see the trucks. Just ask for me.'

I see that Mike's deep in conversation with the girl, probably telling her she's got the perfect look for the role, and I get out of the car and head up Bear Street while

Brindle locks the car and goes to join them. Mike flags down a cab and they get in. I don't feel like going home so I decide to see if Lizzie's at the Kazuko. I walk to the end of Bear Street, go across Leicester Square towards Piccadilly Circus and turn into Rupert Street. I go past the Trocadero and the Chinese restaurants and cross over Shaftesbury Avenue. The Kazuko's on the left hand side and the door's easy to miss as there are no bouncers outside. I say hello to the bloke behind the desk and the cloakroom girl, who both know me, and go into the club.

It's much quieter than the Nite Spot with curtained booths round the edge of the room, for a little bit of private slap and tickle, and small round tables circling a stage, where an older man at a white piano is singing 'The Shadow of Your Smile,' with a nice mellow tone. About half the tables are occupied and waitresses are keeping them supplied with over-priced cocktails and bottles of champagne, which is all the girls are allowed to drink. I can't see Lizzie, but in case she's behind one of the curtains, I sit at a table. When a waitress tells me that Lizzie left a while ago with a German bloke I decide to call it a night and head home.

As I approach the door an older woman in a beautiful sable fur coat walks in. I step aside to let her pass and recognise Marlene Teale. She's wearing very high heels, a blond wig, which gives her a few more inches, and a pair of diamond earrings. She looks at me and her mean little mouth stretches into a smile.

'Just the person I want to see,' she says.

'Go and fuck yourself.'

As I go to push her out of the way, she holds me by the arm.

'I've found her,' she says.

I stop and look at her. She's still smiling in a creepy way.

'Come and have a drink?'

If she's found Dawn I want to know what she's done with her and why she's telling me about it, when the last time she saw me she was ready to kill me. I follow her to a corner table and we sit down. I can see by the light of the table lamp that she's wearing a ton of make-up and powder and looks about ready to go in an open coffin.

'Johnny's talked to you, hasn't he?' she says.

'I don't know what you mean.'

'He's told me the score, so there's no need to fuck about.'

'Where's Dawn?'

'Never mind that now. Are you on for doing Preston?'

I can't believe what I'm hearing. This old slag has thrown her lot in with the man who's punched her son's teeth out, broken his hands, and captured his girl, and she wants to stand beside him while he squares up to one of the most powerful men in London. When George hears this, he's going to put a dead stop to this malarkey and I'm going to help him do it, just as soon as I've found Dawn.

'Could be,' I say.

'Johnny's the coming man all right.'

'Who else has he got?'

'Tony Viner's firm and a few from Birmingham.'

'Danny?'

'Oh yeah.'

'After what Brindle's done to him?'

'Danny'll do what he's told.'

'Where's Dawn?'

'It doesn't matter now.'

She looks round as a bloke carrying a briefcase comes into the club.

'There's my man,' she says.

'Is he in?' I ask.

'No. He's just buying fur coats.'

She puts a dry knobbly hand out to me. 'Here's to better days.'

I shake her hand and she goes off to sell her hoisted finery. I put a ten bob note on the table for the waitress and leave.

9

I'm walking to Shaftesbury Avenue and thinking that the first place to look for Dawn is Danny Teale's. I take a cab to Maida Vale, pick up the Cortina and drive to Harlesden. I park on Scrubs Lane, go through a gate on the left hand side and walk across the cobbled yard to my lock-up.

I open the garage doors, close them behind me, get into my van and turn on the inspection lamp that's taped to the roof. I slip out of my dress, open the wardrobe that's fixed to the side of the van, look among the clothes on the rail and take out a dark blue suit, a Brooks Brothers white shirt, a club tie and a pair of black brogues. I take off my bra, put on the outfit, get some kirby grips from a box where I keep various bits and pieces and put my hair up. I spit on a tissue and wipe off most of my make-up, take a dark grey fedora off the shelf and put it on. The gent who looks at me from the mirror on the inside of the wardrobe door looks a bit camp and dodgy but I reckon I can get away with it in a dark street. I put the Smith & Wesson in my belt, the blade in my sock and the knuckle duster in my jacket pocket, along with a nylon stocking mask.

I drive the van to Notting Hill and park in Talbot Road. As I cross Powis Square I can see lights on in the front room of Danny's flat. The same brass who I saw last time is standing on the corner. When she walks on along the pavement I take off the fedora, pull on the stocking mask, put the hat back on and go up the steps to Danny's. I ring the bell and after a moment the curtain of the bay window twitches, and I turn my head away as it's pulled aside. When the curtain falls back I take out my gun, lower the brim of the fedora and wait. The door opens and I'm looking at Danny's brother Jack. He's smaller than Danny but still a bit lively. I raise the gun and step forward. He sees what's in my hand and backs into the hall. I follow him inside and close the front door behind me.

'Who is it?' says a voice from inside the flat, that sounds like Danny.

I pull back the hammer and motion Jack to go through the open door into the flat. He raises his hands, turns and goes in. When he's through the door I kick him hard in the lower back and crack the side of his head with the gun as he goes down. I close the door behind me, nudge Jack with my foot to make sure he's out, and go into the front room. In the glow from the test card on the TV screen, I see Danny getting up from the sofa.

'What the fuck?' he says, and tries to pick up a wooden chair with his bandaged hands. I put the gun in my left hand, slip on the knuckle duster, step forward and hit him with a straight punch to the knockout point on the side of his jaw. He falls backwards, hits the sofa and slumps onto the floor. I hear Jack give a moan and I go into the hallway and quieten him down with the heel of the gun. There's a corridor which runs the length of the flat with three doors off it and a kitchen at the far end. The first two doors open to empty bedrooms. The third one is locked. When I get near the kitchen I smell bacon cooking. I go in and see a frying pan on the stove and bread under the grill. Dawn is crouching in the corner with her face to the wall.

I take off my hat and mask, turn off the grill and the gas under the frying pan.

'Time to go Dawn,' I say.

She turns slowly and looks at me. Her face is thin and drawn and there are bruises on her neck and arms. She looks at me but doesn't recognise me.

'I was at the cottage,' I say.

Her eyes flicker with recognition and she slowly stands up.

'I remember you,' she says.

'This time you're coming with me.'

I go to her, take her arm and she offers no resistance as I lead her along the corridor. Jack's still lying where I left him and as I step over him I hear a key turn in the front door. I back up and push Dawn through the first door off the corridor. I follow her into a bedroom and hear Marlene's voice.

'Who's left this fucking door unlocked? Oh my Christ!'

The door is slammed shut and there's the sound of face slapping.

'Come on my love, come on…'

Marlene huffs and puffs and Jack starts to gurgle and wheeze.

'My fucking head,' he mumbles.

'Come on, let's get you in here my love,' says Marlene.

I hear what sounds like Jack being dragged into the living room and then a scream from Marlene. I slowly open the bedroom door, pull Dawn after me and we creep into the hallway and out of the front door. As we go down the steps I can hear Marlene shouting at her boys in the front room.

When we get to the van I put Dawn in the passenger seat and head for Harlesden. She doesn't seem to want to talk and by the time we're on Harrow Road she's asleep. I'm thinking maybe she's been drugged with something. When we get to Scrubs Lane, I help her out of the van and put her in the Cortina, while I take the van back to the lock-up and change out of the suit and tie. After I've made everything secure, I go back to the car and drive to Maida Vale. Dawn sleeps all the way and doesn't even wake up when Dennis carries her up to the flat for me. I put her in Georgie's bed and when Dennis asks me who she is, I put a finger to my lips, give him a fiver and tell him to stay awake and not let any old ladies into the building. He pockets the note, gives me a salute and leaves. I turn the keys in all three locks on the front door, close the bolts and go into my bedroom. I take off my clothes and get into bed. I'm so knackered I don't even reach for *Rebecca*.

It seems like moments later when I'm woken by screams coming through the wall. I get up and rush into Georgie's room. Dawn is sitting on the bed holding her stomach and rocking back and forth. Her face is bright red and her eyes are bulging. She sees me and reaches out a hand. As I get to her and hold her, she screams again and throws herself back onto the bed. I run into the hall, dial 999, say I need an ambulance and tell the operator what's happening, then I phone Dennis, tell him there's one coming and to send them up right away. I unlock the front door to save time when they get here and go back to Dawn. She's lying on the bed, holding her stomach and moaning softly. There are tears on her face from the pain that she's in and she's looking up at me imploringly. I kneel beside the bed, wipe her eyes and hold her hands in mine.

'Ambulance is coming. You'll soon be all right.'

Another spasm of pain grips her and she arches back and cries out. When it subsides and she sinks back onto the bed and quietens, I put a hand on her forehead and feel how hot she is. She turns and looks at me.

'Do they know where…?'

'No,' I say.

'Will you be with me?'

'Of course.'

She closes her eyes and clenches her fists as another wave of pain passes through her, then she settles again and her breathing slows. I suddenly realise I'm naked and I tell her I'll be back in a tick and go next door. I put on bra, pants, jeans and a sweater and pull on a pair of socks and my Chelsea boots. I go back to Dawn, put my arm round her and stroke her forehead, until I hear footsteps in the corridor and a knock at the door. I open it and there are two ambulance men holding a stretcher between them. I show them into the bedroom and they take a quick look at Dawn, lay the stretcher on the floor and lift her on to it. I can see blood on the sheet where she's been lying. I ask if I can go with her and get a quick nod from one of them as they pick up the stretcher and carry it into the hall. I grab my keys, open the front door and stand back as they take the stretcher into the corridor. I lock the flat and catch them up in time to open the door to the stairs for them. The man at the front end lifts the stretcher up to his shoulders and holds it with one hand while he turns round, takes it with both hands again and sets off down the stairs, while his mate lowers his end to his knees to keep it level.

When we get to the foyer I see that the back of the ambulance is open and it's parked up close to the glass door. Dennis holds it open while the men put the wheels of the stretcher onto a pair of rails and slide it in. One of the ambulance men tells me to get in the back with him. When he's checked that the stretcher is secure and Dawn's strapped in, I sit beside her and take her hand while the other man closes the back doors, gets into the front, says something into a radio that I can't hear and starts the engine. The sirens wail as we pull out of the service road and accelerate fast down Edgware Road. I get thrown about a bit and have to hold on as the driver swings the ambulance left and right before pulling up at St Mary's in South Wharf Road. As soon as we stop the back doors open and two men in white coats pull the stretcher out, put it on a trolley and take it into the building. I follow them as they wheel it along a corridor to where there are two lifts on each side and men and women in white coats and nurses standing waiting. A lift arrives and the white coats stand back, let the stretcher in first and file in after it. We go up a few floors and they wheel the stretcher out of the lift, along the corridor and into a ward. I follow behind but a nurse stops me and asks me for the patient's name. I tell her that I only know her as Dawn and she says I've got to wait outside. She points to a row of chairs and tells me that someone will come and talk to me when they've examined Dawn.

I sit down and suddenly feel tired. I can see a payphone a good way along the corridor and I'd like to go and phone Lizzie but I don't want to be gone when they come out to tell me the news. I sit back and close my eyes and I'm thinking about what's gone on, and why Dawn was suddenly back in the Teale house, and why Marlene was being all friendly in the club, and telling me she's joined the Brindle team. If Marlene or Jack had found Dawn and had her away, they'd know Brindle would come looking for her and the last place they'd take her is Powis Square. I'm wondering if Brindle's given Dawn back to them willingly, in exchange for them joining him against George, and if he wasn't just using her as bait all along. He could even have them on an earner. George isn't exactly well known for paying his firm top whack. As I'm thinking about the possibilities the door to the ward opens and an Asian bloke in a white coat with a stethoscope round his neck and a clipboard in his hand comes over and sits next to me.

'You are family?' he says.

'Just a friend.'

out, get on and sit downstairs. I tell the conductor I'm going to Clifton Road, give him a shilling and get a ticket from his machine and eight pence change.

A couple of drunks a few seats in front of me start arguing about some fight they've been to. One of them's saying the ref was a wanker and shouldn't have stopped the fight after his man got knocked about, because he would have won it if he'd been allowed to carry on, and he should know because he trained in the same gym as him. The other says he's just pissed off because he's lost a pony on it and the fighter he had money on is the wanker and couldn't punch his way out of a paper bag. The other one calls him a cunt and they start shouting. One grabs the other by the collar and bangs his head on the back of the seat in front and all at once they're grappling with each other and swinging punches. The driver looks back from the cab, sees what's happening and stops the bus. The conductor comes past me, stands between me and the fight and points to the back of the bus. I take his advice, hop off the platform and walk the rest of the way. As I get near home I have a good look round in case there's a Teale about but I don't see anything. I check with Dennis and when he tells me no one's been asking for me, I reckon Fedora man got away with it.

Dennis asks how the girl who went in the ambulance is and I tell him she's going to be all right. He does a great job of pretending he's not interested in what goes on in my life but I can tell he's burning to find out. He knows I'm up to no good but he's too keen on the bung he gets to ask me what's going on and it suits me to keep it that way.

I take the lift, go into the flat and put the kettle on. While it boils, I stand at the kitchen window and watch the dawn break over the rooftops. I think of that poor girl in her hospital bed and wonder if she knows she's lost the baby yet. Perhaps they'll tell her in the morning. I'm just glad she's safe and away from those beasts who have abused and tormented her and I hope she's sleeping peacefully. The kettle boils and I make a cup of cocoa, take it into the bedroom, get undressed and get between the sheets. I fluff up my pillows, sit up in bed and open my book. They're arriving at Manderley and the young bride's a bit overwhelmed by the grandeur and beauty of the house and the estate and she's meeting Frith the butler and Mrs Danvers. When I read that she's "tall and gaunt, dressed in deep black with her prominent cheekbones and a skull's face, parchment-white, set on a skeleton's frame", I shiver a bit and think that compared with Mrs Danvers maybe Marlene's not so scary after all. As the cocoa warms me, my eyelids start to droop and I close the book, turn off the light and snuggle down to sleep.

10

I wake at midday and remember I've got to get to Hoxton Square and see Brindle. I can only hope he hasn't found out that Dawn's been lifted. I make a cup of coffee while the bath's running and think about what I'm going to say to him. If I'm right about him having Danny, Jack and Marlene Teale on his books after he's given them Dawn back, and most of Viner's firm as well, then he's probably got more than enough weight to go against George and get a result. After what he's done to Dawn I'd put him in the ground today, but I reckon George is right to want to find out who he's got with him, in case some other bright spark decides to take over command once Brindle's been done. I finish my coffee, get out of the bath and dry myself, then I go through to the bedroom and put on clean underwear, a pencil skirt, a polo neck sweater and my Courrège boots. I give myself a light make-up, brush my hair, slip the blade into my waistband and put on my suede jacket. When I put the Smith & Wesson in my bag I'm reminded that I need to ask Bert to get me another one to keep as a spare.

I drive the Cortina along Marylebone Road, and then Pentonville, to the Old Street roundabout, turn left and park in Hoxton Street. I get out of the car, walk round the corner into the square and see that one side of it is cordoned off and lined with trucks, a couple of caravans and an old London bus. A bloke in a black anorak and a woolly hat, who's leaning against one of the trucks, steps forward as I approach and asks me what I want. I say I've come to see Johnny Brindle and he tells me I'll have to wait because they are just about to shoot a scene. I can see a small crowd of people on the pavement outside a Victorian terraced house further along the square. There's a camera on a tripod and a trolley nearby with a machine on it and a man wearing headphones sitting in front of it. A beefy bloke is up a ladder adjusting a big lamp on a stand and there's a younger lad holding a long pole with something that looks like a big sock on the end of it. Mike, the director, is standing apart from the group talking to a man holding a megaphone. He sees me, waves and comes over.

'Rina, I'm so glad you could make it,' he says while shaking my hand.

'Hello Mike.'

'You've chosen the perfect moment to visit. Johnny's just about to confront the villain of the piece and give him his just deserts.'

'Oh yeah?'

'They've been working with Ken Merton, the fight arranger, all morning while we've been doing establishing shots of the square. There's Ken now.'

He points to a bloke in a red tracksuit coming out of the front door of the house. The man with the megaphone approaches. 'We're ready Guv.'

Mike nods to him. 'Do come and watch won't you, Rina?'

'Thanks,' I say.

'This is Ed, our trusty first assistant. Ed, this is Rina.'
Ed and I smile and shake hands.

'Can we find a chair for Rina?' says Mike to no one in particular as we walk towards the camera. A woman sitting on a stool, with a folder open on her knee, smiles at me and points to a canvas chair beside her and I go over and sit in it.

Ed raises his megaphone to his lips. 'Stand by!'

The cameraman looks into the camera and turns it until it's pointing towards the front of the house, and the lad holding the long pole raises it above his head and swings the sock thing towards the front door. The man sitting at the trolley presses a button on his machine and says something I don't catch.

'Running,' says the cameraman and someone puts a board with chalk writing on it in front of the camera, calls out a number and smacks the arm at the top of the board down. Mike nods to Ed and he raises his megaphone and pulls the trigger.

'And... Action!'

The door of the house opens and a man with a briefcase, about forty, tall and stocky, steps out. He takes a couple of strides along the paved path and then stops dead as Brindle opens the metal gate from the street and walks towards him. The man turns back to the door and tries to open it. Brindle grabs him by the shoulder, swings him round and catches him on the side of the head with a solid right hook.

'Ouch! That hurt you stupid cunt!' says the man, falling onto the doorstep.

'Cut!' shouts Mike. He leaps forward and bends over the injured man. 'Are you all right Henry?'

'Bloody idiot!' says Henry, holding his head.

Mike helps him to his feet and leads him in my direction. 'Come and sit down. Nurse!'

I stand up and offer my seat. Henry sits down and a woman arrives with a medical bag which she puts down beside his chair. 'Let's have a look at you darling,' she says, putting a hand under his chin and raising his head.

'Ouch!' says Henry as she touches his temple.

'Mmm, yes, he has caught you, hasn't he?' says the nurse.

'Fucking lunatic!'

Mike, Ed and the fight arranger are talking to Brindle by the door of the house. The nurse is giving Henry some pills and a glass of water as Brindle comes over. 'I'm sorry about that mate. I aimed to miss, but you was a bit off balance and I got you by mistake.'

'What the fuck was all that rehearsal for?' says Henry.

'Like I said, you was off balance, so you kind of fell on to the punch. Know what I mean?'

'Now I've heard fucking everything!' says Henry.

The fight arranger comes over. 'You did lose your balance, in actual fact Henry.'

'As for you, you couldn't arrange a piss up in a fucking brewery!'

Mike approaches the happy group. 'How are you doing Henry?'

'I'll live.'

Mike looks at the nurse. 'What do you think Brenda?'

She takes another look at Henry. 'The skin isn't broken. He's bruised, but as it's on the bone I don't think it'll swell very much and make-up ought to hide any discolouring.'

Mike puts a hand on Henry's shoulder. 'I'm very sorry you've been hurt Henry and I'm sure you'd like to rest and recuperate. We're losing the light a bit anyway so we're going to go inside and shoot scene twenty-seven with Johnny and Kim. You get off home now and we'll have another go at the fight in the morning, after you've had a chance to run through it with Ken a couple more times.' He looks round for Ed. 'Can we have a car for Henry please?'

'On its way Guv,' says Ed, raising his megaphone. 'Right boys, we're moving upstairs.'

The cameraman steps back and I move out of the way as one of his team unscrews something under the camera, lifts it off the tripod and carries into the house. A younger bloke picks up the tripod and follows him. While the trolley, the chairs and various boxes and bits of gear are being moved inside, Henry walks rather stiffly to one of the caravans, opens the door and gets in. Mike and Brindle exchange a few words and come over to where I'm standing.

'I'm sorry the first bit of work you saw was a bit of a balls up Rina.'

'That's OK,' I say.

'The next scene is rather more intimate and gentle, between Johnny and his paramour and I hope you'll stay and see how we put it all together.'

'Sure,' I say.

'Good. Right. Well, I'd better go in. Why don't you both relax in Johnny's trailer while we set up?'

Mike heads for the house and a young girl who's been lurking nearby walks up to us. 'Would you like tea or coffee?'

'I'll have a tea love,' says Brindle.

'Coffee thanks,' I say.

Brindle walks to the caravan beside the one Henry got into and opens the door for me. I step inside and Brindle follows, turns on a light, sweeps some clothes off the bed and flops down on it. 'Fucking actors!' he says.

I sit at the table opposite him. 'Did you mean to dot him?'

'Of course I did.'

'How come?'

'He's been asking for it. He starts off all smarmy with how good I am and how well I'm doing, then he starts telling me what I should do and how I should say the lines, but it's all about him looking good and me looking a cunt, and when I won't do what he says he starts calling me a fucking amateur and throwing wobblers.'

'What does Mike do?'

'Strokes his feathers, calms him down and tells him how brilliant he is, the spineless twat.'

'How did you get into this?'

'I met the casting woman in a club and she asked me to test and then Mike's all over me and gives me the part.'

'What happened with the lingerie girl the other night?'

'She was fucking useless. Froze up when he turned the camera on. He still wants you to do it. Told me to try and talk you into it.'

'No chance.'

'I thought so.'

He closes his eyes and lies back on the bed. I look at the smug kid, who's used a pregnant girl like a pawn in a stupid game that he's playing to prove to his old man that he's king of the castle, and for two pins I'd carve him up right now and put a stop to his dirty little tricks.

There's a knock on the door. Brindle gets to his feet and opens it. The girl with the tea and coffee comes in and puts two mugs on the table.

'Cheers Kirsty,' says Brindle.

The girl smiles and leaves. Brindle joins me at the table, selects the tea mug, takes a sip and looks me in the eye.

'Are you going to do Preston?' he asks.

'Maybe.'

'I can slap a good earner into you.'

'It's not about that.'

'Then what?'

'Who have you got?'

'A lot more than I had at the Nucleus.'

'Just as well.'

'I've got all of Viner's now, the Teales and a good few

from Brum, when I give them a shout.'

'What will you do about the rest of George's mob?'

'Put them on the firm.'

'Expensive.'

'I want a clean sweep.'

'You're going to need it.'

'With you, I've got it.'

I look out of the window for a bit, as if I'm considering the offer. When he's waited long enough I turn back to him. 'Fifty-fifty on everything?'

'Sure.'

I do a bit more window time, then look at him again.

'All right,' I say.

'Good girl.'

As I'm stifling the urge to smash my coffee mug in his face there's another knock on the door. Brindle opens it and Kirsty appears.

'They're ready for you upstairs, Johnny,' she says.

'OK love.'

'Wardrobe are up there with a change for you.'

Brindle looks round the caravan. 'Where's my script?'

He finds it on bed and turns to me. 'Coming to have a look?'

We step out of the caravan and follow Kirsty into the house and up the stairs. Mike is on the landing talking to Ed beside the sound trolley. I can see past them into a bedroom where the camera is set up on its tripod with a couple of lights on stands beside it. A door opens and a blousy woman with red hair in a beehive and too much make-up appears and crooks a finger at Brindle. 'Come to me, Johnny my love.'

She stands back as Brindle walks past her into the room.

'I've found you a nice pair of midnight blue undies,' she says, as she closes the door.

Mike turns and sees me. 'Ah Rina. Come and see the set.'

He leads me into the bedroom, closes the door and stands with his back to it. 'I'd like a word, if I may?'

'Sure,' I say.

He goes to sit on the bed, then changes his mind.

'Shouldn't mess it up I suppose,' he says and turns to face me. 'I want to ask you to reconsider taking a short test for the part I talked about last night.'

'I don't think...'

'As soon as I saw you in that club I knew you had exactly the quality I'm looking for. You have a luminous beauty and a purity of presence that I know the camera will love and I think this could be the start of something big for you.'

I've heard some chat-up lines in my time but nothing compared to this. I'm almost tempted to give it a go until I remind myself that in my line of work it might not be too good to be seen in the movies.

'Thanks for asking me Mike but it's not something I want to do.'

'I can't persuade you?'

'No.'

He takes a card out of his pocket and offers it to me. 'If, by any chance, you should change your mind.'

As I'm taking his card from him the door opens and Ed appears. 'Actors are ready to rehearse Guv.'

'Bring them in please,' says Mike, then he turns to me. 'Rina, perhaps you'd take a seat outside while we rehearse and then you're welcome to join us when we're ready to shoot.'

Ed opens the door for me and I nearly bump into a girl with long dark hair that I recognise from the TV. She smiles at me as I stand aside to let her pass. Brindle gives me a wink as he follows her into the bedroom. I sit in a chair next to the woman with the folder. She finishes writing something down and looks up. She's about fifty, slim with dark hair and deep brown eyes.

'I'm Jean, continuity,' she says.

'Rina,' I reply.

'Are you a friend of Johnny's?'

'Yes.'

'Such a nice boy.'

I nod and smile.

'He's doing so well.'

'I'm glad you think so.'

'Apart from nearly knocking Henry out, although between you and me, a few of us have been tempted.'

We laugh and she offers her folder to me. It's got her name, Jean Craven, written on the front cover.

'Would you like to have a look at the scene they're going to shoot?'

'Thanks,' I say.

'Johnny is playing Challoner, and Kim Daley is Mary.'

She passes me the folder and I open it up and read how Mary and Challoner are in bed together and he's comforting Mary and telling her she's safe now and how he's going to take care of her and the baby, and how much he loves her and everything's going to be all right, and I'm thinking it could be a conversation between Brindle and Dawn before he dumped her. The girl says how much she loves him and they start to have a snog and it all heats up, and then the baby starts crying in its cot and she gets out of bed and picks it up, and then they hear the front door opening and Challoner puts his clothes on and reaches for his gun. The girl pleads with him to go down the backstairs and get out, but he stands against the wall beside the door, then they hear footsteps on the stairs and he raises the gun. The door opens and a man walks in and Challoner shoots him.

'Thanks,' I say, handing the folder back to Jean.

'Here comes the baby,' she says, as a woman comes up the stairs carrying a bundle in her arms. The bedroom door opens and Ed appears. 'OK boys, we're ready to shoot.'

Ed opens the door wide and the cameraman, his mate and the lad with the microphone pole go in. Jean picks up her canvas chair and folds it. I do the same and we follow them into the bedroom and wait while Mike and the cameraman discuss where the camera should be. They decide to put it in the corner, and we open our chairs and sit alongside it. The woman with the baby puts the little one in a cot beside the bed. The baby snuffles and whimpers a bit as it's put down and the woman soothes it and strokes it until it quietens. Brindle and the girl are in the bed and Mike is sitting on the side of it talking to them. He sees me come in and says something to the girl. She looks over at me and then shrugs her shoulders and nods to Mike who gives me a smile.

When the room settles, Mike stands up. 'Welcome everyone, we'll do the whole scene for the wide shot and then come in closer. Ed?'

Mike moves to behind the camera, the boy with the pole holds it over where the lovers are and Ed gives a quiet, 'Stand by.'

As before, the soundman presses a button and mumbles something.

'Running,' says the cameraman.

'OK Johnny?' says Mike.

Brindle nods, and Mike looks to Ed.

'Action,' says Ed.

Brindle, who's lying on the far side of the girl gets up on one elbow, strokes her shoulder and whispers something that I can't hear into her ear. She gazes into his eyes and they exchange a few words and then kiss. Brindle pulls back the bedclothes, slides on top of her, fondling her breast, and she wraps her arm round his neck and pulls him closer.

'Cut,' says Mike.

Brindle and the girl stop what they're doing and look up.

'What happened to the baby?' says Mike.

'Sorry Guv,' says Ed.

'It should cry at that point.'

'Edith?' says Ed.

'He's not remote control,' says the baby woman.

'We can do it as a wild track,' says the soundman.

'Put it on afterwards,' says Ed.

'It's not the same,' says Mike. 'I asked for a crying baby and that's what I want!'

Ed turns to the cameraman. 'Are you seeing the floor under the cot?'

The cameraman looks through the lens. 'No.'

'Edith, perhaps you could be under the cot and give the baby a poke, or something, when we cue you?' says Ed.

'No way,' says Edith.

The baby starts crying.

'Oh for God's sake!' says Mike.

'He's a good crier but he's not here to be poked!' says Edith.

Mike gives her a withering look and walks out of the door, followed by Ed. Jean looks at me and raises her eyebrows. Edith goes to the cot, kneels in front of it and comforts the baby. I look at my watch, see that it's nearly four o'clock and realise that if I'm going to get to St Mary's in visiting hours I'd better leave the glamorous world of film making and get on my bike.

I say goodbye to Jean, go past the camera and out of the room. I walk down the stairs and through the front door. Mike is standing by one of the trucks with his arms folded, turned away from Ed, who's talking to his back and looks like he's pleading his case in vain.

11

I park in South Wharf Road and go into St Mary's. I don't know the name of the ward Dawn is in so I ask at the desk. It takes the receptionist a bit of time to locate her as I can't give her surname, but she finally tracks her down to Albert Ward and I go up the stairs and along the corridor until I see the sign. A different nurse is at the desk and when I tell her I've come to see Dawn she tells me the room number and points along the passage-way.

I open the door slowly in case she's asleep but I find her sitting up in bed reading a magazine. Her face breaks into a smile when she sees me. I sit on the bed and she takes my hand.

'I don't know how to thank you,' she says.

'There's no need.'

'I can't think what would have happened if you hadn't come.'

Her eyes moisten and I move closer to her. She puts her arms round me and I hold her while she cries. 'They're so horrible and Johnny's such a bastard. I don't know how he could do it to me and his own baby, and now it's gone and it's my fault because I'm so bad, and I believed all his lies and now it's all awful and horrible and...'

Her head falls onto my shoulder and she sobs in my

arms. I rock her gently from side to side and stroke her back. 'There there, it's all over now and you're safe and sound and everything's going to be all right.'

When she quietens, I put my hand under her chin, lift her head and look into her eyes. 'You're going to be fine my darling.'

I hold her close for a while and then ease her back onto the pillows.

'I'm so glad you're here,' she says.

'How are you feeling now?'

'I'm not too bad, a bit sore where I've been hit.'

I take both her hands in mine. 'Have they said when you can leave?'

'I can go later tonight.'

'Have you got a place you can be where Johnny and them can't find you?'

'I don't know. Marlene knows most of my mates, I reckon.'

I'm wondering how best to keep this girl safe when the nurse comes in, picks up a cup and saucer off the bedside table and turns to me. 'Ten minutes to the end of visiting hours.'

I nod and when she leaves I tell Dawn I'll be back in a tick and follow her into the passageway. 'Excuse me,' I say.

The nurse stops and turns to me.

'I believe Dawn will be leaving tonight.'

'That's right. Nine pm.'

'I'll be taking her home and I wondered if I could take her with me now.'

'I'm not able to authorise early discharge I'm afraid.'

'Only I can't come later and there's no one else who can collect her.'

'What about a taxi?'

'It's a long way.'

'She could discharge herself, I suppose.'

'How does she do that?'

'She has to sign a form. I'll bring one to the room.'

'Thanks.'

I go back to Dawn. She's sitting up and looking better. 'You can come with me now, if you want.'

'Do you mean it?'

'Of course I do.'

'I'd love to.'

'Let's get you dressed then. The nurse is bringing you a form to sign.'

I open a wardrobe in the corner and take out her underwear and the short cotton shift she was wearing when they brought her in the ambulance. She gets out of bed, takes off the hospital nightgown and I can see the bruises she's got from her short stay with the Teale family. As I'm helping her get dressed, the nurse comes in with a form and a biro and shows her where to fill in her name and sign. The nurse takes the form away and I slip off my jacket, give it to Dawn and she puts it on. She's still wearing the hospital slippers and her first few steps along the corridor are a bit wobbly. I hold her arm as we go down the stairs, cross the entrance hall and walk to my car.

Dennis is at the desk when we get to Maida Vale and he scurries across the foyer and calls the lift for us. 'Glad you're feeling better Miss,' he says to Dawn as he opens the lift gate for us. Dawn looks a bit confused until I tell her that Dennis helped her into the ambulance that took her to St Mary's. She thanks him for his trouble and we go up to the third floor and along to the flat.

'Are you hungry?' I ask, as I open the door.

'Not really,' she replies.

'Fancy a drink?'

'Now you're talking.'

I lead her into the lounge, offer her the sofa and go to the sideboard.

'Whisky all right?'

'Lovely.'

I pour two glasses, give one to her and sit in the armchair. She takes a drink, sits back against the cushions and twirls the whisky round in the glass. 'I can't believe what a mug I've been.'

For a moment, I think she's going to cry but then her eyes seem to clear and she takes a couple of breaths and another drink.

'I let them treat me like a bit of dirt until I didn't know which end was up. They made me feel like everything was my fault and I was doing wrong all the time, and I should have stood up to them, or got the fuck out of there, but I just went on taking it and taking it and I don't know why. What was wrong with me?'

I watch as she gets angrier at herself for playing the

victim. The more she feels like this, the more her self-respect will start to build and there'll be less chance of some other evil bastard taking it away from her and grinding her into the ground. I refill our glasses and she carries on blaming herself for what she sees as her weakness and railing against Brindle for using her and then giving her back to the Teales. After a while the whisky slows her down and she starts slurring her words as fatigue takes hold of her.

'Would you like to get into bed and get some rest?' I ask.

'Are you sure you don't mind?'

'Of course not.'

'Then I will. I feel like I could sleep for a week.'

I take her glass from her, 'Do you want one to take to bed?'

'No thanks. I won't be awake long enough to drink it.'

I change the sheets on Georgie's bed and show Dawn where the bathroom is.

'Have a bath if you want. I've got to go out for a bit but I'll be back later. If you wake up, help yourself to anything you want in the kitchen.'

'Thank you.'

As I move to the door, she touches my arm. I turn to her and our eyes meet.

'I don't even know your name,' she says.

I take her hand and put my lips to her ear. 'Rina.'

I go into the hall, try to call Bert to arrange a meet with George but get no answer. No one gets George's phone number, as he arranges everything through Bert. I decide to drive to his house and see if he's there. It's not quite kosher just to turn up there, but I need to tell him what I've got from Brindle and find out what he wants me to do. I'm just hoping he's not in some club or a spieler at the other end of Bermondsey and I can get sorted and back home before morning.

I drive to Lancaster Road, park the car and knock on George's door. Just when I'm thinking there's no one in, I hear shuffling steps and a tapping sound. Jacky Parr, the wizened old boy with the stick who let me in before, opens the door and gives me the once over. 'Are you a fucking treat, or what girl?'

'Hello Jacky. Is George in?'

'He's down the Elgin.'

'Been there long?'

'He's just gone.'

I turn and walk away. 'Cheers Jacky.'

'Aren't you going to stay and make an old man happy?' he calls after me.

I give him a wave as I get into the car.

I drive down Westbourne Park Road and park by the corner of Ladbroke Grove. It's near closing time and the public bar of the Elgin is packed. The piano player they used to have in here has given way to a juke box and Eric Burdon's putting his heart and soul into 'House of the Rising Sun'. I'm guessing George will be at one of the tables along the back wall and I push through the crowd until I see him. He's surrounded by the usual circle of blokes in dark suits trying to look like gangsters. I stand near the table until the man next to George, who I think is called Dave, sees me and says something to him. George clocks me, says something back and Dave gets up from the table and comes over to me. 'Grey Merc, by the Mangrove.'

He goes on past me to the bar and I make my way through the crowd into the street, walk up Westbourne Park Road to All Saints Road and see the car. I hear the pulsing bass notes of ska booming out of the Mangrove as I pass and I wish Lizzie was with me and we could go in there and get wrapped up in it and forget about these stupid men and their crazy battles. I walk past the Merc and wait in a doorway until I see George and Dave come round the corner. I join them as they get to the car and Dave unlocks it and opens one of the back doors for George. I get in the other side and Dave crosses the street and stands in the doorway of a pawn shop.

George takes his fedora off and puts it on the seat beside him. 'All right?'

'Not bad.'

'So?'

'He's got all of Viner's firm on earners and the Teales.'

'You're fucking joking.'

'Brindle offered them Dawn back if they'd go against you and they agreed.'

'If this is a wind up…'

'On my life.'

'You're telling me that Danny and Jack are in with that slag?'

'And their mother.'

'Jesus Christ!'

'It doesn't end there.'

'Go on.'

'Brindle had Dawn away from Danny before because he was beating her black and blue. He'd already been seeing her on the side and got her pregnant, although Danny thought it was his. Brindle's given her back to them in return for their going against you and getting a bite of the action once he's on top, like I said. When I found out she was back at the Teales I've gone in and got her away. One of them had whacked her about and given her a miscarriage.'

'Where is she now?'

'Somewhere safe.'

'I won't ask how you did it.'

George looks out of window. He's opening and closing his right fist and I can see a vein standing out on his temple. He turns to me with his eyes burning and I'm reminded why he's the most feared man on the manor.

'Hurt that bastard.'

'You want me to off him?'

'Do his legs and mark him.'

'You know I don't do that.'

'Maybe you should start.'

'You've got a few can handle that.'

'Like Jack Teale.'

'If you want me to do Brindle I will.'

'Maybe it's the best way.'

'I reckon.'

'It needs to be known he's been done.'

'It will be.'

'Go on then.'

'And I get Dad's money?'

'Yeah.'

'What about the Teales?'

'I'll handle them.'

He raises his hand to Dave across the street and he comes over and gets into the driving seat. I get out of the Merc and it glides away. I walk back past the throbbing bass and sneaky guitar licks, round the corner into Westbourne Park Road, avoiding an old drunk who's swaying along the pavement and snarling and cursing at the world around him.

I leave the Cortina in Hall Road and walk round the corner to the flats. As I'm approaching the glass door, the lift gate opens on the other side of the foyer and Dawn steps out, wearing my Givenchy coat and carrying my shoulder bag. My first thought is to confront her, but then I decide to follow her and try and find out what her game is. I back off to the side of the building and watch from round the corner as she opens the glass door, walks to the road and stands on the pavement. After a moment, she puts her arm out, a taxi stops and she gets in. I run into Hall Road, jump in the car and gun it round the corner onto Maida Vale. There's a cab moving off from the traffic lights ahead. I floor the throttle and just make it through the lights behind it. I can see Dawn's blond barnet through the back window as the cab goes under the streetlights of Edgware Road. It turns left into St John's Wood Road and then along the north side of Regent's Park to Camden Town. When we go up Camden Road I get a good idea where we're heading. Once past Holloway prison, where I spent a couple of months among the charming ladies some years ago, we're almost at Brindle's place.

The cab stops in Parkhurst Road and I pull into a parking space while Dawn gets out and pays the driver. As she walks into Brindle's street, I get out of the car, run to the corner and watch as she approaches the house. She takes a quick look in at the front window and knocks on the door. I can't see who opens it, but when she goes inside I head for the house, creep up the entry at the side, climb over the wall and get to the back window in time to see Dawn take my Smith & Wesson out of the shoulder bag and point it at Brindle's head. He says something to her, then he throws the glass he's holding at her, kicks the gun out of her hand, dives for her neck and she screams as she goes down under his weight. I smash the window with my elbow, scramble over the sill and grab the gun from where it's landed on the floor. As I straighten up with it, Brindle gets up, kicks me in the stomach and I drop the gun and double over. Dawn jumps on his back but he shakes her off, punches her on the jaw and she falls back against the wall. I reach out and pick up the gun but he rips it out of my hand, swings it at my head and it goes dark.

12

I'm lying on a hard floor. It's pitch dark, my wrists and ankles are tied and my head feels like it's been hit with a sledgehammer. I roll over and look around for any trace of light that might give me a clue as to what kind of place I'm in but there's nothing but darkness and silence. I strain against the ropes that bind my ankles, then the ones holding my wrists behind my back, but they're solid. I lie on my side for a while until the pain in my head eases, then I slowly roll over and over until I come up against a wall. When I shift round so I can get my hands to it, I can feel that it's metal and I reckon I'm most likely in the back of a van or a truck. I work my way along the wall and across the floor in search of a sharp edge to cut myself free, but find nothing but a couple of packing cases and some metal rods and poles.

I've almost drifted into sleep when there's a wrenching sound, a door swings open, light floods in and Brindle steps up onto the bed of the truck and stands over me. 'Well well. If it isn't Florence Nightingale.'

He takes out a knife and cuts the ropes binding my wrists and ankles, then he gets down off the truck and beckons me to follow him. I get to my feet and check that he's taken my gun and blade. When my eyes adjust to daylight I can see by the cranes and derricks towering all around, and the big warehouses, that I'm somewhere in the docks. The truck I was in is parked among the rest of the film vehicles that I last saw in Hoxton Square and there are men unloading equipment. Brindle takes my arm. 'Gentle walk to my trailer, like you're visiting the set again, and a nice cup of tea, or would you'd rather I put you back in the truck and cut your tits off?'

'Cup of tea, I reckon,' I say.

As we're walking, a bloke who I recognise as one of the electricians on the film approaches us. Brindle hands him a set of keys.

'Cheers Frank.'

'No worries. Your ears should have been burning last night.'

'How come?' says Brindle.

'Them American producers was in the bar singing your praises.'

'Yeah?' says Brindle.

'They reckon you're on your way.'

The electrician moves on and I can feel the glow of smug satisfaction coming off Brindle as we walk between two tall stacks of pallets to his trailer. When he opens the door there's a moment when I could lamp him, but there are people about and I reckon I need to know more, so I step inside and sit at the table like before. I'm wondering why Brindle hasn't followed me inside and I look out of the window and see him talking to Kirsty. He sticks his head round the door. 'You want a bacon roll?'

He's knocked me out, tied me up and locked me in a truck for the night and now he's offering me breakfast!

'I'm all right thanks,' I say.

He steps into the trailer, slides onto the seat opposite and fixes me with a cold stare. 'You're taking the piss, you are.'

'Where's Dawn?'

'Where you won't find her.'

I'm still holding his look of contempt when there's a knock at the door. Brindle tells the visitor to enter and Kirsty comes in. We exchange smiles as she puts two plastic cups and a paper bag on the table and leaves. Brindle takes a bacon roll out of the bag and bites into it. As soon as I smell the bacon I'm ravenous and wishing I'd had one. I sip my tea while Brindle chews. The silence is supposed to scare me but I've been more frightened by dogs than this nasty little git. He finally swallows the last bite, screws up the paper bag and chucks it on the floor.

'No one's ever going to find the bitch again if you don't do Preston, like you've agreed,' he says.

'I was just about to, until I found out you'd given her back to the Teales.'

'Like fuck you were.'

'Of course I was.'

'I know you've marked Preston's card.'

'Why would I do that when I know you've got a fucking army?'

'Either way, it's time to stop fucking about. You do him quick, or I finish Dawn.'

'How do I know you haven't finished her already?'

He swigs back his tea and stands. 'Come on.'

I follow him out of the trailer and across the dockyard to a tugboat moored at the quay and we get on board. He takes a set of keys out of his pocket, unlocks the wheelhouse, goes inside and opens a padlock on the door to the cabin. Dawn is lying on a bunk. She's turned away but her shoulders are moving slightly as she breathes. Brindle closes the cabin door and locks it.

'You've got two days,' he says.

'It's not that simple.'

'It'd better be, or she gets it.'

I watch his back as he minces off towards his trailer, greeting a couple of crew members on the way, like the big movie star, and I stifle the urge to follow him and put an end his film career right now. I look around me at the stacks of pallets and the rows of forklift trucks. I can see a ship's mast and funnel beyond them and I reckon the place will soon be starting up and the work of loading and unloading will begin.

My head's still throbbing as I walk towards the gate of the dockyard. I put my hand in my jacket pocket and I'm thankful when it closes round my car key. Brindle's had my other gun and I'll need to see Bert to get new ones. There's a small crowd outside the gate and a bloke with a clipboard who's picking men out for a day's work and sending them into the yard. I've no idea where I am when I get out onto the road but I keep walking and soon find myself in Wapping High Street. I check my jeans and find a ten bob note in my back pocket and the keys to the flat. I see a cab and flag it down.

On the way to Finsbury Park I try to decide what I'm going to do about this mess. Dawn was stupid to go after Brindle and I'm chafed with her for nicking my gun and my coat and running out on me. I understand the anger that made her do it, but she's landed herself back where she started, only this time she can't walk away from him. He'll move her from that boat and he could bang her up anywhere. If I kill him without finding her there's no guarantee she'll survive and I haven't got it in me to leave her to take her chances. I could go back and follow him when he leaves the film set but I've no tools and no money and he knows my car. As the cab pulls up beside the Cortina, I begin to get an idea.

It takes a while to drive to Maida Vale through the early morning traffic. When I finally get home, I find them digging up Hall Road and I have to drive round the block and leave the car in Hamilton Terrace. When I get to the flats Dennis is handing over to Keith for the day shift.

'Morning Miss,' he says.

He walks over to the lift and opens the gate for me.

'Cheers Dennis,' I say.

I get out at my floor and knock on Lizzie's door. Moments later she's there, looking soft and sleepy in a silvery silk dressing gown. I almost fall into her arms and she holds me for a moment and then takes me into her bedroom. I sit on the bed and she pours two drinks and gives me one. She sits down and puts her arm round me.

'You look knackered my darling.'

'It's been a bit of a night.'

'Work?'

'Not really, I got caught up in a bit of nonsense and got a slap.'

'Where are you hurt?'

I touch the back of my head where Brindle got me. Lizzie strokes her fingers over the bruise, then she kneels on the bed behind me and massages my shoulders and neck. As she works her fingers into me my head falls forward, and then she's putting me into bed and I'm drifting off.

• • •

I wake from a deep sleep and I can't think where I am. I feel panicky for a moment while I look round the room and then Lizzie opens the door and comes in. She's wearing a black jacket and pencil skirt with a white blouse, sheer stockings and black heels.

'You're looking the business,' I say.

'Signing the lease for the office today.'

'Office?'

'The Escort Agency. I told you.'

'It's all on then?'

'Looks like it. Gerald's really going at it. He's got the office sorted, I've lined up the girls and a photographer's taking their pictures for the brochure this afternoon.'

'Where's the office?'

'Ebury Street.'

'Belgravia?'

'Yeah.'

'There's posh.'

'That's how we want it. I've told him we should do it all on the quiet, by word of mouth, through porters at the gents' clubs and hotels and that, so we don't get any Sicilians wanting a slice if it goes well.'

'Keep it discreet.'

'That's the idea.'

She looks at her watch. 'I should go.'

She sits on the bed and gives me a kiss, 'How's the head?'

'Not bad.'

'You take care now.'

I watch her leave and wish she'd stay and get into bed. I doze for a while, then I get up, put on my clothes, let myself out of the flat and go across the hall to my place. The bed in Georgie's room is messed up and Dawn's left mine in a right state. The wardrobe's open, there are clothes on the floor, the drawers of my dressing table are pulled out and I can see she's been through the contents. I check the top of the wardrobe and find she's taken the few quid I keep in there, as well as the gun. In the bathroom, I'm relieved to see that the bath panels are in place and she hasn't found my real money. I pick up the phone in the hall and dial Bert's number. I let it ring and ring in case the old lush is asleep and eventually he picks up.

'Yeah, what?' His voice is thick and grumpy.

'I need to see you.'

'What time is it?'

'Gone one o'clock.'

'Walmer Castle. Half an hour.'

I put the phone down, go into the bathroom, unscrew the panel on the side of the bath, take out a bundle of fivers and a blade. I turn on the bath and while it's running I tidy the bedroom, put my clothes back in the wardrobe, along with the blade, and straighten up my dressing table. I have a quick dip to wash away the memory of the bed of that truck and put on fresh jeans and my leather jacket. I give my hair a quick brush, put on a lick of make-up, stuff the wad in my inside pocket and head for the car.

I drive to Notting Hill, park in Artesian Road and walk round the corner to the Walmer Castle. As I'm about to go in, Bert's white Jaguar pulls up on the other side of the road. When he sees me, I signal to him to stay in the car and cross over. He opens the passenger door and I get in.

'I need a shooter,' I say.

'All right.'

'Two, in fact.'

'You joining the rodeo?'

'I wish I was.'

'Smith & Wesson again?'

'May as well.'

'I've got a couple of nice Berettas.'

'I don't do automatics.'

'You don't like picking up the casings.'

'I don't like the Old Bill picking them up. Any other revolvers?'

'Only a Colt Python.'

'Too big. I'll have the Smiths.'

'I've got a .38 and a .44.'

'Are they at the yard?'

'Yeah.'

'Ammo?'

'For both.'

'How much?'

'Three hundred for the two.'

'All right.'

'Have you got the notes with you?'

'Yeah.'

'Let's go.'

Bert starts the engine and eases the Jag away. I put the radio on and settle back into the soft leather and I have to put up with Frank Ifield yodelling his way through 'I Remember You' because Bert likes it. When we get to the end of Ledbury Road, he turns right into Westbourne Park Road and pulls up outside the coal yard opposite the El Rio. He tells me to wait, gets out of the car, goes into the yard and I see him go round the back of the shed, which is just inside the gate. A truck is being loaded in the yard and the driver's leaning against the cab having a fag. The digger scoops up a load of coal from the pile and dumps it in the back, the bucket swings away and the digger's engine dies. The driver climbs into the cab, starts up and drives the truck up the slope to the gate. The engine roars while he holds it on the clutch until a bus passes and he's able to pull his load onto the road. I look across at the El Rio. There's a black bloke in a zoot suit, with the long jacket and baggy trousers, standing outside. He's holding a tambourine and tapping it against his leg. He sees me looking at him and comes loping over the road to the car. He leans down to my window and gives me a broad smile. 'Hey honey. You looking for a taste?'

I smile back at him and shake my head just as Bert comes out of the yard carrying two plastic bags. Tambourine man takes one look at him, skips back over the road and goes into the El Rio. Bert gets into the car. 'What did he want?'

'Just selling,' I say.

Bert hands the bags to me. 'Fifty rounds for each.'

I take the .38 out, hold it under the dashboard, break it and spin the chamber. I close it again and check the safety catch, then I do the same with the .44. Both guns are good, so I put them back in the bags.

'Cheers Bert.'

'Fancy a swift one?'

'I ought to get moving.'

He starts the car and does a right turn into Chepstow Road.

'You anywhere near Brindle?' he asks.

'Getting there.'

'George wants it done.'

'Don't we all?'

The car pulls up next to mine. Bert turns to me and puts a hand on my arm.

'Be careful on this one, eh?'

I give him a nod and a smile and we get out of the car. Bert goes round the corner to the Walmer and I drive home.

It's dark by the time I've hidden the .44 under the loose

floorboard in the kitchen, loaded the .38, pocketed my lock picks and a blade and set off for Wapping. I make good time through the City, leave the car a couple of streets away from the film location and walk to the dockyard. As I approach the gate I see one of the film trucks pulling out and driving away. As I quicken my pace two more trucks appear, followed by a Land Rover towing a caravan. The security man, who I saw when I first went to the set in Hoxton, is standing in the road and waving the vehicles out from the gate. I keep my distance in case Brindle's about to make an exit. When there's a lull in the traffic and the security man goes and stands beside the gate, I cross the road and approach him.

'Is Johnny still around?' I ask.

'You've just missed him love.'

'On his way to the new location?'

He nods and waves a car through the gate. I can see Ed the assistant in the back seat. He's reading some file and he doesn't look up as the car passes.

'He did tell me, but I can't remember which one's next,' I say.

'Birmingham.'

'Of course it is, yeah.'

I walk away from the security man until I'm out of sight, then I run to the car. I drive back to the gate in time to see what looks like the truck I was banged up in being waved out on to the road. When it pulls out, I see the bloke Brindle got the keys from at the wheel. The security man stops the one coming after it and waves me through. I get in behind it and hope I've got enough petrol to get me to Birmingham.

13

I have a job keeping up with the truck as we make our way through Holloway and East Finchley and I have to jump a few lights to stay with him. When we get to Watford and on to the M1 he settles into a steady fifty miles an hour in the inside lane and I'm able to relax a bit. There's no speed limit on the motorway and after a while I'm tempted to get in the fast lane and see what the Cortina can do, but that way I'd lose Brindle and never know if my plan would have worked.

After an hour or so I follow the truck onto the M45 to Coventry and then the motorway ends and I haven't a clue if we're going to Birmingham or Bombay as we drag through endless suburbs and then along roads with factories and warehouses and into a poor area with dirty streets, small terraced houses and a bad smell of gas. The truck makes a couple of turns off the main road and slows down. I get the feeling we're at the end of the journey so I stay well back. The truck stops and I pull in behind a van, look out of the side window and see a massive gas holder silhouetted in the moonlight.

The door of the truck opens, the driver's mate gets out and walks across the street to a pair of iron gates that look like the entrance to the gasworks. He goes up close to the bars and says something to a man who's slumped on a chair inside the gate. The man jerks upright, gets to his feet, unlocks the gates and swings them open. As the truck drives through the gates I can make out the vans and trailers of the film unit in the headlights. Once the truck's parked and the driver and his mate have come out of the gate and gone into a pub on the corner of the street, I start the car, drive past the gates and a sign that says Saltley Gas Works.

My throat's parched and I could murder a drink but the local pubs could be playing host to members of the unit and I don't want to be noticed. The area I'm driving through is nothing but mean streets and small factories and I'm wondering how I can find a decent hotel when I see a phone box and stop. I dial Lizzie's number and after a few rings she picks up.

'I'm in Birmingham,' I say.

'What are you doing there?'

'Don't ask. I need somewhere to stay. Do you know a decent hotel?'

'I did a punter there a while back in a good one that was near the station.'

'Can you remember what it was called?'

'Hang on, I'll have a look in my diary.'

I hear her put the receiver down and while I'm waiting I notice a man standing outside the phone box, wearing an old mac and a cloth cap. He's holding a bottle, swaying a bit, and grinning at me.

'It's the Grand Hotel, in Colmore Row,' says Lizzie.

'Thanks.'

'There's a good club there as well, if you're going out.'

'Yeah?'

'It's called the Elbow Room. I saw George Best there.'

'Sounds good.'

'When are you back?'

'Couple of days I reckon.'

'Take care, darling.'

'You too.'

We make kissing noises and I put the receiver down. As I open the door of the phone box the man in the cloth cap lurches towards me and tries to grab my tits. I shove him off me and give him a kick in the knee. He drops the bottle, it smashes on the pavement and he falls over and rolls into the gutter. I get into the car and leave him whimpering.

I drive until I see a pub and stop and ask directions to Colmore Row. The landlord's just closing up, but a bloke who's leaving tells me it's in the centre of town and points me in the right direction. I get well lost on the way but I ask again and finally find Colmore Row. The Grand Hotel is on a corner at the end of an elegant terrace of fine white buildings. It looks a bit posh and pricey but money's no problem at the moment and I feel like a bit of luxury. I park in a side street off the main drag and walk along the side of the building to the main entrance, wishing I'd brought a toothbrush. The clerk looks up from behind the reception desk and smiles politely as I approach and ask for a single room. He says he's got one available and I give him a false name and address and ask if room service is still going. He tells me it closes at midnight and I look at the clock behind him and see that I've got half an hour. He asks me about luggage and I tell him it'll be arriving tomorrow. He gives me the key to a room on the fourth floor and I ask him to send up a bottle of whisky.

I make for the lift on the other side of the lobby and as I pass the entrance to the bar I hear a familiar voice and then laughter. I linger beside the door and look inside. Ed, the assistant director, is at a table on the far side of the bar with the cameraman, Jean the continuity girl and Mike the director. Ed's telling a story of some hilarious episode and the others are laughing and chipping in. I take a detour to the lift so they don't see me.

Soft music plays as I'm wafted up to the fourth floor and I walk along the carpeted corridor to my room. There's a double bed with the covers turned down that looks really inviting, an armchair and a dressing table with a TV set on it. The velvet curtains are closed and I'm delighted to find I've got my own bathroom. There's a knock at the door and a young bloke in a busboy's uniform comes in and puts a tray with a bottle of Bell's whisky and a glass on the dressing table. I sign the bill, remembering to use the false name I gave at the desk, tip him two bob and he thanks me and leaves. I pour myself a drink, look at the room service menu, pick up the phone and order a hamburger, then I turn on the TV and sit in the armchair. All I get is the weather forecast and then the BBC closes down for the night and leaves me with the National Anthem and the test card. I switch to ITV but that's over too, so I turn on the radio and the vicar doing The Epilogue tells me that the Lord is going to "preserve my going out and my coming in", which I reckon is nice of him. I twiddle the knob, find Radio Caroline and Dusty Springfield sings that she only wants to be with me, which is much more like it.

As I'm pouring my next whisky there's a knock at the door. I turn off the radio and ask who it is. I'm told it's room service and I open the door to a quietly beautiful young girl, in a uniform and apron, holding a tray with a silver dome on it. She comes in and puts the tray down next to the TV. She turns, gives me a warm smile, takes a pad and a biro out of her apron pocket and offers them to me. I sign the bill, pick up my jacket off the bed, find a ten bob note in the pocket and give it to her. She looks surprised and then pleased. 'I haven't got any change.'

'It's OK,' I say.

'That's really kind. Thanks.'

She puts the note in her pocket and seems to hesitate. 'Will you be staying long?'

'Only a couple of days.'

We share a look for a moment longer and I'm tempted to ask her what time she finishes, but I remind myself that I'm here on business and go to the door and open it for her. As she walks down the corridor, she senses me watching, turns and gives me a fleeting smile.

I drain my whisky glass, lift the silver dome and set about my hamburger.

• • •

The bed was as comfortable as it looked and when I turn over and reach for my watch on the bedside table I see that it's nearly nine o'clock. I roll out of bed, go into the bathroom, have a long hot shower and shampoo my hair. I discover a little tube of toothpaste and a brush in the cabinet above the wash basin and make full use of them, before drying my hair. I give the bra and pants that I washed in the basin last night a final whoosh with the hairdryer and get dressed. I order breakfast from room service with the faint hope that I might see the lovely girl again, but it turns out to be a young lad with a cheeky smile who arrives with a tray of scrambled egg and toast.

I try to decide what time I should go to the set to find Brindle. I need to catch him when he's finished filming for the day and I need to know when that's going to be. I remember seeing Jean in the bar with the others last night and I realise that I know her second name because it was written on the folder she showed me that day. It's a long shot that she'll be here, but I pick up the phone and call reception. A woman answers and I ask for Jean Craven. There's a pause while she looks the name up and connects me but after a couple of rings Jean answers. She remembers me and I tell her that I've got something I want to give to Brindle and ask if he'll be filming in the afternoon. She tells me that they are not working today as they moved up from London last night but they are doing a night shoot at the gasworks later and that he's in the first scene and should be finished by about midnight. I thank her and ask her not to say anything to him, as it's a surprise.

I go down to reception and ask for a street guide of the city and a local paper. I'm given the Birmingham

Post and an A to Z street map which I take back to the room. I make a cup of coffee and settle down in the comfy armchair. I find Colmore Row and the hotel on the map, then Saltley Gasworks and plot the best route to get there. I've got hours to kill before I go to the set and I'm wishing I'd brought *Rebecca* to read. Maybe I'll go out and buy another copy when I've had coffee.

I look at the newspaper and read that there are local elections on the way and there's a picture of the MP for Wolverhampton on the inside page and some quotes from a speech he's made about the dangers of immigrants outnumbering English people in Handsworth and other places. He looks like a right miserable sod, with a ratty grey moustache and a mean look in his eyes. I turn the pages and notice a story about an accident in a factory called Aston Chain and Hook and there's a picture of the inside of the place which looks as if it might be right for what I've got in mind. There's a Birmingham phone directory on a shelf beside the bed. I look up Aston Chain and Hook and find that it's in Bromford Lane, which I see from the A to Z runs off Tyburn Road, a bit north of the city, and it's only a short drive from the gasworks.

I put on my leather jacket, take the lift to the ground floor and walk along the street to my car. Once I've studied the route on the map, I set off round the one-way system. As I leave the city centre and drive along Aston Road, I pass a dilapidated building that looks like a warehouse, with a faded sign that says Aston Chain and Hook, on the right hand side of the road. It's nowhere near the address

I found for the factory but I decide to stop and have a look. I pull over, get out of the car and cross the road. The building looks deserted, so I walk along a passageway that runs down the side of it, go round to the back and find a set of double doors that are padlocked. I check that I can't be seen, take out my picks, do the lock and ease the door open. I put my ear to the gap and when I hear nothing I slip inside and close the door behind me. There's a mess of old packing cases, piles of rusty metal, a counter at the far end and filing cabinets with the drawers hanging open. When I look up and clock the solid metal beams above, I know I've seen enough, so I get out of there and lock the door. On the way back to the hotel, I buy a length of rope, a pencil torch, a roll of gaffer tape and a copy of *Rebecca*. When I get to my room, I run a bath, pour myself a whisky, slide into the warm water and get back to Manderley.

By the time snobby, skull-faced Mrs Danvers has finished showing her disdain and dislike for our newly married girl and her humble origins, told her how beautiful and talented and accomplished the first Mrs de Winter was and generally made her feel small and unworthy of the position she's married into, it's time for me to get moving. I can't help reading a bit more and I'm glad to find that hubby Maxim is being good to her, Frith the butler seems a friendly sort and she's enjoying the beauty of the great house and grounds.

I close the book, load the .38, put the safety on and slide it in behind my belt. I take the coil of rope I bought earlier, cut about ten feet off it, with the blade I brought

with me, and put it inside my jacket. I put the torch and
my lock picks in my pocket and the rest of the rope back
in the bag with the gaffer tape. I check the route to the
gasworks on the map, pick up the bag and leave.

14

I park the car in a dead end street near the gasworks and walk to the gate. The security man lets me in and tells me they're shooting round the far side of the gas holder. The trailers are parked in a row beside a long shed near the fence. I approach Brindle's, look round to make sure there's no one about and knock on the door.

'Hang on,' he shouts from inside.

Moments later he opens the door. 'What are you doing here?'

'I've got something you might want to see.'

'Is it done?'

'Yeah.'

'So why haven't I heard?'

'No one knows yet.'

'Why should I believe you?'

'Because he's in the boot of my car.'

'You got George Preston into the boot of a car?'

'I didn't say he was in one piece.'

'What the fuck did you bring him up here for?'

'To show you it's done and so you can help me get rid.'

I turn and walk towards the gate and Brindle follows me. He nods to the security man and we go along the street towards my car. As we get near and I can see there's no one about, I hand him the keys. 'Help yourself.'

He bends to unlock the boot and fumbles with the key

for a moment before getting it into the lock. When the lid opens, I take out my gun and smash the butt down on the back of his head. He falls forward, I grab hold of his ankles and stuff him head first into the boot. I have another look round to make sure I haven't been seen, then I get the rope from my pocket and tie his hands behind his back. I turn him over, take the gaffer tape out of the bag, tear a strip off and stick it across his mouth, then I shut the boot lid and lock it.

The journey to Aston Chain and Hook takes about ten minutes and I don't hear any thumping or bumping from behind on the way. I drive the car onto the pavement, back up close to the passageway beside the building and open up the boot. He's still out cold, so I take out the bag with the rope and the tape and tie it to my belt. After I've checked for sightseers I lift Brindle out onto the pavement. I put one end of the rope that's binding his wrists over my shoulder, drag him along the passageway and leave him by the back door, while I go back to the car and park it properly. When I get back to Brindle, he's moaning and twitching a bit so I give him another whack on the head with the gun and put him out again. I take out my picks, do the lock, pull the door open, drag Brindle inside and lock up again.

There's enough light from the street coming through the front windows for me to make out the piles of metal and old packing cases that are lying about. I leave Brindle by the door and drag a filing cabinet that's lying on its side into the middle of floor, until it's directly underneath one of the metal beams, and stand it up. I find a couple of empty packing cases of different sizes, put them next to the filing cabinet and climb on top of it. When I stand up, the metal beam is about three feet above my head.

I go to where I've left Brindle and take the coil of rope out of the bag. I make a noose at one end with a slip knot, put it round his neck and pull it tight. I take him by the shoulders, drag him to the packing cases and manage to lift him up and sit him on the smaller one, then I bend low, pick him up in a fireman's lift, climb up the packing cases and lay him on his back on top of the cabinet. I get up beside him, grab him by the collar, sit him up and throw the end of the rope that's round his neck up and over the beam. I catch the end and pull it tight enough to hold him sitting upright. I keep hold of the end of the rope and climb down off the cabinet just as he opens his eyes. He looks wildly around him, tries to turn his head, feels the noose round his neck and screams into his gag. He twists his body about as if to shake it off and then he sees me below him and becomes still. I show him the rope in my hand and give it a tug, which pulls his neck. He looks up, sees the rope over the beam above him and gets the message.

'I'm going to take that tape off you and you're going to tell me where Dawn is,' I say.

He nods his head as much as he can and makes a sound like a pig in labour. I tie the rope off on one of the drawer handles, climb up to him and rip the tape off his gob. He gives a gasp of pain, takes a couple of deep breaths and looks at me with pure hatred in his eyes.

'Well?' I say.

'You fucking slag.'

I pull on the rope and his head jerks forward.

'All right!' he squawks.

'Yeah?'

'Lozells.'

'What?'

'She's in fucking Lozells!'

I remember seeing it on the map now, and thinking it was an odd name.

'Where in fucking Lozells?'

'Burbury Street.'

'Number?'

'Forty-nine.'

'What's there?'

'Fran.'

'What?'

'My Auntie Fran.'

For a moment, I'm looking down at the little boy from the orphanage who's desperately lonely and just trying to get noticed by the world and I almost feel sorry for him, then I think what he's done to Dawn and what he'd do to me if he had the chance. I turn his face to mine, reach behind his head and tighten the rope. His eyes bulge and he goes a deeper red.

'If she's there and she's all right, I'll be back to get you. If she isn't, I won't.'

I let the rope go, put the tape back over his mouth,

make sure his wrists are tied tight and climb down onto the floor. Once I've checked that he can't move without hanging himself, I open the door, let myself out and lock it behind me.

Burbury Street in Lozells is mostly small terraced houses, with a couple of factory yards and a pub called the Queens Head on the corner, where I leave the car. There are no lights on at number forty-nine as I walk past and I can't see a way of getting round the back, so I decide to take a chance. I put my hand on my gun and knock on the door. There's no answer, so I wait a bit and try again. Eventually a light goes on and I hear a woman's voice. 'Who is it?'

I bend down and open the letter box. 'Fran?'

'Who is it?'

'I've come from Johnny,' I say.

I see a pair of mules approaching and I shut the letter box. The door's opened by a little old woman with a round face and a frizz of grey hair.

'Who are you?' she asks.

'I'm Noreen. I'm sorry to get you up but it's Johnny. He's down the Elbow Room and he's asked me to come and get Dawn and take her to join him there.'

She sighs and puts a hand on her hip. 'That boy'll be the death of me, he will.'

'Only I don't like to say no to him,' I say, trying to look a bit pathetic.

'I know love. Come on in.'

She ushers me into the hall. As soon as I'm inside

she slams the door behind me and locks it. 'Gerry!' she shouts.

A door opens on the landing and a big bare chested man appears and lumbers down the stairs. I take out my gun, grab hold of Auntie Fran, put my back to the front door, pull her to me and hold the gun to her head. The man stops at the foot of the stairs.

'Get Dawn or I shoot,' I say.

He stares at me and doesn't move. I put the muzzle up against Fran's temple and pull back the hammer. She starts to tremble.

'Go on Gerry,' she says.

'Where's the key?' he asks.

'Kitchen table.'

Gerry gives me an evil look, goes to the back of the hall and opens a door. I keep a firm grip on Auntie Fran.

'He told me all about you,' she says.

'Oh yeah?'

'I said he was mad to trust you.'

'You got it right then.'

'He'll have you for this, you fucking slag.'

The door at the back opens and Dawn appears in a pair of skimpy pyjamas. Gerry pushes her forward and stands behind her. Her face is bruised and she looks shocked, as if she can't quite make out what's in front of her.

'Put a coat on Dawn. You're coming with me,' I say.

She takes a breath, her eyes clear and she recognises me. I point at the coats on the hall stand and she takes one off its peg and puts it on. I move away from the door, gently push Fran towards Gerry and point the gun at the pair of them.

'Open the door and walk to the right,' I say to Dawn.

She does as I tell her and I back out after her and along the street with the gun aimed at the door of the house. I put Dawn in the car, get behind the wheel and fire up the engine. As we move away I look in the mirror. Gerry comes out of the house and I switch the lights off so he can't get the number plate.

'What are you doing?' says Dawn.

'I've got Johnny where he can't hurt you and I'm getting you away.'

'Where to?'

'I'm not sure yet.'

'After what I did?'

'Don't worry about it.'

'I stole from you.'

'It's OK. I just want you safe.'

She looks away and out of the window and I can tell she's crying. I reach over and take her hand.

'How you can be so kind to me?' she says.

'I know what you've been through.'

'I woke up at your flat and you weren't there, and it hit me that my baby was dead, and I was so angry at him for what he's done to me and all I wanted to do was get hold of him and tell him what a bastard he'd been, and I looked in your wardrobe for something to wear and I found the gun and I decided to kill him.'

'I don't blame you.'

'I'm really sorry I stole from you and got you into even more bother.'

'It's all right.'

I feel her relaxing and I concentrate on trying to find the way to the hotel. I get back to Aston Road, turn right and drive into town. I see some familiar landmarks, make a couple more turns and get to a station called Snow Hill that I recognise from earlier. I turn into Colmore Row and park in front of the hotel.

The night receptionist looks a bit confused when I tell him Dawn's sharing my room, but after I give him a quid for his trouble he alters my booking in the register, we get into the lift and climb to the fourth floor. We enter the room and I lock the door.

'All safe now,' I say.

'I don't know how to thank you.'

'Just stay away from bad men.'

'I intend to.'

I pick up the whisky bottle. 'Drink?'

'I'd love one.'

'Why don't you hop into bed and I'll bring it to you.'

'Lovely.' She takes her coat off, puts it on a chair and gets between the sheets while I pour her a whisky and one for myself. I sit on the bed and hand her the glass.

'What was Auntie Fran like?' I ask.

'She tried to come on all mumsy and nice while she locked me in that back room – "Just for your protection my darling". She's all over Johnny like he's her little baby boy and now he's going to be a film star she's fancying herself on the red carpet with him at the Oscars.'

'Gerry?'

'Never said a word.'

'Did he try anything?'

'No. He's probably too scared of Johnny.'

She finishes her drink, lies back and stretches. 'It's lovely here isn't it?'

'It's a nice hotel.'

'Are you getting into bed?'

'I need to go out for a bit.'

'Must you?'

'There's something I need to see to.'

'Will you be long?'

'I shouldn't be. You go off to sleep and I'll see you later.'

'All right.'

I put on my jacket and go to the door. 'I'm going to lock you in, just in case. Is that all right?

'I'm used to it,' she says, with a smile.

• • •

The roads are almost deserted apart from a few cars and vans and a couple of dustcarts. It's just getting light as I park in the side street off the main road. I walk to the Aston Chain and Hook building and along the passageway to the side. I'm excited by what I'm about to do and my hands are trembling as I take out my lock picks, but when I bend down to the keyhole, I find the door's unlocked. I get a firm grip on my gun and go in.

The filing cabinet's on its side, the rope is lying on top of it and Brindle's gone. Some night watchman or security bloke must have found him on his rounds and I kick myself for choosing a warehouse. As I walk forward I hear a rustling sound in the far corner. I bolt out of the door, run to the main road and along towards the car. There are footsteps behind me and I glance round to see Brindle coming after me. I turn into the side street and stop. As he comes round the corner I trip him up and he falls onto the pavement. He gets to his knees and I swing a kick at his head which puts him on his back. I'd like to shoot him now, but even though there's no one watching, there could be after a gunshot. I make a dash for the car and turn it round. As I move off he starts to get up and I'm tempted to drive onto the pavement and smash into him, but I can't be sure of killing him that way and I can see someone walking along the other side of the main road.

15

I drive down Aston Road with an eye on the mirror to make sure he didn't have anyone watching the place, who might be following me. I turn off the main road and look for a car to swap for the Cortina. Brindle's going to be hot to get me now and I need to be wide awake. Not only him, but Gerry and Auntie Fran have got my number and seen the car. I reckon he'll be expecting me to take Dawn and go back to London, which is why I'm going to stay here and try to do him on his home turf.

I turn up a side street, looking for an inconspicuous motor and spot a grey Hillman Minx that's seen better days and looks boring enough. I park the Cortina, give it a wipe over for prints and wait for a bit to make sure there's no one around. When I reckon the coast is clear, I take the wallet with my lock picks out of my pocket, walk along to the Hillman and kneel down beside the driver's door. I've never done a Hillman before but most car locks have three wafers to turn and I'm hoping this one does, as that's the only rake I've got with me. I take the tension tool out of the wallet and work it into the lock. I slide the rake in beside it, feel for the wafers and find I'm in luck when the lock turns. I open the door and have a look for the ignition wiring. I have to use my knife to prise off a panel under the dash to get at the wires, but when I twist the reds together and touch the browns, the engine starts first time.

I drive until I see a phone box and look up car breakers in the directory, but I can't find any. As I'm opening the door, an old bloke in overalls walks past and I ask him if there's a yard anywhere about. He says there's one in Bracebridge Street and tells me how to get there. He seems like a nice old chap so I thank him and offer him a lift, but he says he's going in the opposite direction and toddles off on his way.

It's just gone eight o'clock when I turn into Bracebridge Street and find the yard. The gate is shut but I can see a tall thin type on the other side of it walking towards a shed, carrying a kettle. I jump out of the car, call to him and he comes to the gate and gives me the once over and a leery smile.

'What can I do for you, young lady?' he says, in a broad Brummie accent.

'I want a set of plates,' I say.

'Do you now?'

'Old ones.'

'If I were to give you them, I'd be breaking the law.'

'A tenner do it?'

'I dare say so.'

He opens the gate, I follow him to the shed and he puts the kettle on a gas ring, strikes a match and lights it. He opens a cupboard on the far wall, takes a pile of number plates off the bottom shelf and puts them on the desk.

'Take your pick,' he says.

'Are these all dead?' I ask.

'And buried.'

I look through the plates. The number on the Hillman is KON 297 and I want something similar so it's the same sort of age. I find LRB 934, take two fivers off my roll and put them on the desk. The kettle whistles and our man takes a teapot and a packet of Typhoo off the shelf. 'Cup of tea?'

I could murder a cup but I need to get moving. 'No thanks,' I say.

'Suit yourself.'

He picks up the notes and slips them in his pocket. I put the plates under my arm.

'Cheers,' I say.

'Sure you won't have a cup?'

'I've got to go,' I say, as I move to the door.

'Bye love,' he says.

I drive round a few corners until I find a deserted street of terraced houses that are half way through being demolished and pull over. I take the needle-nose pliers out of my pick wallet and change the number plates. I bury the old ones in a pile of rubble on a demolition site and set off for the hotel.

Breakfast's happening in the dining room when I get there and I wait at the front door and check there are no film people about before crossing the foyer to the lift. When I get to the room I open the door quietly and see that Dawn is sleeping. She's lying on her back in the middle of the bed with her blonde hair fanned out on the pillow. Her breathing is slow and regular and she looks perfectly at peace. I sit on the bed and feel grateful that she's here and away from the monsters. As I look at her, so still and calm, I suddenly feel very tired and I know I've got to sleep. I go to the door, put the 'Do not disturb' sign out, take off my clothes and put the gun and blade on a shelf in the wardrobe. When I get in beside Dawn she opens her eyes and she's far away for a moment before she recognises me. 'Mmm… you're here,' she mumbles as she snuggles up to me. I put my arm round her, gently rub her back and feel her sliding back to sleep, as I close my eyes.

I'm running down a street. The houses on each side of me are being smashed to pieces by huge cranes and wrecking balls and people are escaping through doors and windows, as the houses collapse around them, and fleeing down the street. Auntie Fran comes out of a house wielding a huge number plate and she's bashing me over the head with it and I go down and people are trampling over me and I grab her ankle as she runs away and then she's lying next to me on the pavement and shouting in my face and I can't hear her above the noise and it's getting louder and louder. A phone box crashes down on the pavement and the door flies open…

I wake with a jolt and sit up. The phone by the bed is ringing but it stops as I reach for it. I look round for Dawn and feel like I've landed back on earth when I see her sitting in the armchair, holding a cup and saucer.

'Afternoon,' she says, as she gets up and switches on the kettle.

'What time is it?' I ask.

'Just gone two.'

I feel panicked for a moment as last night comes back to me and but then I realise that I just have to do two things, get Dawn away from here and kill Johnny Brindle.

'Sugar?'

'Just milk.'

She brings the coffee to me and sits on the bed. 'You were dreaming.'

'I often do.'

'I've given you nightmares.'

I laugh and sip hot coffee.

'It's not just you, believe me.'

'What are you going to do about Johnny?'

'I'll think of something.'

'He's an evil bastard. If he catches hold of you...'

'I'll be all right.'

'If there's anything I can do.'

'You'll be the first to know,' I say, as I drain the coffee cup and pull back the bedclothes. 'The sooner you get out of here the better, so let's find you something to wear and get you on a train.'

'Aren't you coming too?'

'I've got a couple of things to do here,' I say as I head for the bathroom. I'm sure she'll have an idea that there's bad stuff on the way, but after what she's been through I reckon she'll have the sense to stay out of it and let it happen. I have a shower and get dressed. When I put on my bra and pants I remind myself to buy some fresh underwear when I'm shopping for Dawn. I put on my jeans, shirt and leather jacket, with the gun in my belt and the blade in my boot.

I ask her if she wants a shower but she says she's had a wash. I'm not sure we can get away with her wearing pyjamas when we go out but when she rolls the trousers up to her knees and puts her coat on she looks OK. I find a pair of hotel slippers in the wardrobe for her bare feet and we take the lift downstairs. I ask the receptionist where we should go to buy women's clothes and she suggests a shop called Rackhams in Corporation Street. There's a cab for hire waiting outside so we jump in and I tell the driver to take us there. I sit low in the seat with my head turned away from the window on the way and tell Dawn to do the same.

Rackhams is a nice looking store that sells everything, so we go straight to the shoe department and buy Dawn a pair of suede slip-ons, then it's up the escalator to Ladies Fashions for a dark grey trouser suit by Cresta, that doesn't break the bank, and I get myself a slinky lurex mini dress in a metallic grey. Dawn's all over me with gratitude and it's good to see her happy in her new threads as I drag her to the underwear department and get myself an Emilio Pucci bra and three pairs of pants. I take her to the café on the top floor and leave her with coffee and toast while I go to the menswear floor and buy a belted raincoat and a tweed cap.

I go and collect Dawn and we go down to the ground floor, where I pick up a hairbrush, a few bits of make-up and some kirby grips, and we score a couple of blasts of free perfume from the testers on the counter on the way out. I hail a cab on Corporation Street and it takes us round the block to Snow Hill Station. I pay the driver while Dawn has a look round for familiar faces. When she gives me a nod we get out of the cab and go into the station. The ticket office is round to the right and we join a short queue.

'Is there somewhere you can go which is out of the way of the Teales?' I ask.

'I don't know. Like I said before, Marlene knows most of my mates, but I'll think of something.'

'Outside London?'

'I don't know anyone.'

'What about your parents?'

'My dad's dead and my mum's in a home in Barking.'

I can't give her the key to my flat after what she did before and I can't ask Lizzie to take her in, for the same reason. She'd be too close to the Teales with us anyway. She sees me looking concerned.

'It's OK, I'll find a squat. Highgate or somewhere.'

'Will you be all right?'

'I'll be fine.'

She looks into my eyes and I feel that strength and purpose in her that I saw when I first tried to get her away from the house in Leighton Buzzard.

'You've done enough for me, and I love you for it, but I can take it from here.'

She's still got me with her eyes and for a moment all I want to do is get on the train with her, but then the ticket man is tapping on the window. I ask him when the next train to London leaves. He says there's one to King's Cross from platform 6 in ten minutes and I buy Dawn a single ticket.

We say goodbye outside the office. I watch her striding towards the platform and I reckon she probably can take it from here.

It's not far along Colmore Row to the hotel and I decide to risk walking it. When I get there, I go up to the room, put my hair up and hold it in place with the kirby grips. I put on the tweed cap and the raincoat, put the collar up and turn to the full length mirror. The jeans are a bit odd, but apart from that I'm satisfied that I don't look like me. I check my gun's loaded, put *Rebecca* in my pocket, go downstairs and try to remember where I left the Hillman.

I drive to Saltley and park where I can see the entrance to the gasworks and film people going about among the trucks and vans inside. I can just see the back of Brindle's trailer and the light on inside tells me he's here. I reckon he's got some bottle, turning up for work after the bashing he took last night. I keep an eye on the gate for a bit, but I don't recognise anyone from the unit among the few people who are coming and going, so I take out *Rebecca*, put it on the steering wheel and read about our girl being so overwhelmed by Manderley and the formality of it, and thinking that the servants are laughing at her and feeling out of place and unworthy of the grandeur of it all and not being as good as the famous Rebecca, Maxim's first wife. Then her sister-in-law visits and she's nice to her and tells her to stand up for herself and buy herself some new clothes and then she goes for a lovely walk with Maxim and she's feeling better until they get to a beach and he gets all tearful and buggers off and leaves her to find the dog that's run away.

Just as I'm finding out that this is where Rebecca drowned, I look up and see a black Ford Zodiac approach the gasworks and stop near the gate. Gerry's at the wheel and there are three men in the back. I pull my cap down and back the car further away from the gate to where I can still see them. It's getting dark now and people from the unit are leaving in ones and twos. Brindle comes through the gate by himself and a big bloke in a dark suit gets out of the Zodiac and opens the front door of the car for him. Brindle gets in and the bloke closes the door and gets in the back. As they drive past me I see Brindle turning to the back seat and saying something which gets a laugh from the others.

I turn the car round and follow them at a distance as they go towards the centre of town. I almost lose them a couple of times but manage to stay with them. We go past the Town Hall which is a big building with pillars across the front that looks more like a Roman temple than a council building. I catch sight of a poster that says Dizzy Gillespie is playing there, and I'm glad I'm not going. The Zodiac turns off, goes down a hill and pulls up outside a shop called Chetwyns, that has Mod suits in bright colours and short Crombie coats in the window. Brindle and the lads get out of the car and he's rather dwarfed by Gerry and the other three as they walk past the shop five abreast and looking dangerous.

I drive past in time to see them turn a corner and go into a doorway. I leave the car and walk back, just as a couple of girls in flared skirts and halter tops get out of a taxi and go to the same door, where a bouncer checks them out and then lets them in. I put my hands in my raincoat pocket and go back to the car, wondering if I'm wasting my time trying to do Brindle on his own manor, where he's obviously well protected and where I'm known to him and a few others. My only chance would be to pick him off in the street, which is about as dangerous as it gets, and where there's no chance of getting rid of the body, which is the vital part of a sound hit.

I start the engine and drive back to the hotel. As I go through the front door and walk past the bar, I see Mike, Ed and Jean sitting together. They've got their backs to the door so I go straight to the lift and call it. As I climb to my floor it occurs to me that Brindle was on his own when he left the gasworks location and that he never had anyone with him when he was filming in Hoxton either. By the time I get to the room, I've decided how I'm going to get to him.

16

I pick up the phone, dial reception and ask to be put through to the bar. While I'm waiting to be connected I realise that I don't know Mike's surname so when the barman answers I ask for Jean Craven. When she comes to the phone I say who I am and ask if I can speak to Mike. There's a pause and then he picks up.

'Rina, my dear girl, how nice to hear from you. How are you?'

'Very well thanks.'

'How can I help?'

'You know that part in the film that you talked to me about?'

'Tell me you've had a change of heart!'

'Well…'

'You have?'

'Yes.'

'That's fantastic!'

'If it's still…'

'It certainly is. I cast someone and we shot one scene but it didn't work out. I wasn't happy, neither was she, and we've just agreed to part, so this is perfect timing.'

'I thought about it and…'

'I'm very glad you did and I'm delighted you want to do it. Jean said you were up here to see Johnny and I was going to have another go at persuading you. Would you mind doing a short test? I'm sure it'll only be a formality but I just need to show it to Don, our producer, who keeps us all fed and watered.'

I'm wonder what the hell I'm letting myself in for and thinking I must be mad, but I can't pull out now.

'Yes sure,' I say.

'Could you come to our hotel? We're at the Grand on Colmore Row.'

'I'm here now.'

'Oh that's wonderful. Hold on one second darling.'

He puts the receiver down and I can hear the buzz of conversation in the bar and the odd chortle and laugh before he picks up again.

'Ken the cameraman is here and so is Jean. If you'd be willing to have a look at a short scene, Jean could bring the pages to you in your room and explain a bit about the context, and then if you'd like to come along to mine in about half an hour, I've got a Super 8 video camera and a cassette recorder and we can put something on tape. There's no need for you to learn the lines, you'll be able to read them. Don's coming up later and I'll be able to show it to him when he arrives and with any luck we can wrap it up tonight.'

'Sounds good,' I say, even though my stomach's just turned over twice.

'Excellent. I'm in 243. See you soon.'

I put the phone down, sit on the bed and try to calm down. It's only a silly film and I'll probably fail the test anyway but if I get the part I'll be near to Brindle without his heavies in the way, which is my best chance of finding a way to off him and get away with it. I change into the lurex mini dress that I got in Rackhams earlier and wish I'd bought some shoes. I put on some make-up and I'm just brushing my hair when there's a knock at the door and Jean's there with a script under her arm. She looks pleased to see me.

'Mike is so excited about this,' she says.

'I only hope I'm worth it.'

'Have you done a test before?'

'I've never acted.'

She looks at me for a moment. 'If Johnny's anything to go by that's probably a distinct advantage on this one.'

We sit down and she opens the script and takes a couple of loose pages from the front of it. 'The main character is called Mary, and you're playing Ella, her younger sister.'

'A lingerie model?'

'That's right. In this scene, Ella has come to see Mary and finds her with a black eye and bruises and the baby crying in its cot. She comforts the baby and asks Mary what happened, but Mary won't tell her anything at first. Ella guesses that Challoner, that's Johnny, has hit her and Mary admits that he has. Ella takes her and the baby to their mother's flat in Islington, to get them out of danger.'

She passes the pages to me and I read through the scene. The words all make sense and when I look at the description of her calming the baby down I'm reminded of our Jack when he used to wake up in the night in the bed that he shared with me and Georgie, and how I used to pick him up and take him into the kitchen and give him a bottle, so as not to wake Georgie.

'Would you like to try some lines?' asks Jean.

'I would,' I reply.

'OK,' she says.

I look down the page at the lines with Ella in front of them and Jean opens the script and finds the place. 'So, you've arrived at the door, which is unlocked, you hear the baby crying and let yourself in. Mary's slumped on the sofa and…'

"Oh my Christ!" I read.

'And you go and pick up the baby,' says Jean.

She looks at me and I think of our Jack and read on. "There there, it's all right my love… mmm… up you come… there there. Auntie Ella's here and everything's all right."

'Mary wakes up and you see her black eye,' says Jean.

"What's happened to you?" I read.

"I had a fall," says Jean.

"Do I look stupid?" I reply.

We read on through the whole scene and by the end I'm quite enjoying it, especially when she starts slagging Challoner off and calling Mary a mug for taking it.

'You're a natural,' says Jean.

'Was that OK?'

'I'll say.'

She closes the script and stands. 'Shall we go to Mike's room?'

I look down, see that I've still got my boots on and remember that I've got nothing else to wear with this dress. I can see that Jean's feet are about the same size as mine. 'You couldn't lend me a pair of shoes, could you?'

'Certainly I can. My room's on the way to Mike's,' she says, as she opens the door.

I pick up my pages and follow her. We go up one floor in the lift and along to her room where she offers me a pair of low heels that work with the dress. They're a bit tight but they'll do. Jean gathers up my boots and we take the lift to the top floor.

Mike ushers us in to his luxury suite and I say hello to Ken who's sitting on the sofa fiddling with a video camera. Mike offers us a drink and I'm glad to accept a whisky which I knock back in a couple of swigs while he's showing Jean how to work the cassette recorder. When Jean's got the idea, Mike offers her a chair.

'How are we doing Ken?' he asks.

'Ready to go,' says Ken.

'Did you have a look at the scene Rina?'

'I did.'

'Are you happy with it?'

'I think so.'

'Shall we give it a go?'

'May as well,' I reply.

He goes and stands beside the door. 'So. You've heard

the baby crying from outside the door and you come in, look around, see him in his cot and go and take him in your arms,' he says, indicating an upright chair with a cushion on it. 'Ah, sorry,' he says, picking up the cushion, 'I should have introduced you. Rina, this is your niece Amanda.'

'Pleased to meet you Amanda,' I say, shaking hands with a corner of the cushion. Jean and Ken chuckle encouragingly as Mike goes on. 'Then you see Mary, on the sofa, and you cross to her, still holding the baby, and we have the rest of the dialogue. Jean will be on the sofa giving you Mary's lines and holding the script up for you to read the words.'

I nod in agreement. Jean moves into position and Mike goes to the middle of the room. 'Ken if you're somewhere here and panning with Rina, so we get her full length, then we can go again, with you in closer.'

'Sure,' says Ken.

'Right. If you're ready Rina?'

'How do I read the lines for the first bit with the baby?'

'Good point, yes.'

'I can be behind the chair with them and then move to the sofa?' says Jean.

'Will that work for you Rina?'

'I think so.'

'Good. Then let's try it. I'll say "action" when you're outside and you come in when you're ready.'

I go and stand in the corridor and when I hear him say

the word, I think of our Jack, then I go in and pick up that cushion.

By the time we've done it again for the close-ups and he's played them back on the camera, Mike is in a lather of excitement and convinced I'm the new Marilyn Monroe. Considering she topped herself a couple of years ago, I'm not sure it's quite what I want to hear. He's looking at the shots again and playing the cassette recording back when the phone rings and he picks it up.

'Don! You've made it... I've got something to show you... 579?... Stay there and I'll come to you.'

He picks up the camera and the cassette recorder and heads for the door. 'Help yourselves to drinks. I'll be back soon.'

We pour drinks from a good collection of spirits and beers on a side table and sit back with our glasses. Ken takes a swig of his lager. 'Have you worked with Mike before?' he asks.

'No,' I reply.

'This is Rina's acting debut,' says Jean.

'You could have fooled me,' says Ken.

'Thanks.'

'What you did was really smooth.'

'I'm glad you think so.'

He seems like a straight up bloke, so I feel good hearing this.

'You know Johnny?' he asks.

'I do, yeah.'

'He's enjoying himself now he's got into his stride.

Quite the leading man, eh Jean?'

'Oh yes. Did he tell you about the agent who's after him Rina?'

'No, he didn't mention it.'

'International Talent want to sign him.'

'ITM are good, aren't they?' asks Ken.

'One of the best, I believe.'

'That's nice,' I say.

'I bet Henry's not pleased,' says Ken.

'Slightly tinged with green, I'd say,' says Jean.

'He'll probably come in wearing that gold medal he won at Rada.'

I wonder who they're talking about until I remember it's the actor that Brindle smacked in Hoxton.

I'm becoming aware of Ken's eyes lingering on my legs when the door opens and Mike comes in followed by a tall, good-looking man with black slicked back hair and dark brown eyes, wearing a sharp suit and a silk tie.

'Don, this is Rina. Rina, this is Don Keeble, our executive producer.'

Don shakes my hand and flashes a smile. 'A great pleasure to meet you. I just saw your test. I loved it, and I want to welcome you to the show.'

'Thanks,' I reply.

The door opens and Ed enters. Mike turns to him, 'Ed, just so you know, Rina is now playing the part of Ella.'

Ed shakes my hand. 'Glad to hear it.'

Mike looks at Don. 'We'll need to reshoot Rina's scene at Hoxton.'

'Of course, but you're going back there anyway.' says Don.

'I'm afraid not,' says Ed.

'What?' says Mike.

Don turns to Ed. 'What are you talking about?'

'I've just had a call from Lenny. The owner's pissed off about the way we left the place, apparently there's some damage. He's changed the locks and won't let us back.'

'Oh for fuck's sake!' says Mike.

'The good news is that the exteriors at Hoxton are all fine and Lenny knows a house up here that'll be a match for the interiors,' says Ed.

'Where is it?' asks Don.

'Erdington,' Ed replies.

'When can you get in there?'

'Anytime.'

'You finished the exteriors at Hoxton didn't you?'

'We did.'

'How long to reshoot the interiors, including Rina's scene?'

'Two days?'

'Mike?'

'Should be enough,' says Mike.

'You've finished at the gasworks?'

'Yes.'

Don turns to Ed. 'Can you get into the Erdington house for the reshoots tomorrow?'

'We can.'

'Then get it organised.'

'Will do,' says Ed.

'That'll put you two days late starting at the high rise in Islington,' says Don.

'Shouldn't be a problem. The Islington flat's empty,' says Ed.

'Good. The second unit can pick up Rina arriving at Hoxton when she's not needed in Islington.'

'As long as the owner...'

'Fuck him! Just get over there with a tripod and steal it!'

Everyone laughs and Don gets up to leave. 'Really glad you're with us Rina, I look forward to seeing more of your work.'

We shake hands and he leaves. Mike closes the door behind him. 'OK, so we move the unit to Erdington in the morning and hope to be ready to start after lunch. We'll shoot the scenes in story order which means that we should get to Rina's scene, which is the one we've just done, sometime in the late afternoon. Ed will arrange a car for you at about one o'clock Rina, which should give you time to read the script and learn your scene.'

'If you'll excuse me, I've got some calls to make,' says Ed, as he heads for the door, followed by Ken.

'Jean darling, would you be an angel and see if Deidre's around so that she can talk to Rina about costume?' asks Mike.

'Certainly,' says Jean and goes into the bedroom, as Mike goes on. 'Colette will be taking care of your make-up Rina and she'll be at the location when you get there.'

'Right,' I say.

Jean opens the bedroom door with the phone in her hand. 'Deidre would like to see Rina in her room now so that she can take her measurements and talk about clothes.'

'Is that all right with you Rina?' asks Mike.

'Yes.'

Jean tells Deidre we'll be along shortly, puts the phone down and rejoins us.

'Any questions Rina?' asks Mike.

'Not at the moment,' I reply.

'Very good,' says Mike, as he opens the door. 'See you all on the morrow.'

I slip out of Jean's shoes and give them to her, then I put on my boots and we walk along the corridor to the lift.

'How are you feeling?' she asks.

'A bit nervous.'

We get into the lift and she slips her arm round my waist. 'You're going to be fine. I promise you.'

Deidre's room is two floors down and she opens the door in her dressing gown, smoking a cigarette in a holder.

'Sorry to be a bit déshabillé ladies, I was about to go to beddy byes. These early starts will be the death of me. Do come in, won't you?'

She stands back and we go into her room, which smells of booze. The TV's on with the sound turned down and there's a half empty bottle of gin beside it which Deidre picks up.

'Care for a drinky?' she says, pouring herself one. I can't stand gin so I shake my head.

'I'm going to leave you to it,' says Jean. 'I'll see you both in the morning.'

'I gather we're in sunny Erdington,' says Deidre.

'It's standing in for Hoxton,' says Jean.

'Where the fuck is Erdington?'

'No doubt we'll find out. I'll see you tomorrow Rina.'

Jean takes a script out of her bag, passes it to me and makes a quick exit. Deidre downs her gin and gives me a big smile.

'So. You're Ella mark 3.'

'Yes.'

'Can't say I'm sorry to see the back of the last one. Right little madam. Anyway darling, you're taller than her and so I'm afraid we'll need to start again, although I rather like what you're wearing.'

'I got it in Rackhams this morning.'

'Did you now?'

'They've got some good stuff.'

'And it's a perfect fit.'

She pours herself another splash of gin. 'Why don't we go to Rackhams in the morning and kit you out? We need three outfits and some undies. It's going to bend my budget, but if they will recast... What time are you called tomorrow?'

'I'm being picked up from here at one o'clock.'

'If we leave for Rackhams at ten you should be back in good time. Shall we meet in reception?'

'Yes.'

'Sure you won't have a nightcap?'

'I think I'd better get some sleep.'
'OK darling,' she says.
As I'm closing the door I hear her pouring another one.

17

The alarm call wakes me at eight and I make coffee and get back into bed. The script is on the bedside table, where I left it after I finished reading it last night. I've never read a film script or a play before and I was quite gripped by it in places.

It's the story of a brass from a poor East End background called Mary, who's being kept in a flat in Dolphin Square by Harold, a rich client who's fallen in love with her. Mary's older sister Jane is mentally ill and living with their mother in a high rise council flat in Islington. Jane falls pregnant and has a baby. When the mother, who was looking after the baby, dies suddenly and Jane is put in a mental home, the council want to put the baby in an orphanage but Mary steals it and takes it to Dolphin Square. Harold turns nasty and threatens to throw her out if she won't get rid of the baby.

Mary meets a villain called Challoner, who we see receiving a shipment of drugs at the docks and fighting off a rival gang. Mary falls for him and Challoner takes her and the baby to his flat in Hoxton. Harold comes after Mary but Challoner kills him and dumps his body in the tar pit at Kensal Green Gasworks. All goes well in Hoxton until Challoner begins to drink heavily, take drugs and abuse Mary and the baby.

Mary's younger sister Ella, played by me, who models

underwear, and has always helped Mary out, goes to visit her, finds her badly injured and takes her and the baby from Hoxton to their mother's flat in Islington to escape Challoner and stays there with her to help look after the baby. Challoner breaks into the flat, looking for Mary, but she's at the hospital with the baby. He finds Ella's portfolio of underwear advertisements and looks through it. When Ella arrives and discovers the unlocked front door, Challoner pulls her into the flat and rapes her. Mary walks in on them and tries to pull Challoner off her sister, but he gets up and throws her into the kitchen. Mary hits Challoner with a cast iron frying pan and accidentally kills him. When the girls are trying to think how to dispose of the body, Ella remembers an underwear shoot she did at a farm in Essex and they take the body there and feed it to the pigs.

It reads like a really good story, apart from the pigs, because they would only eat the flesh, and maybe the bones, but not the skull, which could be identified. I might tip Mike the wink about that, but then again he might wonder where I've got the expert knowledge, so maybe I won't. I'm not too sure about the underwear pictures for the portfolio either, it's more Lizzie's game than mine, but I suppose I can grit my teeth and do it, if we get that far.

I go over my lines, which I learnt last night, and find I can remember them. I say them again while I'm in the shower to make sure, then I put on my jeans, shirt and boots and order some breakfast from room service, hoping the lovely girl with the dark hair and the soulful eyes will bring it. After a while there's a knock on the door and a matronly lady with a big arse bustles in, puts the tray down, proffers the bill for me to sign and sweeps out again.

I make short work of the scrambled eggs and a couple of pieces of toast and go down to the foyer. There's no sign of Deidre so I sit in an armchair near the front door. There are papers and magazines on a table so I pick up a *Daily Express* and leaf through it until I notice a report about a couple of murderers who were hanged yesterday, one in Strangeways and the other in Walton Prison in Liverpool. It says they killed a bloke while robbing him and one of them left his coat behind, with a note to him in it, and they were arrested the next morning. The judge described them as being of "low intellect" in court, which is putting it mildly. I'm reading how the Labour Party under Harold Wilson are trying to abolish the death penalty, but that the Tories remain all for it, when Deidre appears in front of me.

'Ready to go?' she says.

'Sure.'

I drop the paper on the table, follow her through the front door and we get into the back of one of the cabs that's waiting outside. She tells the driver to take us to Rackhams and sits back. 'Sleep well?' she asks.

'Yes thanks. You?'

'I was so pissed I went out like a light and slept through the alarm call. I could cut glass with this headache.'

'I'm sorry if you've had to get up on my account.'

'Don't be, darling. It serves me right. I'm not a big

drinker normally but there's something about hotels.'

'I know what you mean.'

She closes her eyes and rests her head back. I have a look out of the back window in case there's any sign of a black Ford Zodiac with Gerry at the wheel, but it's clear.

The cab stops outside Rackhams. Deidre wakes up, pays the driver and we go inside and up the escalator. When we get to the Ladies Fashion department I take a quick look round in case Auntie Fran is refreshing her wardrobe and follow Deidre to the dress racks. She goes straight for Mary Quant and takes a black and white striped skirt and blouse off the rail, holds them up against me and nods. She does the same with a pair of Emilio Pucci check trousers, a silk blouse and a short Ashleigh Verrier dress in a red chiffon. I follow her to the fitting rooms, she puts me in a cubicle and asks me what size bra I take. I tell her, she asks me to try on the Mary Quant and disappears. By time I've changed she's back carrying an armful of frilly bras, pants and suspenders. She dumps them on the chair in the cubicle, stands back, looks me over, tells me to do a twirl and nods her approval. I change into the trousers and blouse, which get the OK, as does the Verrier dress.

Next it's the underwear, and as a few people have now come into the changing rooms, she joins me in the cubicle to view the items she's found for me and shuts the door. Now she's close to me I can smell last night's booze on her breath and I feel embarrassed to be taking all my clothes off in front of her. She senses my discomfort and turns away as I start to undress. I put on different bras, pants, chemises and suspenders, and most of them find favour apart from a few that she rejects for being "far too mumsy and boring darling". When she's seen me in the whole lot she collects everything up, leaves the despised underwear on the floor and tells me to get dressed and meet her at the till.

We go down the escalator to the shoe department and buy a pair of medium heels and some Courrège boots. Deidre decides that we've got all we need, picks up the carrier bags and heads for the escalator. I follow her out of the store and she hails a taxi. When we stop at the hotel she rummages in her handbag, finds a piece of paper and gives an address to the driver. She tells me she's going on to the location in Erdington and that she'll catch up with me later. I get out of the cab and as it drives off I see her take a hip flask out of her bag and have a swig.

I've got an hour before I'm being picked up so I go to my room and run through my lines a couple of times, then I lie on the bed with *Rebecca* and read about Maxim getting grumpy with our girl after they've been to the beach where Rebecca drowned, and him saying he should never have come back to Manderley and stomping off. She follows him back to the house and meets Frank Crawley the estate manager who's nice to her and tells her to forget about trying to measure up to Rebecca and enjoy Manderley, and that no one wants to remember the past. Just as I'm thinking she should have married Frank, the phone rings and I'm told that my car is waiting. I put on my leather jacket, take the Smith & Wesson out of the pocket and wonder if I should take it with me. It could be awkward if someone finds it, but even more so if I need it and haven't got it, so I put it in my handbag along with my knife and go down to reception.

There's a tubby little bloke in a brown suit that's seen better days, standing by the front door. He sees me and raises his hand.

'Miss Walker?' he says, as I approach.

'Rina,' I reply.

'My name's Harry. I'm your driver.'

'Nice to meet you,' I say, as he opens the door and leads me to a Ford Consul parked outside. I settle into the back seat and he drives off.

'Your first day then?'

'Yes.'

'Are you from here?'

'No, London.'

'Like me.'

Rather than give Harry any more information, I take out my script and open it.

'I'd better look at my lines.'

'Sure,' he says, and drives on. As we go down Aston Road, past Chain and Hook, I remember what a mess I made of finishing Brindle the other night and wonder if I'll have any chance of getting to him today. He's an evil bastard and there's no telling what he'll do when he knows I've muscled in on his movie.

We pass a sports ground on the left, go up a long hill, turn right at the top into a tree-lined street with terraced houses on each side and I see the trucks and trailers of the film unit. Harry pulls up alongside the catering van, gets out and opens the door for me. Kirsty is standing by the table with the tea urn on it and she sees me and comes over.

'Good morning Rina.'

'Hello Kirsty,' I reply.

'Shall I show you to your trailer?'

'Please do.'

I follow her along the pavement to a row of four caravans and she opens the door of the first one for me. As I'm about to climb in, Brindle steps out of the one next door. He sees me, stops dead and fixes me with a look of pure loathing. I thank Kirsty, go into the caravan and close the door. Moments later it's yanked open and Brindle walks in, slams the door shut and stands glaring at me, rigid with rage. I open the clasp on my handbag, put my hand inside and wrap it round my gun.

'What the fuck are you doing here?' he snarls.

'I finally thought it over.'

'You're not…?'

'I should be learning my lines.'

He takes a step towards me. 'I wouldn't bother. You won't live long enough to say them.'

While I'm slipping the safety catch, there's a knock on the door.

'Come in,' I say.

The door opens and Mike steps in behind Brindle. 'Good morning Rina, my darling.'

'Morning Mike,' I say, taking my hand out of my bag.

Mike sees Brindle and claps him on the shoulder. 'Johnny, I was just on my way to tell you the good news but I see you're ahead of me. Isn't it great that Rina's decided to join us and play Ella?'

Brindle grins and grasps Mike's hand. 'I'm over the fucking moon about it!'

'I'm sure you had a lot to do with persuading her,' says Mike.

'If you only knew. I begged, pleaded, blackmailed, plied her with presents and she only agreed to do it when I promised to take her to Monte Carlo after we wrap.'

Mike laughs. 'Well I'm very grateful to you and I hope you enjoy the trip. She did an excellent test last night, and with the wonderful work you and Kim are doing, I now feel I've got the cast who can make this film the success it deserves to be.'

'She's going to be great,' says Brindle, putting his arm round me. 'We've known each other for years and she knows the lay of the land, like I do,' says Brindle, winking at me.

'I can't wait to see you working together,' says Mike, turning to the door. 'By the way Johnny, Hal Wallace the American distributor is calling at five o'clock our time and he wants to talk to you about your availability for a promotional tour of the States with Kim in the spring, so would you mind going over to the Grand to take the call in Don's room?'

'Sure,' says Brindle.

'We should be ready for you in an hour or so Rina,' says Mike, as he leaves.

Brindle's looking at me as if he'd like to tear me apart with his bare hands.

'I never knew you could act that well,' I say.

'Just wait till the rape scene, bitch.'

As I'm feeling for the gun again there's another knock on the door.

'Come in,' I say.

'Can I get you some lunch?' asks Kirsty.

She hands me a menu and waits by the door. While I'm looking at it, Brindle gives a kind of snort and leaves.

When I've eaten some very tasty lamb cutlets with mashed potatoes and peas, Kirsty takes me to the make-up trailer and introduces me to Colette, who's slim and elfin with auburn hair in a pageboy cut and about my age. I find out she's from Shepherd's Bush and while she's putting foundation on me we talk about the clubs and pubs we've both been to and different bands we've seen. She does my eyes really nicely so they look a lot bigger. I note the way she's done the lines and lashes, and when I ask her what she's used, she tells me what the various products are and where to get them. She does a great job on my hair as well, with different gels that she also gives me the names of. When I'm done, Kirsty takes me to wardrobe, which is in a room on the top floor of the house.

'Come in darling,' says Deidre when she sees me

through the open door. 'Ooh I like the make-up. Very modelly. Colette?'

'Yes,' I say.

'She's so good.'

Deidre looks through the clothes on the rail. 'I think it's the Quant for this scene darling. OK with you?'

'Sure,' I reply.

Deidre holds the suit for me while I take off my clothes. When I'm in my underwear she looks me up and down. 'Do you know, I think we could do with a bit more "lift and separate" in the bosom department.'

She picks a Rackhams bag up off the floor, searches through it, pulls out a black lace Playtex bra and hands it to me. I put it on, she does up the clip and makes another inspection. 'Yes, much better darling. Jayne Mansfield had better watch out!'

She gives me a white blouse and the Quant skirt and jacket to put on, then a black velvet jacket that she takes off the rail. When I'm dressed, she walks round me once. 'I think we've got it. How do you feel my love?'

I look in the mirror. 'Good.'

'Excellent. Not sure if you'll need the jacket but we'll have it there in case. See you later darling.'

I leave the jacket with her and follow Kirsty across the landing and down the stairs. As we come out of the house I nearly bump into Kim Daley. She's smaller than she looks on the screen but her eyes are that clear blue, her skin has a lovely glow to it and her hair is a rich mixture of deep reds.

'Oh, hello. It's Rina, isn't it?' she says.

'Yes,' I reply.

'Great to meet you. I'm Kim, playing Mary.'

'Good to meet you too.'

'I'm late for costume I'm afraid but I'm sure we'll have time to talk on the set.'

'See you then,' I say.

She gives me a big smile, goes into the house and up the stairs. Kirsty and I walk to my trailer. As she opens the door for me, a long car sweeps past. It turns at the end of the road and I see Brindle sitting in the back seat.

18

I'm sitting on a canvas chair between Jean and the sound trolley. Mike has introduced me to some of the crew and they seem like a nice bunch of people. Some of the lights are being adjusted and the camera's being moved to a new position. Mike and Ed are talking together in a corner.

'I love that costume,' says Jean.

'It's nice, isn't it?' I say.

'You should keep it afterwards.'

'Do you think I could?'

'As long as you keep Deidre sweet.'

'Buy her a drink?'

'Or ten.'

As we're having a quiet laugh Kim appears. I'm shocked to see she's got a black eye and blood on her face and I nearly run to her, but then I realise that she's made up for scene. Mike sees her and comes out of his corner. 'Thank you everyone, if you'd like to give us the room for rehearsal.'

'There's tea downstairs, boys,' says Ed, as he opens the door.

The crew start to leave except for Jean who stays seated. I stand up and Kim comes over to me and points at her face. 'Another glamour part.'

'At least it washes off,' I say as the last of the crew leave.

Mike closes the door and turns to us. 'We'll rehearse

without the baby first.' He stands in the middle of the room. 'So, if you're over there by the cot Rina, and you've just settled Amanda down. Let's take it from where you see Mary lying on the sofa, and going to her.'

Kim goes to the sofa and lies on it.

'Perhaps you should be turned away from the room Kim, so that it's more of a shock when your face is revealed,' says Mike.

'OK,' says Kim, turning her face to the cushions.

'When you're ready Rina.'

I go and stand by the cot and I suddenly feel cold and a bit faint and I want to be anywhere but here with Mike and Jean looking at me. I take a couple of deep breaths, remind myself why I'm doing this and look over at Kim. I walk to the sofa, kneel down and touch her shoulder. She turns to me and I'm looking at her ruined face. I know I've got to speak but I can't think what my first line is. I feel all frozen up and Kim's looking at me and Jean says something and more time passes and my mind's blank, then an arm goes round me. 'It's all right Rina my love,' says Mike, in a soothing voice. 'Just relax for a moment and we'll try it again.'

I stand up and move away from him. I look at Jean sitting in her chair with the folder on her knee and she smiles and then I feel calm and I know I can do this.

'Sorry about that. It's "What's happened to you?" isn't it?' I ask Jean.

Jean nods and smiles and I go back and stand beside the cot, looking down to where the baby should be. I look up and see Kim, then I go to her and this time the words come to me and I'm really feeling sorry for her and she's crying and I'm trying to wipe the tears and the blood away and comfort her. When we get to the end part where she's sitting up and defending Challoner, saying she still loves him and I'm having none of it and making her pack up and leave, the sparks are flying and it feels like real life.

We get to the end and Mike is dead pleased. He tells us where we should go a bit slower in a couple of places and build up the argument at the end a bit more gradually. We play the scene again with those changes and when we finish he says it's really good and asks us if we feel ready to film it. We say we do and he explains how he's going to shoot it and he tells me that we'll do it a few times with the camera in different places, then he opens the door and calls to Ed that he's ready to shoot.

The crew come in and watch us rehearse the scene again, with the bit with the baby added on at the beginning, and then Ed tells Kim and me to wait on the landing while they set up. Kirsty offers to bring us tea and one of the crew puts chairs against the wall for us, as the mother and baby come up the stairs, to be greeted by Ed and taken onto the set.

'I'm sorry about the false start there,' I say to Kim.

'Please don't apologise. I forget my lines all the time.'

'But you've done so much.'

'Every time I start a job I feel as if I've never acted before.'

'You're kidding.'

'God's truth.'

I know she's only saying it to make me feel better but I appreciate it all the same.

'First days are horrible,' she says.

'All of them?'

'Without fail. I'm always convinced that I'm going to get found out this time.'

She's saying all this with a slight smile and I really can't tell if she means it or not. Colette appears with her make-up bag and starts to touch up Kim's black eye and bruises. She gives me a quick dust over with powder and Kirsty tells us they are ready for us on the set.

Mike explains that they will do the whole scene as a master shot and then how it's going to be broken up for the different camera angles after that. I see the mother sitting by Jean in the corner and I go over, introduce myself to her, ask the baby's name and if I can hold her. She gives me the baby and tells me her name's Susan. She's a lovely little thing and I get a smile from her when I stroke her cheek. Mike sees me with her. 'Ah, good Rina, I see you're forming a relationship with Amanda.'

'She's lovely,' I say.

'Indeed she is. By the way, the crying will be on tape, but will be cut when you start to speak, so you'll have to imagine it thereafter. Unless of course young Susan chooses to give tongue herself at that point.'

'I understand,' I say.

'If you'd like to put her in the cot, I believe we're about ready to go.'

He gives a nod to Ed, who checks with Ken and the soundman and tells us to stand by. I put the baby down gently in the cot and as I let go she starts to cry. I look at Mike and he shakes his head and points to the door. Once I'm outside I hear him say, 'Action,' and the baby stops crying. I'm not sure what to do so I wait a bit and then I hear a different baby crying, which I suppose is the tape, so I go in, cross to the cot, pick up the real baby and she starts crying again.

'Cut!' shouts Mike. He turns to the soundman. 'Forget the tape. All right?'

The soundman nods and Mike looks at me. 'Just come in and pick her up, whether she's crying or not, and we'll put it on afterwards if necessary.'

She's still crying and I want to go to her now but Ed gives the stand by call again so I go outside. Mike says 'Action,' and the crying stops. I enter, go to the cot, pick her up, give her the soothing dialogue and she stays silent. When I see Mary on the sofa and put her back in the cot, she starts crying again.

'Cut!' says Mike. He's red in the face now and clearly not happy.

Ed comes forward. 'If we cut where the baby goes back in the basket, take it away and pick up from the look at the sofa, we'll get a clean track.'

Mike shakes his head. 'I don't want to cut there.'

'If you're not going to cut you'll have to post-sync all of Rina's dialogue,' says Ed.

'And Kim's,' says the soundman.

They've lost me completely. Mike paces back and forth with his eyes closed for a bit and then he stops. 'All right. We cut there, do a close up of the baby going into the cot and then we're on a close up of Rina's look at Mary,' says Mike.

I haven't a clue what they're on about but everyone seems happy with the plan and we do it again. This time the baby cries when Mike says action and stops when I calm her down and put her in the cot. We stop there and Mike looks even more frustrated but we go on and do another couple of takes and then the rest of the scene with Kim. I've noticed that with all the stopping and starting I'm not feeling nervous at all. I just need to think about our Jack for a moment before I go to the baby and then, when I really look at Kim's damaged face and listen to what she's saying to me, the right feeling seems to come over me.

By the end of the day we've done it so many times and from so many angles that I'm knackered. Mike says he's really pleased with it and that I won't be needed again until the day after tomorrow at the high rise flat in Islington. Another assistant called Bonnie asks me if I want a car back to London in the morning and I tell her I'm going to drive myself. She asks for my phone number so she can tell me the schedule and pick-up time for Islington but I decide to be careful, just in case it's not safe for me to be at home, and I tell her I'm staying with a friend whose number I don't know. Bonnie gives me hers and I agree to phone her later to get the call time.

I share a car to the hotel with Kim and we have a good laugh about Mike's prima donna side and she tells me that she enjoyed acting with me today, which makes me feel good. When we get to the Grand she suggests having a meal together. I'd really like to get to know her, but I reckon the sooner I put some distance between me and Brindle and his chums the better, so I tell her I have to drive to London tonight and suggest we go out together soon.

I go up to my room, put *Rebecca* and my few bits and pieces in a carrier bag and go back down to reception, to pay the bill. As the girl is adding up my account, Don the producer gets out of the lift and comes over. 'Checking out?'

'I have to get back tonight,' I say.

'That's a shame, I was hoping we could have dinner.'

'Another time, perhaps.'

'Absolutely. How did it go today?'

'Quite well, I think,' I reply.

'I look forward to seeing it.'

The girl lays my bill on the counter and I have a quick look at it and open my handbag. Don picks it up, glances at it and turns to the receptionist. 'Charge this to Millbank Films.'

He takes out a pen, signs the bill and hands it over the desk. The receptionist takes it and puts it in a file. I'm relieved Don hasn't noticed the false name I signed in with.

'That's kind, thank you,' I say.

Don walks with me to the front door. 'I just realised, you've just done your first day and we haven't even talked about your fee.'

It hadn't occurred to me that I'd be paid to be in the film and if I can get to Brindle I doubt if I'll be around to collect my wages.

'Do you have an agent?' he asks.

'No.'

'Do you want to get one?'

'Not really.'

'How would it be if we offered you the same as we'd agreed to pay the lady you're replacing?'

'Sounds fair,' I reply.

'I'd have to look it up to make sure, but from memory I think it was four hundred pounds.'

'That'll be fine.'

'Are you sure?'

'Yes.'

'Good. I wish it was always this simple to negotiate fees with actors. You wouldn't believe the bullshit I get from agents sometimes. My client this... my client that... it can take weeks to agree a deal.'

'Sounds frustrating.'

'Believe me, shooting the film is the easy bit.'

He opens the door for me. 'See you in Islington.'

'Bye,' I say, as I head for the car.

19

The Hillman is getting on a bit and she makes hard work of the trip out of Birmingham, through an area called Spark Brook, and on towards Coventry. She won't do much more than sixty-five on the motorway and the radio's dead, so I sit back and try not to fall asleep after what feels like a long day. It's almost dark and I'm looking forward to getting home, and hoping Lizzie's there, when I glance in the mirror and notice a van coming up quite fast in the middle lane and then slowing down and pulling in behind me. I let him sit there for a bit then I move into the middle lane and he does the same. I go back to the inside and when he follows I take the gun out of my handbag and lay it on my lap.

I go on for a few miles with the van behind me until I see a sign for the exit to Northampton. I leave the motorway at the slip road and the van follows me. When I come to a roundabout I take the road to Northampton and turn off onto a country lane with the van close behind. After a few twists and turns I get to a straight downhill run and floor the accelerator. The car surges forward and the van drops back and then catches up quickly. At the bottom of the hill I brace myself against the wheel and stamp on the brake. The van rams into the back of me and we shudder to a stop. I grab the gun, open the door, hit the tarmac, roll into the gutter and fire three shots at the van. The windscreen shatters, the driver's door opens and a man staggers out and falls onto the road. I hear the back doors open, a shot's fired and a bullet whistles past me. I claw my way through a hedge and run across a ploughed field. There are voices behind me and I'm barely making headway across the muddy soil when I see a row of small huts with pointed roofs ahead of me. I can hear my pursuers gaining on me as I reach one of the huts and crouch down behind it. I look over the top and make out a shape coming towards me out of the darkness. I aim a shot at him, he goes down face first in the mud and another shape appears beside him. I fire again but the shape keeps coming. I turn, run towards a line of trees and fall arse over tit into a trench. As I struggle to get up, hands grab my shoulders and ankles. I roll over, kick out with both feet, get one of them in the stomach and he falls. The other one lands on top of me and goes for my neck. I grab his hand, put a finger in my mouth, bite it hard and while he's screaming like a little boy, I push him off me and get up. As he rolls on his back I stamp on his bollocks, kick him in the head and hoof it back towards the road. I can hear the other one coming after me but I manage to stay on my feet and get through the hedge. He's too close behind for me to make it to the car so I take the knife out of my boot and crouch down in the ditch. When he comes out of the hedge I stand up, plunge the blade into his stomach and he falls into the ditch moaning.

I go to the van and pull on the handbrake. The Hillman's still ticking over, so I get in and put it in gear.

There's a screeching sound as I let the clutch out and the back of the car tries to tear itself away from the front of the van and fails. After a couple more attempts, I get out and have a look at the damage. The front of the van has pushed the rear end of the car right into the back seat, the tail lights are a few bits of glass on the road and the Hillman's going nowhere.

I get my carrier bag out of the car, wipe it over for prints and run up the lane towards the main road. When I reckon I've put enough distance between me and the enemy, I slow down to a walk and think about how I'm going to get home. I'll never find a cab out here so I'll have to try and get a lift to a station. When I get to the main road I turn towards Northampton, walk along for a bit, until I'm out of sight of the turning into the lane, and put my thumb out.

A few cars pass and then a grey Morris 8 slows down and I can see the driver having a look at me. He stops, reaches over and opens the passenger door. He's a tubby middle-aged man in a tweed suit, with grey wavy hair, a blotchy red face and piggy eyes.

'Need a lift?'

'Are you going to Northampton?'

'I am indeed.'

'Anywhere near the station?'

'Right past it. Hop in.'

'Thanks.'

I get in, close the door and he takes his eyes off my body and drives.

'What happened?' he asks.

'My car broke down.'

'Ah.'

'My brother's a mechanic and he'll come and get it in the morning.'

'That's handy.'

After we've driven in silence for a bit I feel his hand on my leg. After what I've just been through he's lucky that I just put it back on the steering wheel, shift along the seat and cross my legs.

'Sorry. I thought that was the gearstick,' he says.

'I'm often mistaken for one,' I reply.

He laughs. 'I hope you won't blame me for trying. You are extremely beautiful.'

'Thanks.'

'You won't tell your brother, will you?'

'Not if you drop me at the station.'

On the way, he tells me about how his wife left him for a younger bloke, and his business is going down the tubes, and he's got a bad heart, and he's lonely and depressed, and I'm just about losing the will to live when we get to the station and he stops the car. I wish him luck, thank him for the lift and head for the ticket office.

There's a train to London in half an hour and I buy a first class ticket and head for the station bar. As I walk in I get a couple of strange looks and I catch sight of myself in a wall mirror and see that my face and my jacket and jeans are muddy from the field. I go to the ladies and clean myself up as much as I can, then I go back to the bar, down a large whisky and then another one. The train is announced on the speakers and I go to the platform, find the first class carriage, settle back in my seat and close my eyes.

• • •

I'm flying through the air in a white van. I'm at the wheel and I can see miles of ploughed fields far below. I swoop and dive and climb up again and I'm loving flying the van through sky and then the bodies in the back are waking up and clawing at the metal grill between us and snarling at me. I pull the wheel back hard and we go into a steep climb. I press a button on the dash and the back doors fly open and the men all slide along the floor and fall out, screaming as they plunge down through the air, making strange shapes on the muddy fields when they land and then a pack of wolves are on them and tearing them apart and eating them. I hear laughter and I look round and Kim, with her lovely red hair, is on the seat next to me. She comes close, puts her arm round me and whispers sweet things in my ear and then she's stroking my stomach and then her hand moves between my legs and I'm tingling all over and I take the van down to land it in a grassy field and we touch down with a bump.

'Watford Junction,' says a rasping voice.

I sit up and look out of the window at a deserted rain-soaked platform. A uniformed guard walks past the window. I watch him go all the way along the curve of the platform until he reaches the end of the train, where he blows his whistle, raises a flag and gets on board. The engine gives a long sigh and then chuffs and puffs and pulls us on towards London.

I'm wondering if it's safe to go home. Brindle's going to get the news about his men getting shafted and he could well put the Teales after me, or whoever else he's got in London. I really want to get home and see Lizzie but I decide to be careful and when we get to Euston I take a cab to Covent Garden and tell him to drop me on the corner of Shelton Street where I know there are a couple of small hotels. I walk along the street until I see one called The Vincent, which looks suitably discreet, and I go up the steps and into reception. The clock on the wall says midnight and the man behind the desk is half asleep, but he rouses himself enough to book me into a room that costs seventeen and six. He gives me a key, tells me where the bathroom is, and I go up the stairs and let myself into the room. After the Grand in Birmingham it's pretty bare and basic with a narrow double bed, a wardrobe, a small dressing table and an upright chair. There's a phone on the bedside table so I wake the receptionist again and ask him to call Lizzie's number.

Just when I'm about to hang up she answers. I tell her where I am and ask her if she'll come over. I think she senses that I might be in danger, and like the diamond she is, she says she'll be on her way once she's squared it with Gerald. I put the phone down, pick it up again, ask the man to get me Bonnie's number and when I get through she tells me my pick up time is 2pm on the day after tomorrow. I call reception again, ask if I can buy a bottle of whisky and he says he'll bring one up to the room. I take my leather jacket off, put it on the back of the chair and lie on the bed, until there's a knock at the door and the bloke's there with a bottle of Johnnie Walker. I tell him I'm expecting a visitor and I'll need two glasses.

'You never said you was working,' he says.

'It's just a friend.'

'That's what they all say. It's a quid extra.'

'It's a woman.'

'I don't care if it's a fucking donkey.'

As it's quite possible Lizzie'll stay the night I take a pound note out of my pocket and give it to him.

'And fifteen bob for the whisky,' he says.

I give him a quid to keep him sweet and he thanks me, lumbers off downstairs and comes back with another glass.

I pour myself a good drink, take *Rebecca* out of the carrier bag, lie on the bed and read about our girl breaking a glass ornament in the drawing room and being too embarrassed to admit it, and then owning up, after horrible Mrs Danvers blames a servant, and how husband Maxim thinks the whole thing's funny, even though she's really upset about it, and she tells him how uneducated and out of place she feels. Maxim tries to reassure her but she's worried that the marriage is going to fail. Just as I'm thinking she'd be better off out of it, I hear a tap on the door and I jump off the bed and open it. I look at Lizzie and feel such a wave of relief and love that I have to pull her inside and throw my arms round her. We hold each other and kiss and I'm so grateful she's here I start to cry. She sits me on the bed.

'Easy now, my darling,' she says as she puts my head on her shoulder.

I take a deep breath and wipe the tears from my cheeks. 'Thanks for coming.'

'Don't be silly.'

'You had Gerald there, didn't you?'

'I can't get rid of him.'

'I thought he was living at his brothers.'

'He's supposed to be but he reckons he's in love with me and he can't bear to be apart and all that bollocks.'

'How's the escort business shaping up?'

'He's done really well with it. Had our first date tonight. A fiver commission up front. They met for dinner at the Savoy and they're probably doing the business about now.'

'That's great. Who was the girl?'

'Cute little thing from Murray's.'

'How's the office?'

'Great. I feel really serious and important at the desk, answering the phone.'

'Will I have to call you Miss Jenson?'

'Madam will do. You can give me a drink an' all.'

'Sorry,' I say, as I pour a large one and hand it to her.

She takes it and reaches for my hand. 'So why are you shacked up here?'

'Just a bit of aggravation.'

'Is it about Dawn?'

'Kind of.'

'Do you want to tell me about it?'

'Probably best if I don't.'

'I worry about you, you know.'

I'd love to share my troubles with her and tell her about the film and everything, but I don't want to put her in any danger. I know she'd be shocked if she knew what I get up to and the less she knows the better.

'It'll be sorted in a couple of days,' I say.

'Why don't you stop being a gangster and come and help me run the agency?'

'Believe me I'd love to.'

'Well then?'

'Just let me try and sort out this bit of malarkey, then we'll see.'

She puts her arm round me, pulls me close and puts her lips to my ear. 'Very good Miss Walker,' she whispers.

We put our glasses down and lie back on the bed.

• • •

Lizzie gets up early to get to the office and asks me to go with her. I've got nothing I need to do until I'm filming in Islington tomorrow, and I reckon I can learn my lines later, so we have a quick breakfast downstairs, served by a woman who's even grumpier than the bloke was on reception last night, and get a cab to Harrods. I buy a new pair of jeans and a dark blue suede jacket, and then it's on to Belgravia.

Ebury Street's looking immaculate in the sunshine and the cab drops us outside number forty-seven.

'Brass plate's coming tomorrow,' says Lizzie, as she unlocks the front door.

'What are you called?' I ask.

'I suggested "Hump and Dump", but he wouldn't have it.'

'I'm not surprised!'

'We've gone for "VIP". The company'll be in Gerald's name and he wants to keep it discreet.'

We go up to the first floor and I follow Lizzie through a door off the landing. Gerald's sitting at a desk turning the pages of an album of photographs. He looks up and sees me. 'Ah, Rina. Hello again.'

'Hello Gerald,' I say, as we shake hands.

'I've just picked up the brochure from the photographer, darling,' he says.

'That was quick,' says Lizzie.

'I know,' he says, standing up and offering the album to Lizzie. 'Have a look, while I make some coffee. How do you take it Rina?'

'Just milk, thanks.'

He opens a side door and goes into a small kitchen. Lizzie sits at the desk, opens the album and I go and look over her shoulder. The girls are in evening dresses on one page and swimsuits on the other, and they're all giving it a come-hither smile and a promise of a good time to come. I recognise a couple of them from round the clubs. As we get to the end of the book the phone rings and Lizzie picks it up. 'VIP. Can I help you?'

She winks at me and I try not to laugh.

'Certainly sir. Would eleven-thirty this morning be convenient?... We're number forty-seven Ebury Street... We look forward to seeing you then, good day,' she says.

Gerald comes in holding a tray with three cups on it. 'Did I hear the phone?'

'Punter at eleven-thirty,' says Lizzie.

'Did he say where he heard of us?'

'The Athenaeum.'

'Now we're motoring!' says Gerald, handing me a cup of coffee and putting one on the desk for Lizzie. 'I don't suppose we could persuade Rina to join our little fold of beauties?'

'Not exactly her line of work,' says Lizzie.

'Talking of which, I really ought to be going,' I say, taking a swig of coffee.

Lizzie says to call her later and gives me a VIP card. I say goodbye to Gerald and I can hear the phone ringing again, as I go downstairs.

I want to go home but I reckon it could be dangerous until I've settled Brindle and discovered where it leaves the Teales and maybe a good few others. I phone Bert from a call box, in case there's anything I need to know, and he tells me George is getting impatient for me to off Brindle. I tell him I'm nearly there and I'll be in touch, then I get a cab to the hotel.

20

Harry picks me up at 2 o'clock the following afternoon and drives me to the location in Islington. It's the Brunswick Close Estate, which they finished building a few years ago. There are three massive tower blocks, standing one behind the other with a balcony for every flat, and I count fourteen storeys in each. It reminds me of Berlin when I was there a couple of years ago. There are three other blocks that aren't so tall and one with a curved front. Harry says he grew up nearby and did a bit of labouring on the site in the fifties. The estate already looks run-down and neglected even though it's not been there long. The film trucks and trailers are parked on the road in front of one of the big blocks and I can see men, carrying lamps and equipment, heading for the entrance.

Harry stops the car and Kirsty appears and opens the door for me. She takes me to my trailer and shows me my costume, which is laid out on the bed. She says she'll let me know when make-up are ready for me and asks if I'd like tea or coffee. I say yes to coffee and change into the underwear and the Mary Quant skirt, blouse and jacket that I wore in the last scene with Kim. I sit at the table and check on the call sheet that Brindle's not coming in until later, then I open the script and look at the scenes we're doing. There's the one where me and Kim arrive at the flat in Islington, on the run from Challoner. We put the baby to bed and I tell her that I'm going to move in with her and help her look after the little one, then we talk about whether we should try and find our sister Jane who's mental and got committed after our mum died. I learnt the lines last night and when I run through them I find I can still remember them. The next scene is the one where Brindle rapes me and then gets killed by Kim. I don't speak until the end, after she's done him, and I'm just checking my lines when Kirsty arrives with the coffee and tells me that I'm wanted in make-up.

Colette's looking bright-eyed and lovely today, and while she's making me up and telling me how she can't wait to pick her cat up from her mother's, where it's been while she was in Birmingham, Mike comes into the trailer and stands behind me. 'I've just seen a rough cut of your scene in Erdington and it works incredibly well. There's a real chemistry between you and Kim. The way you fight your corner at the end, and make her take the baby and leave with you, is perfectly played and completely believable.'

'That's good to know,' I say.

'See you on the tenth floor,' he says, as he opens the door and leaves.

Colette picks up her mascara brush. 'I only saw the rushes, but I thought you looked really great.'

'Oh, thanks.'

She puts the finishing strokes on my eyelashes and brushes on some powder and then Kirsty's there and it's time to go to the set.

The lift smells of stale piss, and as we grind up to the tenth floor, I read on the walls that Doreen Macy's a slag and Kenny R is going to get his head chopped off. The doors open and a ginger-haired woman with a pram and a couple of young boys are on the landing. The boys rush into the lift and stand in front of us. I try to pass between them and the woman shouts at them to come out of the way and let us get off. They push past us to the back of the lift and start jostling and punching each other. We get out and I smile at the woman as we pass her.

'With this filming lot, are you?' she says.

'That's right,' says Colette.

'Tell them to keep the noise down will you? I'm next door and it's driving me bleeding mad.'

'We'll try.' I say, as she wheels the pram into the lift. The doors close and we can hear her shouting at the boys as it descends.

Kirsty leads me along the corridor to the flat we're filming in. Various crew members are standing around the tea and coffee table, which is outside the door, and Mike and Kim are sitting on canvas chairs on the far side. Deidre turns from the coffee urn and sees me.

'Good morning loveliness. How are we today?'

'Very well thanks.'

'Cozzy all right?'

'Feels fine.'

'I think we'll use the Verrier dress for the nastiness scene with Herr Challoner that we're doing later darling.'

'OK.'

'I've bought a couple of spares for backup in case it gets ripped or damaged,' she says, and goes into the flat. While I'm hoping I'm not going to get ripped or damaged, Mike sees me and comes over. He smiles, takes me by the arm and we walk a short way along the corridor.

'I wanted a quiet word about the rape scene,' he says.

'Oh yeah?'

'As you saw when you came to Hoxton, Johnny can get a little carried away on occasion.'

'I did notice.'

'These scenes have to look frightening and horrid and one of the great qualities that Johnny has as an actor is the realism that he brings to his work. Having said that, I want you to promise me that you will not permit him to hurt or injure you in any way and that you will feel free to stop the scene at any point if you are not comfortable with what's happening.'

'Understood.' I say.

Ed appears at his elbow. 'Ready for you to take a look, Guv.'

Mike smiles, squeezes my hand and follows Ed into the flat.

I go and sit next to Kim.

'What was that about?' she asks.

'Storm warning about Johnny in the rape scene.'

'Quite right too.'

'How have you found him?'

'The most selfish, competitive, scene-stealing toad I've ever had the misfortune to work with.'

'It's gone well then?'

'I hate his fucking guts and I wish he'd choke on his own conceit and die a very painful death.'

Even though I'm laughing, I'm a bit surprised to hear this kind of poison from the beautiful girl with the glistening eyes that I'm sitting next to, but I'm glad she shares my opinion. Kirsty tells us we're needed and we follow her into the flat where Mike shows us the moves. We're to enter the flat with Kim holding the baby and me with the carrycot and a suitcase. We then go to the bedroom and I take the baby, put her in the cot and sing her a little song, while Kim unpacks the suitcase. When she's finished, we move into the kitchen, where Kim finds a bottle of gin in Mum's old hiding place, and we have a drink and talk at the kitchen table.

The baby's asleep when the mother gives her to me and she stays that way while we shoot the first part, where we walk in the front door and go to the bedroom. After they've set up the shot in the bedroom and we're rehearsing it, she wakes up, starts to cry and we have to stop. Mike gets a bit tetchy and tense but once mum's given her a feed she drops off again and stays asleep while I put her to bed. When I tell Mike I'm worried that me singing 'Hush little baby' is going to wake her, he tells me to try just humming a few bars quietly, because he wants to see Ella's maternal side. When I do it, the little thing opens her eyes and gives me a lovely smile and it's all I can do to stop the tears welling up.

We do the scene a few times with the camera in different

positions, until Mike says he's got it, and we move into the kitchen. It's really cramped in there but apart from a bit where Kim and I can't stop giggling after I say "this flock of bats" instead of "this block of flats", we get it done and break for a meal.

Ed announces that the bus the crew normally eat in has been held up and won't arrive until tomorrow, so the caterers have put a buffet on the table in the corridor. Everyone files out and Kim and I follow. The food looks really nice but when Brindle gets out of the lift my appetite disappears. He gives me a cold look and walks into the flat. Kim nudges me. 'What's up with Laurence Olivier?'

'Search me,' I reply, and pour myself a glass of water. Kim is looking at me. 'Are you OK?'

'I'm fine,' I say and pick up an egg sandwich.

'The stupid little twat's probably having a strop because nobody opened the car door and bowed and scraped and brought him his dinner.'

'Probably,' I reply.

Kirsty approaches and tells Kim she won't be needed for a while and she can go back to her trailer, if she'd like to.

Kim puts her plate down, puts an arm round me and gives me a peck on the cheek, 'I'll see you later. Good luck with Stanislavski,' she says, and walks off towards the lift.

I've no idea who this Stan person is, but I'm still feeling a nice little shimmer from the kiss when Kirsty tells me that Deidre wants to see me. I follow her into the flat next door to the one we're shooting in and into a bedroom.

'Time to slip into this little number my darling,' says Deidre, holding up the Verrier dress.

I take off the Mary Quant jacket and skirt, Deidre hangs it on her rail and slips the dress over my head. I smooth it over my hips, look in the mirror and see that it looks clingy and elegant.

'Mmm... very tasty,' says Deidre.

We decide that the stockings I'm wearing will do, so she gives me a pair of medium heels to put on and declares herself satisfied. Kirsty tells me I've to wait while they finish shooting in the corridor and takes me to the kitchen, where Colette freshens up my make-up and brushes my hair.

When they've shot Brindle doing the lock on the front door, they move the camera into the flat and I watch from the lounge while they shoot the bit where he finds my modelling portfolio in the hall and has a good look at it. It's actually blank pages, because I haven't done the photo shoot yet, but apparently the editor will add the pictures later. Mike takes me into the corridor and explains that he wants me to put my key in the lock, find that the door is open, come in cautiously and call out for Mary. Brindle will then come out of the bedroom, grab hold of me, pull me into the lounge, chuck me on the sofa and leap on top of me. He says he's going to stop the scene there and then move the camera nearer. While Mike's explaining this Brindle's leaning on the wall with his head down looking like he'd rather be somewhere else.

'Is that OK for both of you?' asks Mike.

'I reckon,' I say.

Brindle gives a slight nod and goes into the bedroom.

'Right, so, let's mark it through in slow motion, shall we?' says Mike.

I go out of the front door and we wait while Ken and the boys move the camera to the far end of the hall beside the kitchen. When Mike calls action, I push the front door open slowly and say Mary's name. Brindle glides out of the bedroom, takes hold of my wrist and pulls me to him, then he takes me by the shoulders, lifts me off my feet, carries me into the lounge and lays me gently on the sofa. When he lies on top of me and looks into my eyes, I get a whiff of foul breath as he whispers in my ear, 'I'm going to hurt you.'

He gets off me and Mike comes over to us. 'I'm afraid I'm not happy with the positions on the sofa. It looks contrived and wrong. If we fit you with a good back pad Rina, would you mind if Johnny puts you on the floor?'

'Let's try it,' I say.

'Thank you. We'll get you fitted up right away.'

Brindle wanders back into the bedroom and Kirsty takes me back to wardrobe in the flat next door. Kim is there trying on some trousers. I tell Deidre that I'm to have a back pad and she takes a weird looking metal frame, with a padded plastic panel in the shape of a back, out of the wardrobe.

'That's the one I wore, isn't it?' says Kim.

'It is,' says Deidre.

'It's great. He slammed me into a wall and I didn't feel a thing.'

Deidre helps me off with my dress and straps me into the contraption. Once she's pulled it about a bit it feels quite comfortable and I put the dress back on.

We do another slow motion rehearsal, using the floor instead of the sofa and when Mike's satisfied that the pad can't be seen, Ed tells everyone to stand by and I go and wait in the corridor.

Mike calls action and I open the door and move slowly inside. When I say Mary's name Brindle flies out of the bedroom and grabs me round the neck with both hands and starts to throttle me. I bring my knee up into his balls and he grunts and lets go. I could nut him easy, but I remember what I'm doing and turn back to the front door. He grabs me round the shoulders, drags me across the hall and throws me into the lounge. I hit the floor, he lands on top of me and pins me down.

'Cut,' says Mike.

Brindle gets off me, stands up slowly and puts his hand to his crotch while I roll over and get up. Mike looks to Ken and gets a nod from him.

'Are you all right Rina?' he asks.

'Yeah. This pad's the business,' I reply.

'Johnny?'

Brindle sits on the sofa and opens and closes his legs a couple of times. 'I'm OK.'

'That was terrific, particularly the neck and goolies bit you put in at the top, although you might have warned me.

We might need to pick up a reverse on you, Rina, for when you turned back to the door, but we'll move into the living room now that it's dark.'

Ed announces a fifteen minute break and I go into the corridor, pour myself a cup of coffee and sit next to Kim.

'One of the prop boys said you gave him a good kick in the knackers,' she says.

'Least I could do,' I reply.

'Wait till I get hold of that frying pan.'

Kirsty comes and tells Kim that Deidre wants to see her again and she gives me a wink and goes to wardrobe. I sip my coffee and look round for Brindle but he's not about. Ed comes out of the flat and the crew follow him and head for the remains of the buffet. Mike appears behind them, deep in conversation with Ken, and they move along the corridor. Ed picks up a sandwich and joins them.

I've suddenly got a feeling that I need to know where Brindle is. I wait until no one's looking, then I slip in through the front door of the flat, creep into the lounge and see him on the balcony. He's leaning on the parapet looking out over London and I know this is my chance. I open the glass door and step onto the balcony. He goes on staring into the distance and I walk slowly towards him and tap him on the shoulder.

He turns to me and I punch him on the point of his jaw. As he staggers back, I bend down, take hold of his ankles and tip him over the balcony.

I move fast out of the flat, into the corridor, and sit in my canvas chair.

21

It's a while before he's found. We've gone back in after the break, Mike and Ken are deciding on a camera position and the sparks are setting lamps. Mike asks me to lie on the floor so that they can look at the shot, and just as he calls for Brindle, a siren starts wailing, and then another one, and suddenly there's lights flashing, the sound of tyres squealing and a voice shouting at people to stand back. Someone goes onto the balcony, says there's a body down below and they all pile out and have a look. I follow them, go to the end of the parapet and lean over. Two police cars are on the pavement and Brindle's in the headlights, spread out on the concrete with his head in a pool of blood. One copper is kneeling beside the body and another two are stringing crime scene tape around the area. A small crowd of people have gathered and two other plods are keeping them at a distance.

Mike runs out of the flat followed by Ed and the rest of the crew. I get to the corridor as people are piling into the lift. Deidre appears from the flat next door and grabs my arm. 'What the fuck happened?'

'I don't know,' I say.

'Were you shooting on the balcony?'

I shake my head, follow the rest of the crew towards the other lift, which has just arrived, and squeeze in between a couple of prop men. Nobody talks while we creak down

224

to the ground floor. When we get to where Brindle landed, a police van pulls up beside the cars and two crime scene officers in the white suits and hoods get out. One of them photographs the body from various angles, then he puts the camera back in the van and they both kneel beside the body. One takes a sample of the blood and puts it in a test tube, while the other takes Brindle's fingerprints. Mike and Ed are talking with two coppers by one of the police cars. After a while Ed comes over and tells us we're to go back up to the flat where the police will speak to us.

On the tenth floor the senior plod tells us to wait in the corridor and goes into the flat. After a while Kirsty calls us in one by one. When it's my turn, I go in and they ask me where I was and if I saw anything. I tell them I was in the corridor with everyone else during the break, went into the lounge to shoot the scene and had no idea what had happened until the alarm was raised. They've got me down on a list as Rina Walker, but I say that's just my stage name. I tell them I'm really called Gloria Wilkins and give them an address in Chiswick.

After everyone's been questioned Don the producer arrives. When he's had a confab with Mike and Ed, he calls us together and tells us to go home and that we'll be contacted as soon as it's been decided what's going to happen after this terrible tragedy. As people are packing up and leaving Kim comes over to me, looking shocked and pale, and we walk towards the lift. 'What do you think happened?'

'I've no idea,' I reply.

'Was he OK when you rehearsed?'

'He was quiet, but he seemed all right.'

I keep my eyes down and don't say anything in the lift and when we get to the trailers I tell Kim I need to go and she says she understands, gives me her phone number and we kiss goodbye. I go to the trailer and change out of my costume. As I step out, Kirsty sees me, tells me the car's ready and asks me for my phone number to give to production. I make one up for her, say goodbye and head for the car. Harry starts talking as soon as I get in the back, but when I sob and sniff a bit he shuts up and drives.

I get out of the car at Marble Arch and walk up Edgware Road feeling clear and light headed as I always do after a job. I pass by the Arab shops and cafés with the men sitting outside, smoking the hookahs and drinking coffee, and I sniff the rich cooking smells on the air. An American convertible with the roof down pulls up at the lights and I get a wolf whistle and the offer of a lift from a couple of young blades in sharp suits.

As I walk on to Maida Vale I'm remembering when I was little and my Grandpa taught me that knockout punch, that I got Brindle with, and how he made me keep hitting him again and again at that exact spot beside the point of his chin until my knuckles bled. I'd come home bruised one day, after I'd been bullied by some older girls in the playground, and he swore he was going to teach me how to look after myself and make sure it would never happen to me again. He was only a small man but he was one of the best fighters around Notting Hill in his day.

He taught me that speed, not strength, was the vital part of winning a fight and always to go for the weakest point first. I really loved him and Grandma and I still miss them.

As I approach the flats I slip into a doorway and check there's nobody sitting in a parked car watching the building, just in case the news of Brindle's death has got to some of his little friends. I can't see anything to worry about so I go along the service road and into the foyer. Dennis is on the phone behind the desk. He sees me, holds up a piece of paper and I go over and take it from him. It's a message from Bert telling me to call him. Dennis holds the phone away from his ear and points at it. I can hear a high pitched voice jabbering away. He mouths the words 'the wife' and raises his eyebrows. I smile, wish him goodnight and go and call the lift.

I stop at Lizzie's door and wonder if I should see if she's awake. It's gone two o'clock and now she's got an office job I reckon she needs her sleep but I knock anyway. When there's no response I leave it and unlock the door to my flat. There's an envelope with the crest of Leavenden School on the mat and I pick it up and open it. It's the programme for the school Sports Day which is happening the day after tomorrow. I write a note for Lizzie, asking her if she wants to come with me and telling her to drop in or phone me in the morning. I slip the note under her door, then I go into my bedroom, peel off my clothes and get between the sheets with *Rebecca*, but I'm asleep before I've even opened the book.

• • •

It's just gone eight o'clock when the phone wakes me. It's Bert saying George wants to see me. I tell him to pick me up in an hour, then I phone Lizzie and ask her about going to Georgie's Sports Day. She says she'd love to, as long as Gerald can mind the office, and she'll call me back later. I make coffee, have a quick bath, and as soon as I'm dressed, Keith the porter's on the phone telling me that Bert's waiting. I knock on Lizzie's door on the way past, in the hope of a quick cuddle, but she must have left for the office.

Bert parks the Jag in Lancaster Road and rings George's bell. We wait a bit and then old Jacky opens the door in his pyjamas, sways a bit and steadies himself against the doorframe. 'You were well out of order last night, Bert Davis.'

'That's the thanks I get for saving you from a fucking good hiding?' says Bert.

'That streak of fucking piss couldn't punch his way out of a paper bag.'

'That streak of fucking piss is a hundred years younger than you. He punishes the heavy bag for an hour a day, and you go and call his mother a slag.'

'I fight my own fucking battles.'

'I'll leave you alone next time then.'

'Fucking right. Making me look a cunt.'

'Go back to bed Jacky,' says Bert, walking past him and opening the door of the lounge. George is sitting in his usual armchair wearing a maroon silk dressing gown with a velvet collar. He points to a chair opposite him and I sit.

'Were you in Islington last night?' he says.

'I was,' I reply.

'And that was Brindle who took a tumble off that balcony?'

'It was.'

'With a bit of help from you?'

'Just a bit. How did you know about it?'

'Bert got it from one of the crew who came in the pub.' Bert nods.

'How did the Bill book it?' asks George.

'Accidental, I reckon. Maybe suicide,' I say.

George broods for a moment, looking at the fireplace. 'It's not ideal.'

'He was hard to get to.'

'It'll have to do, I suppose. Do you want a drink?'

'I want my money.'

'Not yet.'

'What now, for fuck's sake?'

'I need you to find the Teales.'

'What's gone on?' I ask.

'We put the frighteners on Danny and Jack and got the story that they only told Brindle they'd go with him against me so they'd get Dawn back and they were going to do him once they'd got her.'

'They don't give a fuck about her,' I say.

'I know that now.'

'So where are they?'

'No one knows. I need you to find them and get rid of

them, then you're on a pay day.'

I know it's a waste of time to argue as he's holding all the cards. I look him in the eye. 'I want your word you'll give the money to Georgie if I get toasted.'

'You've got it,' he says, and I know he means it.

'What about Marlene?' I ask.

'She just got done for fencing.'

'Gone away?'

'On remand.'

'Nice.'

While I sip my whisky, I'm thinking that George is right to want the Teales gone, in case they've got notions about wasting him and taking over the firm. I doubt if they've got it in them, but they have done a runner and it's not worth the risk.

'What happened to Dawn?' George asks.

'Brindle had her banged up in Birmingham but I got her out and she's safe and away.'

'Nice one. Give the girl a lift home Bert.'

'I want expenses.'

'Bert'll see you right.'

'Could you drop me in Harlesden?' I ask.

'I don't mind,' says Bert.

I leave George pouring himself another drink and follow Bert to the car. On the way to Harlesden we talk about the Teales and agree that even though Danny is the better fighter, Jack is the more devious and dangerous of the brothers and he can get Danny to do anything he wants.

Bert drops me beside the second hand car lot in Scrubs Lane, gives me three hundred quid and I walk between the rows of motors looking at what's on offer. I stop beside a Sunbeam Alpine and while I'm looking it over, a familiar figure in a trilby hat hoves into view. 'Hello again. Bored with the Cortina already?'

'Wrote it off, didn't I?'

'I hope you weren't hurt.'

'No, I was lucky,' I say.

'This Alpine is a very nice car indeed.'

While he goes into his spiel about the one careful owner and all that blarney, I decide the car is a bit too distinctive and I look round for something a bit less conspicuous. There's a dark blue Ford Anglia in the next row that looks like it might do, so I wander over and have a look. It's a couple of years old, done fifteen thousand miles, it's taxed for six months and only two hundred and fifty quid. Trilby runs off to get the key while I check that it's got a radio. We go for a drive and I have to listen to the history of the Ford Motor Company all over again, but this time the Anglia is the best car they've made since the Model T. After a couple of miles on the North Circular I reckon it handles pretty well, the brakes are good and it seems quite pokey. Back on the forecourt I talk him down to two twenty-five and a full tank of petrol, give him the cash, pocket the log book and drive down Scrubs Lane, with the Beach Boys, Surfin' USA.

22

The phone's ringing as I open the door to the flat. It's Lizzie saying that Gerald can't mind the office tomorrow but they've decided to give one of the escort girls a go at handling it because she's got a posh accent. Lizzie's shown the girl what she needs to do already and she's picked it up fine, so she can come to Sports Day with me. I'm so happy Lizzie's going to be with me and when she says that Booker T & the MGs are at the Marquee tonight and asks me if I want to go, I feel even happier and tell her there's nothing I'd like better. She says she's got a bit of business at the Kazuko and asks me to pick her up from there at about eight.

I go into the kitchen and look in the cabinet for something to eat. The bread's gone mouldy and when I unwrap some sausages they smell bad too so I chuck them in the bin along with the bread. I can't be bothered to go to the shops so I open a tin of spaghetti, dump the contents into a pan and put it on the stove to heat up. There are a couple of eggs left so I light the gas under the frying pan and drop them in once the fat's melted. I pick up a kitchen knife, go into the bathroom, unscrew the panel on the side of the bath, take out a few notes and put them in my pocket.

When I've gone back to the kitchen and discovered why no one eats fried eggs with tinned spaghetti, I chuck the remains in the bin, put the dishes in the sink and go into the lounge with *Rebecca*. I lie on the sofa and read about our girl going to the beach again and meeting a man who's a bit loopy who asks her if she's going to put him in the asylum and tells her that Rebecca was like a snake. She goes back to the house feeling confused and meets the dashing Jack Favell who takes her for a spin in his sports car and chats her up, and she gets a bit frightened of him. Then Mrs Danvers tells her about Rebecca being drowned, and how she thinks she's haunting the house, and it's all getting creepier and more horrible for her and the words on the page start to swim in front of my eyes and I fall asleep.

I'm woken by the phone ringing, but as I get up off the sofa, it stops. I pick *Rebecca* up off the floor where it fell. I'm about to carry on reading when I notice the time and realise that I must have slept for ages and I need to get ready if I'm going to pick up Lizzie from the Kazuko in time to catch Booker T.

I decide on my black Anne Klein V-neck dress, sheer stockings and the Alberto Fermani heels. I freshen up my make-up, give my hair a light spray of Aqua Net and wonder whether I need to take a tool. I don't want a blade in my suspenders if I'm dancing so I slip the knuckle duster into my shoulder bag and put on my sway-back jacket.

Dennis is behind the desk in the foyer. 'Out on the town Miss?'

'Looking that way,' I reply.

'That's what Friday night's for, eh?'

'I hope you won't go too wild in here Dennis. I know what you're like.'

'I'll try and keep it down Miss.'

Through the glass door I catch sight of a cab for hire waiting at the lights. I say goodnight to Dennis and get to the road in time to flag him down. I jump in and tell him to take me to Rupert Street.

The West End's warming up nicely as we drive down Regent Street and into Shaftesbury Avenue. I get out of the cab at the corner of Rupert Street and walk towards the Kazuko. A couple of Mods stop me and ask if I know where the Scene Club is and I tell them how to get there. The Scene is a hot little basement club in Ham Yard, off Great Windmill Street, that I've been to a couple of times. They sometimes have bands on but it's mostly a DJ who plays really great soul, R&B, blues, ska and rock'n'roll records to a sharply dressed crowd of Mods full of lager and pills.

When I get near the Kazuko I can see a man in a grey raincoat and fedora talking to the man behind the desk. He doesn't look like a punter and something tells me not to go in. As I walk past, the doorman gives the man an envelope which he slips in his coat pocket. I stop and look at the menu outside a Chinese restaurant a bit further down the street, and once the man in the mac has gone past me, I go back to the club. The doorman knows me as a friend of Lizzie's and although I'd like to know how much he's just bunged the Vice Squad, I reckon it's best not to ask. I pass my jacket to the cloakroom girl, put the ticket in my bag, give the doorman a smile and he waves me into the club.

All the tables are occupied and the waitresses are busy weaving their way through the punters and delivering bottles of champagne and brandy. The pianist has a bass player and a drummer with him tonight, helping him through something hot and jazzy that I don't recognise. One of the waitresses opens the curtain that's across one of the booths at the end of the room and I get a glimpse of a girl in a bra going down on a Japanese man. It takes me a minute to spot Lizzie at the bar talking to an older woman in a gold lamé dress, a beehive hairdo and a ton of make-up. It looks like they're having a pretty intense conversation so I catch Lizzie's eye, sit on a stool at the other end of the bar and order a whisky. After a while the gold lamé one walks through the tables to the back of the club and goes out through a door. Lizzie comes and sits on the stool next to me, looking a bit peeved.

'Who was that?' I ask.

'The old cow who owns this dump.'

'What's her problem?'

'She's found out we've got a couple of girls from here working as escorts and she's demanding a taste.'

'They can work where they like can't they?'

'Of course they can, but the old bat's so fucking greedy she can't see an earner go by without kicking up a fuss.'

'What are you going to do?'

'Probably throw her a fiver to keep her quiet.'

'You're making a few quid though?'

'Yeah. It's going really well. We've got toffs queuing up for girls.'

'That's great.'

'Apart from lover boy slobbering all over me.'

'Is he still smitten?'

'Not half. He says he wants to marry me when his divorce comes through.'

A couple of gents in suits appear beside us and one of them asks us if we'd like to join them for a drink in a weird accent that might be Swedish. Lizzie tells them we're just leaving but we'd love to have a drink with them another time and they move on. We go to the cloakroom, collect our coats, Lizzie gives the girl half a crown and we walk up to Shaftesbury Avenue.

There's a show called 'Robert and Elizabeth' on at the Lyric Theatre, with a big poster of June Bronhill and Keith Michell looking all romantic, and Keith's wearing more make-up than June. I remark that I could fancy Miss Bronhill and Lizzie says she wouldn't kick Keith out of bed either. We turn into Wardour Street and when we get to the Marquee there's people milling around outside and a rich smell of hash. There's a poster on the door for Booker T and a support band called Blues by Five. We pay six bob each to get in and leave our jackets in the cloakroom. As we go down the narrow corridor, I can hear a tasty version of 'Cross Road Blues'.

The club is packed tight and it's hot and sweaty, with a hundred cigarettes stoking up the fug. The band are sounding really bluesy and sexy and the guitarist is weaving a great solo as we squeeze through the crowd, until we can see four of them in a line at the front of the stage with the drummer behind. They look all clean cut in white shirts and straight trousers, and not much like rock musicians, but they can really play the blues. The singer's moving well with a hand mic and the crowd are loving it. I put my arm round Lizzie, we swing our hips to the beat and I start to relax and let go. We get a couple of slow ones then they finish up with 'Shake Your Moneymaker'. We have a bit of a jive and the crowd give them a big send off. The roadies come on and start shifting the speakers and we move to the bar.

When I can finally get served, I buy two treble whiskies and we go back to the main room to get a spot near the stage. On the way there a scuffle breaks out between a couple of young blokes. One of them is accusing the other of bumping into his girlfriend and nicking her purse out of her pocket and they're squaring up to each other and throwing punches. As we move back out of the way I tread on something. I look down and see it's a leather purse, so I pick it up and offer it to the girl. She takes it off me and as her boyfriend staggers back after collecting a right hook, she waves it in his face and he looks at it, mumbles an apology to the other bloke and things simmer down. As we get near the front of the stage Lizzie says she thinks she's seen the tough guy before, playing drums with some band from Shepherds Bush.

The music from the speakers fades and the singer from the support band comes on and announces Booker T &

the MGs. The audience clap and hoot and Booker Jones walks on and sits at the organ, followed by the drummer, bass player and the guitarist, and they kick off with 'Time is Tight', really funky and loud. The organ sound is hard and edgy and so is Steve Cropper's guitar. Steve and the bass player don't move much but they play really tight and the music's loud and punchy, but somehow smooth at the same time. Me and Lizzie move back through the crowd to where we can dance. I'm shaking and twirling and lost in the joy of it, when a couple of young West Indians with snaky hips start moving with us and we open up and let them in. The music goes on and on with hardly any breaks and by the time we get to 'Green Onions' and it's all over, I'm about ready to collapse. The audience are still clamouring for more but Booker's not coming out again, so we say goodnight to the dancing boys and head for home.

When the cab drops us off on Maida Vale we go into the foyer and find Dennis fast asleep behind the desk. We creep past him so's not to wake him, ease the lift gate open as quietly as we can and go up to our floor. Lizzie puts a finger to her lips as we get out of the lift, and it's another creep past her door in case Gerald's still awake. When we get into mine I pour us both a nightcap and look at the programme for Sports Day at Leavenden. The final of the inter-house lacrosse tournament starts at 2.30pm, then there's the track and field events, after that an MP presents the prizes and we're all invited to tea in the marquee.

'Sounds like fun,' says Lizzie, downing her drink, taking me by the hand and leading me to the bedroom.

23

It's a warm day and the sun's shining as we sit outside the French café in Clifton Road with coffee and croissants. Gerald had left by the time we got up and Lizzie was able to go to her flat and put on a summer dress and a cashmere cardigan. I'm wearing a light grey suit with a blue paisley silk scarf and we reckon we're dressed about right. Lizzie's bought a paper and she shows me a story about 300 people getting injured when 150,000 turned out in Liverpool to welcome the Beatles back from their world tour.

I leave Lizzie to get the bill while I go to the newsagent and buy a road map. We walk round to Hall Road, get into the Anglia and I work out the route to Leavenden and show it to Lizzie on the map. It's over the river to Elephant and Castle, down the A20 and the school's just beyond Tonbridge. I put the radio on and the reception from Caroline is even worse than usual so I change to the Light Programme and we listen to Saturday Club with Brian Matthew, as we head into town and over the river.

A couple of hours later I swing the car through the tall gates of Leavenden School for Girls and we roll up the long gravel drive. There are wide immaculate lawns on one side and trees on the other that seem to bow to us in the wind. We round a bend and there is the school, a large red brick Victorian mansion with a long side wing that looks more recent. As we approach we see a marquee on the lawn near to the house and the sports field in front of it with the white lines of the running track and a pitch marked out, with goals at each end. There's a large crowd of parents there already. A few girls are jogging on the track and some others are trotting about on the pitch with lacrosse sticks. I see a sign for the car park, with an arrow pointing round to the side of the house. I follow its direction and park the Anglia between a Rolls Royce Silver Cloud and a Bentley Continental.

'I told you we should have come in the Lagonda darling,' says Lizzie, as we get out of the car.

'And worn a hat,' I say, looking at the parents walking towards the sports field and the array of elegant bonnets. As we're crossing the car park, a black Daimler pulls in and drives past us.

'Oh fuck!' says Lizzie, taking my elbow and steering me round the corner of the house.

'What's the matter?' I ask.

'Gerald and his missus.'

'What?'

'In the Daimler.'

'Have they got kids here?'

'Must have. She's liable to kill me if she sees me. It's best if I leave you to it.'

'Don't be daft.'

'It'll only be embarrassing and you're here to see Georgie, not referee a fight.'

'You've come to see Georgie too and she'll be so glad you're here.'

'I don't know.'

I look round the corner of the house and see Gerald get out of the car and open the rear door for a tall brunette in a blue dress and a pillbox hat with a feather. An older couple get out of the other side and the four of them make their way across the car park towards us.

'It's too late now.' I grab Lizzie's arm and lead her off towards the playing field. I head for the marquee, in case there's a drink on offer that I can get down her, but as we get near the tent a heavy set woman in a pair of brown culottes, knee socks and plimsolls comes out of the house followed by a line of girls carrying lacrosse sticks, who form up in front of the marquee. I get a rush of pride when I see that Georgie's among them, and I want to wave and try to catch her eye but a group of more soberly dressed women have now come out from the marquee, and an older one among them is mounting a small platform in front of the tent. The parents all gather round and the lady on the platform welcomes everyone to Leavenden School Sports Day, says how lucky we are with the weather, tells us that the final of the lacrosse tournament will now be played between Richmond and Hazelwood houses and asks us to make our way to the pitch, where the game will begin in ten minutes. I look round at Lizzie. 'Are you OK?'

'Yeah. Fuck'em,' she says. A stiff looking gent standing next to her turns and raises an eyebrow and we head for the touch line. We catch up with Georgie on the way, wish her good luck and I can tell she's glad we've come. She runs off onto the pitch and I turn round and bump straight into Gerald.

'I do beg your pardon… Oh,' he says, as he recognises me.

His wife is standing very still, staring icily at Lizzie, and the older couple are either side of her. 'Aren't you going to introduce us?' says the older man.

'Oh, yes of course,' says Gerald. 'Erm… Elizabeth and Rina, this is Lord and Lady Hackett and er… my wife Jessica.'

'You're both a bit young to have a daughter here, aren't you?' says His Lordship as he shakes my hand.

'My sister,' I say.

'Ah. In the team?'

'Yes.'

'Which house?'

'Richmond.'

'Our two are Hazelwood.'

'I think the game's about to start. Let's go over the other side, it's less crowded,' says Gerald, taking his wife's arm and moving off.

'Won't you join us? I have a small flask,' says His Lordship, with a twinkle.

'We'll stay this side thanks. I think these might be the Richmond supporters,' I reply.

'Probably wise. Wouldn't want any hooliganism breaking out, eh what?'

Her Ladyship favours us with a smile. 'Come on Eustace, we're going to miss the start,' she says, walking off after Gerald and the woman who's about to take him for every penny he's got.

The referee blows her whistle and Lizzie and I find a place behind the touchline, while the teams form up in each half. Richmond are in blue and Hazelwood are wearing white. Georgie's standing with one foot slightly in front of the other, balanced and ready to go as the referee calls one girl from each team to the centre spot. The girls raise their sticks and bring them together so that the netted ends are touching. The referee places the ball in between the two nets, steps back and blows her whistle. The girls wrestle with the sticks for a moment until the Richmond girl gets the ball free and hurls it down the far side of the pitch. It's caught by a Hazelwood girl and she runs forward, until her stick gets whacked by an opponent's and the ball falls out, to be scooped up by a Richmond girl, who tries to get it in the air, but a jab from a Hazelwood stick makes her drop it. Several girls fight over the ball with a clattering of sticks, until one of them snaffles it, has a quick look round and skies it to our side of the pitch. Georgie belts past us in a blur, catches the ball and has a shot at goal. The keeper blocks it and passes it straight out to her winger on the far side who gets tackled hard and hits the ground. The referee blows her whistle and runs to the girl who's gone down, but by the time she reaches her she's on her feet again.

The game restarts. Richmond get possession and make

good ground towards goal. Georgie's in the thick of it and I'm so glad to see her getting stuck in to something that isn't just her schoolwork. Lizzie and I are shouting encouragement and a woman beside us with a really deep voice is bellowing at Hazelwood every time they make a mistake. Richmond are still in their opponents' half and looking like they're going to score until a defender digs the ball out, whacks it up the other end and a couple of Hazelwood forwards dance it round the goalie and put it in the net.

I look across the pitch and see His Lordship doing a victory jig, Gerald's cheering and clapping his hands and even the wife has cracked a smile. The game starts again and Richmond fight really hard but in spite of several attempts at goal, with Georgie leading a couple of them, Richmond fail to score and it's 1-0 at half time. We walk away from the pitch and sit down in some long grass nearby.

'I'd no idea it was such a rough and tough game,' says Lizzie.

'Nor me,' I reply, lying back and chewing on a blade of grass.

'Hardly ladylike, eh?'

'Good fun though.'

'I'll say.'

'Looks like Gerald's wife is doing the martyr bit, so you're all right.'

'If she sucks her cheeks in much more she'll swallow herself.'

'Are those her parents?'

Lizzie nods. 'Lord and Lady Hackett, they own Yorkshire.'

Lizzie's just lowering herself down beside me when we hear three blasts on a whistle. We get to our feet and go back to the touchline as the teams form up for the second half.

The two captains touch sticks in the centre and the referee puts the ball between the nets and blows her whistle. This time the Richmond captain wins the ball and passes it to the winger who catches it, cradles in her net, runs down the touchline and lobs it into a space in front of the goal where about six girls dive in and fight for it. There's a tangle of bodies and a clashing of sticks until one of them hikes it out to Georgie, who's been hovering nearby, and she whacks it past the goalie and scores. We whoop and cheer as the referee blows her whistle and the woman with the deep voice lays into the Hazelwood defence.

The game restarts and it's looking fairly equal with play moving from one half to the other and a few failed shots from each team until Hazelwood score again, then Richmond equalise with a brilliant shot by a very tall girl, from almost the halfway line, and then a few minutes before the end, Georgie sends a great pass across the goal from the corner, the keeper dives for the ball and misses, and a Richmond girl scoops it up and hooks it into the back of the net. The referee blows the final whistle, the parents give a massive cheer and everyone claps the teams as they walk off the field towards the house.

Next there's some races on the track and Georgie comes second in the hundred yards. The last event is the high jump, and the tall girl who was in the lacrosse match wins it easily. She gets a big round of applause and then there's a general move by the spectators towards the marquee. We follow on, keeping a good distance between us and Gerald's party. As we're entering the tent, the lady who made the speech before the game comes up to me. 'Are you Georgina Walker's sister, by any chance?'

'Yes, I am,' I say.

'Margot Rainsford, I'm the headmistress,' she says, holding out her hand.

We shake, and I introduce Lizzie to her.

'I just wanted to say how delighted we are to have Georgina at the school. Her academic performance has been exemplary, we think it's highly likely that she'll get into Cambridge and now, as you'll have seen, she's distinguishing herself on the sports field as well.'

'It's nice of you to say so,' I reply.

'I'm very keen to have more pupils of her type at Leavenden and I very much hope that Georgina will be the first of many. Do enjoy your tea.'

I almost feel like tugging my forelock as she sweeps off, approaches a woman with a lorgnette, who's bending forward studying the top tier of a cake stand, and taps her on the shoulder.

'Snobby cunt,' says Lizzie.

'Just the sort of language I'd expect, from a girl of your type.' I say.

As Lizzie laughs and gives me a dig with her elbow, I see Georgie come into the tent. I give her a wave and she comes over.

'Here's our goal scorer!' says Lizzie.

'We only just did it,' says Georgie.

'You were great out there,' I say.

'Thanks.'

'And you almost won your race.'

'Natalie got a better start.'

'Make sure you beat her next time,' says Lizzie.

Margot Rainsford mounts the podium, taps the microphone, congratulates the athletes and calls upon Harriet Cooper, member of parliament for Eastbourne to present the prizes. Harriet tells us how she owes her success to the fine education she received at Leavenden, dishes out the cups and medals and we all line up for tea and cakes.

'Where's Annabelle?' I ask Georgie.

'She's not well.'

'That's a shame. I hope it's not serious.'

'Just a bad cold, but the matron's made her stay indoors.'

'Did you have a nice time at hers?'

'It was amazing. We went riding and they've got a swimming pool.'

'How lovely,' I say, adding it to the list of things the new house is going to have.

When tea is finished, the headmistress tells us that the art room is open, if we would care to visit before we leave, and that she hopes she will see us all again at the forthcoming performance of 'Romeo and Juliet' at the end of term. Georgie takes us to the art room, which is in the main house, and we look at the girls' paintings, some of which are really good, and then she comes with us to the car park, thanks us for coming and we say goodbye.

As I pull the car out onto the drive I see her walking across the lawn towards the school and I feel sad to be leaving her. Lizzie senses it and puts her hand on my knee.

'She's fine,' she says.

'I know… it's just…'

'She's fine, really.'

• • •

After a pleasant run through the Kentish countryside we settle in among the traffic on the A20 and head for London. We talk about the day and how rude the headmistress was and Lizzie says it's lucky that Gerald's sort don't go in for scenes in public, considering the mayhem his wife caused when she caught them in bed together, and we have a laugh about how furious she looked, and how the feather in her pill box hat was shaking. When we get into London we decide to go home and change, then go out for a posh meal and on to a club. I park the Anglia on Hall Road and we walk round the corner to the flats.

As we arrive at the front door, it swings open and a man in a grey suit comes out followed by two uniformed police and a WPC. The uniforms grab me and push me face first against the wall. One of them cuffs my wrists, the other one turns me round and the plain clothes man stands in front of me.

'Katherine Walker. I am arresting you for the murder of Jonathan Brindle. You do not have to say anything, unless you wish to do so, but what you do say may be given in evidence.'

24

They walk me to the kerb and put me in the back of an unmarked car between the WPC and one of the uniforms. Lizzie follows us to the pavement and I see her stricken face as we drive away. With my wrists cuffed behind my back I have to sit forward in the seat and I can feel the woman's breath on my cheek as she looks me over. The driver bombs along Marylebone Road, does a left turn onto Penton Street, goes round a corner and stops outside Islington nick. I'm pulled out of the car, walked in through a side door, my cuffs are taken off and I'm told to sit down at a desk. A sergeant comes in, sits opposite me and asks me to confirm my name and address. After he's written them down he asks me if I want legal representation. I tell him I do, he says that a solicitor will be appointed, shown the evidence against me and that I will receive a visit from him shortly. He asks me if I want anyone informed of my arrest. The only person I'd want to know is well aware of it already, so I say no and the sergeant picks up his paperwork and leaves.

The WPC steps forward and takes me to another room where my fingerprints are taken. The contents of my shoulder bag are tipped onto a table and inspected by the male copper, and I'm glad I took the brass knuckles out before I went to Sports Day. He puts the bits and pieces back in the bag and leaves. Another WPC comes in, leans against the wall and watches while the other one makes me hold my arms out and gives me a body search, which she clearly enjoys, while getting a couple of knowing looks from her mate.

When they've had their little bit of entertainment they take me downstairs to the cells. I walk past a couple of old blokes lying on bunks and a young lad standing behind the bars, looking lost and sorry for himself. They take me to a cell at the far end of the block, unlock the door and tell me to take my shoes off. I step out of my slingbacks and go into the cell. One of them picks up my shoes, the other locks me in and they walk off down the corridor.

I stand by the bunks, clasp my hands together and press my wrist against the edge of the metal frame until I'm feeling nothing but the pain. When it's driven the anger away I let go, lie on the bottom bunk and massage my wrist while I try to work out how I can have got nicked. It can't be anyone on the film because they were all in the corridor when it happened and if someone on the ground saw anything they'd be too far away to identify me. As I'm trying to think of any other angle I hear footsteps and the WPC appears and unlocks the door.

'Your brief's here,' she says, swinging the door open and jerking her head in the direction of the corridor. She gives me my shoes and I follow her upstairs to a room with a desk and a couple of filing cabinets. She tells me to take a seat and leaves. Moments later a short man in a suit and tie, wearing horn-rimmed glasses and carrying a briefcase comes in.

'Katherine Walker?'

'Yes.'

'Duncan Mayfield. I've been appointed your solicitor.'

'That was quick,' I say.

'My practice is nearby and I happened to be working late.'

He opens his briefcase, takes out a file, opens it and puts it on the desk in front of him. 'You are charged with the murder of Jonathan Brindle on the 18th of June 1964. The police have shown me the evidence they have to support that charge and I must tell you that they have a statement from an eyewitness who claims she saw you throw Brindle off a tenth floor balcony at the Brunswick Close Estate, Islington.'

'I didn't do it.'

'Very well,' he says, looking at me steadily for a moment before writing something down.

'Were you present in the building at the time of Brindle's death?'

'I was in a film that was being made there.'

'Ah yes, the film. I believe the death occurred during a break in filming?'

'That's right. Brindle was in the flat on his own while we were all in the corridor.'

'Are there those who can testify that you were in the corridor the whole time?'

'I reckon.'

He writes something down and then looks past me for a moment, tapping his pen on the desk.

'You will shortly be questioned by the police, and in view of what you've told me, I would advise you to remain silent, which you have the legal right to do. I shall be present and able to intervene should there be any departure from correct procedure.'

'OK,' I say as he puts the file in his briefcase and bangs on the bars. Moments later the WPC arrives and unlocks the door. Duncan Mayfield gives me a courteous nod and leaves.

When I'm taken back to the cell, I lie back down on the bunk, wondering who on earth this eyewitness can be. I'm thinking that maybe one of Brindle's mob or the Teales are trying to nail me.

My next visitor is a man in white overalls, who parks a tray with a bowl of soup, a piece of dry bread and a cup of tea on the shelf opposite the bunks. He leaves without a word and pushes his trolley on along the corridor. I sniff the soup and decide to give it a miss. When I've drunk the tea, I'm taken back up to the office where I met my brief and told to sit at the desk. The same sergeant who took my name earlier comes in, sits opposite me and opens a notebook. He's followed by Mayfield who takes the chair next to me. The sergeant asks me where I was on the night of Brindle's death and I say nothing. After a few more questions that I don't respond to, Mayfield tells him that I've got nothing to say to the police at this time and the sergeant snaps his notebook shut and walks out. Mayfield stands up, says he'll be back to see me soon and I'm taken back to my cell. I lie on the bed, close my eyes and listen to the boy in the next cell crying softly.

The man in white overalls is back the next morning with a bowl of porridge and tea. The uniform who lets him in tells me that there's an identity parade in half an hour and I'm in Bow Street magistrates court at midday. I wait for him to leave, use the bucket in the corner, then I drink the tea and try the porridge. It's just about edible and by the time I've finished the uniform's back with a WPC. They take me upstairs and a long way through the building, to a room with a tinted window along one wall, where five or six women, all with blond hair and about the same height as me, are standing talking in a group. They fall silent when they see me. The WPC asks them to form a line against the wall opposite the tinted window and she tells me to stand in third place from the left. When I've joined the line, a voice comes through a speaker somewhere and tells us to stand still and look at the window. A few minutes later the voice thanks us and tells us we're done. The women troop out and I'm taken back to my cell.

Mayfield arrives after a bit, looking gloomy. 'I'm afraid they've got a positive identification.'

'Who from?' I ask.

'Her name is Doris Webb. She lives in the flat next door to the one you were filming in and she's given a statement to the effect that she saw you strike Brindle and throw him off the balcony.'

I remember the ginger-haired woman with the pram and two boys who got into the lift and I wonder how much Brindle's team must have paid her to offer me up.

'She's lying,' I say.

'In that case I would advise you to plead not guilty.'

'I intend to,' I say.

'There is a prima facie case against you, which means there is no need for the evidence to be tested, so your matter will be sent straight to the Old Bailey. I shall make an application for bail on your behalf, but I doubt it will be granted.'

'Do your best.'

'Very well. I shall see you in court.'

Mayfield leaves, and it hits me that I'm going to be hanged, or spend the next twenty years of my life in prison.

• • •

At Bow Street, I'm taken from the paddy wagon and put in a cell. About an hour later I'm brought into court by an attendant and told to sit on a bench with some iron railings in front. It's a big wood panelled courtroom and there are three older gents sitting opposite me who look like the magistrates. There's a silver-haired one in the middle, on a high backed chair, talking to a clerk who's standing beside him. I can see Mayfield sitting at a table on the floor of the court. He's deep in conversation with another serious looking bloke, in a dark suit and tie, who glances over at me now and again. The silver-haired magistrate clears his throat and taps on the desk with a little wooden hammer. The clerk comes over to me and tells me to stand. 'Are you Katherine Walker?' he asks.

'Yes,' I reply.

'Of 22 Welby Court, Maida Vale, London West 9?'

'Yes.'

'Sit down.'

I do as I'm told and he goes and sits at the table. The man Mayfield was talking to stands up and turns to the magistrates.

'Sirs, I represent the Crown in this matter. The defendant Katherine Walker is accused of murder and has been identified in the act by an eyewitness of good character. I would respectfully suggest that in view of the serious nature of the charge and the weight of evidence to support it, the matter be committed for trial at the Old Bailey.'

The magistrate looks to his left and right and receives nods from the two others. 'Thank you very much. We commit the matter to the Old Bailey,' He taps the desk with his hammer and the prosecutor sits down. The magistrate writes something and then looks up. 'Is there an application for bail?'

'Indeed there is sir,' says Mayfield.

The prosecutor stands up again. 'I oppose bail on the grounds of seriousness of offence, possibility of absconding due to likely length of sentence if found guilty, and risk of interference with witnesses.'

Mayfield stands. 'The accused has no previous record, has agreed to occupy an alternative address until trial and will accept any conditions that the court might wish to put in place, including curfew,' says Mayfield.

The magistrate confers briefly with his colleagues.

'Bail denied. For the reasons cited by the prosecution. Take her down.'

25

Holloway hasn't changed since I was on remand here eight years ago. It looks like a big ugly medieval castle and it's a maze of corridors and different wings. I get fingerprinted, then I'm told to strip and a mean-faced screw with a bald patch gives me a rough body search. I get a white overall and grey cardigan to wear, and a pair of uncomfortable leather shoes. I'm taken across the yard to a wing on the far side and put in a single cell on the first landing. There's an iron bed, a bucket in the corner and a small sink with one tap that gives a measly trickle of water.

After a while Mayfield comes to visit me and tells me it'll probably be a month before I get my trial date and I ask him to contact Lizzie and tell her where I am. I'm so shattered by what's happened that I lie on the bed and stare at the ceiling, wondering how I can survive this and cursing George Preston for making me do a job that I knew was too risky, on the promise of Dad's money. I must talk to Lizzie and tell her where the cash is for Georgie's school fees that need paying for the extra term she's doing, and ask her if she can look after her when she's alone in the flat in the holidays, and help to get her sorted out in Cambridge, if she's going there. I know Lizzie will do everything she can for Georgie, and for me, and I thank God for her.

My head's full of a million thoughts about how I

can defend myself in court, and if I'll be able to get any witnesses on my side, when I hear the lock turning. There's the sound of doors opening and shutting all over the landing and the screw opens mine and says it's exercise. I don't feel like moving but it's the only chance I'll have to get any fresh air for the rest of the day, so I get off the bed and follow the prisoners walking along the landing, round the corner and down the centre stairs to the floor of the wing. We're made to wait until all the prisoners have come down and then the screws open the doors and let us out.

It's a bright day and I'm glad to be out of the cell as I walk round the outside of the yard. I haven't spoken to anyone yet and I'm wondering if I should talk to a slim dark-haired girl, about my age who's walking near me, when something sharp jabs me in the back. I turn round and Marlene's there with a toothbrush in her hand. She looks about ten years older and a foot shorter than when I last saw her.

'You're going to wish you never come in here, you evil bitch, and if you ever get out my boys'll be waiting to tear you apart!' she snarls.

'Fuck off Marlene,' I say, and walk away. She follows me and jabs me in the back again. There's a screw near so I keep walking, with Marlene behind me. When I get to the corner of the yard I turn on her and snatch the toothbrush out of her hand. I throw it on the ground, take hold of her skinny arms and look her in the eye. 'If you give me just one bit of aggravation in here Marlene Teale, you won't see your next birthday.'

I walk away before she can reply. The girl I was thinking of speaking to before comes alongside me. 'She's a nasty little cow, but you need to be careful,' she says.

'Yeah?'

'She's got a couple of screws well satisfied, so she gets away with a lot.'

'That's good to know, thanks.'

'And she's got a team.'

We walk on a bit and then a scuffle in the middle of the yard turns into a fight, women start cheering and I see Marlene scuttling towards the action. Whistles are blown and the screws move in, drawing their truncheons, and pull the fighters apart. More staff come onto the yard from different doors and order the rest of us back inside.

'That was a couple of hers, in the ruck,' says the dark-haired girl as we go up the stairs. We get to the landing and she goes one way and I go the other. When I get to my cell, I see that hers is opposite mine, on the other side of the wing.

The screw who's been standing by the door locks me in and I go to the window and hold the cold bars. I look across the yard at the rows of barred windows in the wing opposite and think of how many women are banged up in here and all the anger and frustration and loneliness these buildings hold. Someone swings a line with a paper bag on the end from one window to another, a hand catches it and a shout goes up. I lie down, close my eyes, listen to the sounds of the prison and drift off.

The wooden walls of the courtroom are bulging

inwards towards me and the dock I'm sitting in shudders and starts sinking. I try to stand up but I can't. The silver-haired magistrate is rising up out of his chair and floating towards me with his arms outstretched. His hands are claws and they're reaching for me, and Mayfield's jumping up and trying to catch hold of him, but I'm sinking so fast the magistrate can't reach me. I'm plunging down a long dark shaft, past flaming windows, where women with screaming faces are trying to escape through the bars. My chair starts burning. I leap out of it and I'm falling faster and faster, and now I'm in the sky, and I can see the prison below me, and there's a blinding bright light, and I crash through the roof and it goes dark. I open my eyes and see a pair of black shoes in front of me.

'What are you sleeping on the floor for, you daft little cow?'

The black shoes turn and I watch the screw walk onto the landing. I get up slowly and go to the door. Prisoners are walking past and I follow them downstairs and across the hall. When everyone's down from the landings the screws open a gate and we file along a corridor to the dining hall. I get in the queue for food, look round for the girl I spoke to in the yard and see her a little way back in the line. We exchange smiles, and as I turn back I see Marlene coming through a door behind the counter. She hands a paper bag to one of the women serving, then she goes and stands at the head of the queue. They start dishing out the food and everyone moves forward. When Marlene's been served, she turns and stares at me for a second, then she picks up her tray, goes to a table of younger women and sits down among them. I recognise one of them from the fight in the yard.

The women behind the counter are giving out plates of some kind of stew with mashed potato. When it's my turn the one serving hands me my tray without looking at me. I take it, pick up a plastic cup of water off the end of the counter and make for an empty table. I don't feel like eating, but I know this will be the last chance I'll get until morning, so I sip some water and try a bit of the mash. It's a bit dry but I've had worse. I'm just about to attempt the stew when I see the dark-haired girl coming towards the table.

'Join you?' she says.

'Please do,' I reply.

She puts her tray on the table and sits down opposite me.

'I'm Trudy.'

'Rina.'

'How are you doing?'

'Not bad.'

'First time?'

'Second.'

'Me too.'

'How long have you been in?' I ask.

'Just a month.'

I notice Marlene clocking me from her table. She says something to the girl opposite, who turns and looks at me.

'Remand?' I ask Trudy.

'Yeah.'

'Same as me. Have you got your trial date?'

'It's three months away.'

'Could be worse.'

'I suppose.'

I'd like to ask her what she's in for, but I don't want her to know why I'm here just yet, as she seems nice and it might frighten her off. She pays attention to her plate, and I give the stew a try and find the meat tough and gristly. When I put my fork into the mashed potato it touches something hard in the middle. I use my knife to investigate and uncover something brown and revolting, which gives off a foul smell. Trudy reels back as I spit the stew out of my mouth, pick up my plate, stride to the nearest bin, open the lid and dump the contents into it. A screw standing by asks me what I'm playing at. I tell her I've just thrown away a shit sandwich and she walks away, not wanting to get involved. I sit back down and see Marlene and the girls at her table pointing at me and laughing. Trudy has a quick look round at them. 'That's one of her favourite little tricks.'

'Does she work in the kitchen?'

'She doesn't work at all. She's got her fingers everywhere. Fancies herself as running the place. Why is she after you?'

'It's a long story.'

'OK.'

While Trudy finishes her meal, I'm thinking that if I'm going to get any respect in here and be left alone I'll have to settle Marlene. I could well do without it as I've got enough on my mind already and I don't want to end up in solitary.

We get taken back to the wing and the cells are left open for association. Trudy invites me to hers and when we get up the stairs to the landing I look over and see prisoners putting up a table tennis table down below. People are smoking and playing cards in the cells. When we get to Trudy's she jumps on the bed, sits cross-legged on the pillow and I sit at the other end.

'What are your neighbours like?' I ask.

'This one's all right,' she says, pointing at the wall behind her. 'In for robbery with violence, but she's gentle as a lamb. The other side's a bit tricky, going up for GBH next week I'm told. She hardly speaks, just mumbles a lot and looks scared when a screw comes near her. Screams in the night as well. I reckon she ought to be in the mental wing. How are yours?'

'I haven't seen them yet.'

'What are you in for?'

I hesitate and then decide to tell her as she's bound to find out anyway.

'Murder.'

I can see she's shocked although she's trying not to show it.

'How about you?'

'Drugs. I got caught at Heathrow with some Thai Sticks.'

'That was bad luck.'

'I never knew I had them. My boyfriend put them in my rucksack.'

'What a cunt.'

'Yeah.'

'You said you were in before.'

'That was just shoplifting. What was your first time?'

'Same thing, but I got off.'

'Do you think you will this time?'

'I'm not so sure.'

I can tell she's not as easy with me now she knows why I'm here. She seems like a nice kid and it's probably best if she's not seen with me too much until I've sorted Marlene, so I tell her I'm tired and go back to my cell.

• • •

The doors are banging and the screws are shouting for us to slop out and there's plenty of effing and blinding going on. It's only just getting light outside so it must be about six o'clock. I put my overall and shoes on, pick up my bucket and join the ladies on the landing. The stench is horrible and the screws are grumpy, standing with their heads down and snapping at prisoners to get a move on. As the line moves along the landing I feel something dripping down the back of my leg that can only be one thing. I turn and it's one of Marlene's girls.

'Oops, sorry,' she says, with a sneer.

It takes all my self-control not to smash her in the chops and empty my bucket over her, but I know it'll be a one way ticket to solitary if I do. I give her a warning look, get to the toilet, empty my bucket, go back to my cell and shut the door.

After everyone's slopped out, the porridge trolley comes round. I swallow a cupful and lie back down on the bed. About an hour later a screw comes in and tells me I've got a visit. I jump up and follow her down to the hall praying that it's Lizzie. After I've walked what seems like a mile and the screw's unlocked half a dozen doors and locked them again behind us, she finally lets me into the Visitors Room. It's crowded but I see Lizzie, over on the far side, sitting at a table by herself. She stands up when she sees me and I can't help running to her and putting my arms around her.

'No contact!' shouts one of the screws, stepping forward. I let go of Lizzie and we sit at the table. I try not to cry as I look at her lovely face and think how long it could be before we can hold each other again.

'Thanks for coming,' I say.

'I couldn't wait to see you.'

'You're everything to me.'

Her face softens and she reaches for my hand.

'No contact!' shouts the screw.

We smile at one another as she pulls her hand back.

'You know I love you,' she says.

The tears well up again but I manage to hold them back.

'So what is all this?' she asks.

'It's a bit complicated.'

'You're on a murder charge?'

'Yes.'

'Is it to do with Dawn, and Danny Teale and that?'

'Partly.'

'I heard him say Brindle's name when they charged you.'

I look round and see the screw who was near us walking away. I wait until she's out of earshot then I lean forward and tell Lizzie the whole story. By the time I get to the end, I know I've shocked her.

'I can't believe what you've been through, you poor thing. There you were bopping away the other night with all this swirling round your head?'

'You're such a hot dancer.'

'Does your brief think you've got a chance?' she asks.

'I haven't got down to it with him yet.'

'Five minutes,' says the screw, walking past us towards the door.

'If there's anything I can do.'

'Could you help out a bit with Georgie?'

'Of course, anything.'

I tell her about the school fees that need paying and ask her if she'll look after Georgie when she comes home for the holidays. She says she'll be happy to and I tell her where the money for the fees is, behind the bath, and the phone number for the school and the registrar's name so that she can arrange it. I ask her how the escort agency's going and she's just telling me that it's OK but that Gerald's been a bit strange, disappearing in the night and such, when the screws call the end of the visit.

Lizzie says she'll come back as soon as she can and I watch her walk away and out of the door.

26

We're locked up for twenty hours a day. There's an hour in the morning for slop out, a wash, breakfast and cleaning the cell, then we're banged up till lunch. Out for an hour's exercise in the afternoon and banged up again until supper and association, then back in the cells for the night by eight o'clock. The volunteer woman with the library trolley came round and I was hoping she'd have *Rebecca* but she didn't. She said she'd try to get it for me and I had a look at what she'd got. It was mostly romance stuff so I picked *The Cruel Sea* by Nicholas Monsarrat which looked like it could be an adventure story.

It's nearly two weeks after Lizzie's visit when I get my chance to square up to Marlene. She's had her girls giving me some kind of grief every day, either tripping me on the stairs or throwing some muck in my cell or jogging my tray in the dining hall so something gets spilt, and Marlene's always there gloating and making sure it's seen that she's tormenting me. I've kept my temper and not reacted so far, as I want to stay off punishment.

One afternoon a screw opens my door and tells me I'm out for a bath. Once a week every prisoner gets a bath in about four inches of nearly cold water, but at least it's a chance to get clean. There are three tubs in the bathroom, and when I grab my towel and follow the screw onto the landing, two of Marlene's girls are leaning on the rail giving me sly looks. One of them is big and plump with short black hair, the other is scrawny and quite tall with light brown curls and a pale face. I follow the screw along the landing and down the stairs with the girls behind me. She leads us across the hall to the bathroom and unlocks the door. We go in and the screw, who's an ugly old bag of about fifty, comes in after us, locks up and leans against the wall.

I know it's going to kick off and I can tell by the look on the screw's face that she's in on it. The girls circle round me and I stand still and wait for it. When I feel the skinny one make a move behind me I drop to the floor, grab the fat one's ankle and ram the heel of my hand into her kneecap. She screams, falls backwards and I get on top of her and punch her hard in the face. The skinny one jumps on my back and I roll sideways, crush her against the wall and jab my elbow into her ribs. The fat one's up first and she lands on top of me grabs my throat with both hands and presses hard. I grab her tits, shove her sideways, bring my knee up into her crotch, get hold of her head and smash her face against the stone floor.

The screw's laughing as I get up and face the skinny one who's coming at me with a chiv in her hand. She swings the blade at me and I jump back to the wall and get behind a bath. She lunges at me and I dodge sideways, jump onto the edge of the bath and kick the chiv out of her hand. As I fall into the water, I grab her hair, take her in with me and push her head under. The screw comes over, still laughing, pulls out her truncheon and holds it over my head. 'All right now, that's enough, we don't want her drowned.'

The fat one's getting up off the floor as I climb out of the bath, followed by the skinny one. The screw stands back by the door swinging her truncheon. 'You three going to get clean, or what?'

'I thought you wanted some,' says the fat one, holding her head.

'Fat chance, with you two wallies.'

'Give her a clout and we'll hold her for you.'

'Maybe I will,' says the screw, coming towards me. I move sideways but the fat one grabs me, then the other one's at my legs, the screw's truncheon is swinging towards me and I go out.

I come round and I'm on my back on the floor. My wrists are cuffed to something behind my head. The girls are holding my ankles apart and the fat one's dripping blood from a broken nose. The screw's face is between my legs and she's got one hand up her knickers. I twist sideways and the fat one comes and sits on my chest. I can barely breathe and I feel like I'm going out for good, and with what the screw's doing to me, it might not be soon enough. Moments later, when I'm thinking I really am for it, I hear the lock turning and the door opening. Before I can see who's there, it shuts again. The screw scrambles to her feet and tells the girls to get off me. She unlocks the cuffs, pulls me up off the floor, opens the door and two other screws walk in.

'Forced to restrain Prisoner Walker after she attacked

two prisoners and myself. Taking her to be booked on a charge of violent assault on a prison officer. These two to the hospital wing,' she says.

'You've got it Doreen,' says one of the others, barely hiding a smile.

Doreen marches me out of the door, across the hall, along a corridor and into an office where I'm charged with assault and the rest of it. When the woman behind the desk has typed it all out and put the sheets of paper in a pigeon hole, she picks up the phone and asks for an escort to the punishment block. Two screws arrive minutes later and march me to another wing, down two flights of stairs and along a dark narrow corridor, with barred cells on one side that you can see into. They lock me in a dark cell with a low metal bunk and a bucket. I lie on the bunk, roll into the wall and press my aching head against the rough brick until the throbbing pain takes me over and kills my thoughts.

• • •

Two days later I've seen no one except the old woman with the food cart and the screw who slops me out to the toilet at the end of the corridor. The other cells are all empty and I'm beginning to feel like I've been forgotten, when I'm woken from a deep sleep by a loud whack on the bars.

'Governor's office!'

I recognise one of the screws who came into the bathroom. She unlocks the door and stands swinging her truncheon while I drag myself off the bunk and reach underneath for my shoes.

I'm handcuffed and marched along the corridor and up the stairs. It's a relief to see daylight and breathe some fresh air as we go across the yard towards the turrets and towers above the main gate. The screw leads me to an oak door to the right of the gate and knocks twice with her truncheon. A panel in the door slides open and a face appears.

'Prisoner Walker up before the Governor,' says the screw.

The door's opened by a miserable looking woman with mousy hair and bags under her eyes. We go in and she tells me to sit on a wooden bench while she goes to a table in the corner, opens a big book and writes in it. She beckons the screw over, points to a place in the book and the screw writes something. She closes the book, puts it under her arm and goes up some stairs. The screw strolls past, looks me over and leans against the wall, twisting her truncheon in her hand.

'If you weren't so fucking filthy you might make a decent bit of skirt,' she says.

I decide that this is not the time or place to teach this cow a lesson and look at the floor. After a while the one who let us in comes down the stairs and goes to the table in the corner. As she puts the book down there is a knock on the door. She slides the panel open, has a quick look and opens up.

'All right Doreen?' she says, as my accuser walks in and sees me.

'I'll be all right when I've put this cunt downstairs for a few months,' she says.

'Put your moniker on here,' says the mousy one, going to the table and opening the book. Doreen joins her, signs her name and Mousy hands her a sheet of paper. 'Governor's there. You can go up if you want.'

'Cheers Jean,' says Doreen, as she goes up the stairs.

The screw points after her with her truncheon and I follow Doreen up two flights to a landing, where she knocks on a door which is opened by a dark-haired young woman in a uniform skirt and blouse. Doreen hands her the sheet of paper and she stands back as we file in to a long oak-panelled room with a desk at one end. Doreen places me in front of it and she and the other screw stand on each side of me while the young woman puts the sheet of paper on the desk and goes out through a door at the side. She comes back moments later and tells us that the Governor has received a telephone call and will be with us when it's finished. She leaves and a few minutes later a tall posh-looking middle-aged woman, in a dark brown suit and black brogues enters. She takes a quick look at us, sits behind the desk and puts on a pair of glasses that are on a chain round her neck.

'Good morning,' she says.

'Morning ma'am,' say Doreen and her mate.

The Governor looks at me and then at the paper in front of her. 'What have we got?'

'Remand prisoner Walker ma'am. Violent assault on two prisoners and assault on an officer,' says Doreen.

'Where did it take place?'

'Washroom ma'am.'

'Witnesses?'

'Yes ma'am,' says the screw beside me.

'You were present?'

'I was.'

The Governor looks at Doreen. 'What took place?'

'An argument started between Walker and one of the prisoners. Walker punched the prisoner in the face, threw her on the ground and attempted to strangle her. The other prisoner tried to intervene and Walker kicked and punched her. I attempted to restrain Walker, who kicked, punched and bit me, and I was forced to use my truncheon to put her unconscious.'

'Just as well, by the sound of it,' says the Governor.

'Walker has been involved in other violent incidents ma'am.'

'Indeed,' says the Governor, writing on the paper in front of her. 'Anything to say Walker?'

'No ma'am,' I say.

The Governor finishes writing, takes off her glasses and gives me a stern look. 'In the short time that you've been here you have shown yourself to be a considerable danger to others. Violence against prison officers cannot be tolerated and you are to remain in solitary confinement for a period of eight weeks from this day. Should you still be with us after that date, any further incidents of this nature will be dealt with most severely. Is that clear?'

'Yes ma'am.'

'Prisoner dismissed.'

She picks the paper up off the desk and sweeps out. I'm feeling like a lead weight has landed on me as Doreen grabs my shoulder, turns me round and pushes me towards the door. The other screw opens it and goes onto the landing. I follow her down the stairs with Doreen behind me and the mousy one lets us out into the yard.

'Let's get her back to the playpen and have a bit of fun,' says Doreen, pushing me in front of her.

'Nah. She's filthy dirty,' says the screw.

'Ooh, I like 'em a bit grubby, me.'

'Suppose we could hose her down.'

'Fancy a nice cold shower girl?'

As I'm thinking which one of these slags I'm going to hurt first, I hear footsteps behind. I turn and see Mousy hurrying towards us.

'Governor wants her back,' she says.

'What for?' asks Doreen.

'Don't know.'

'Ah fuck it,' says Doreen and pushes me back the way we've come.

The young girl is waiting inside the oak door and we follow her upstairs. She knocks on the office door, opens it and makes way for us to go in. The Governor's standing behind her desk and she's talking to my brief, Duncan Mayfield. She sees us come in and sits down. Mayfield looks at me, gives me a flicker of a smile and moves away from the desk. While I'm wondering what can be happening, the Governor picks up some papers in front of her.

'There's no point in prolonging this. I have received notification from the Clerk of the Assize Court at the Old Bailey that the charge of murder made against you, Katherine Walker, has been withdrawn and you are therefore eligible for immediate release from this place.'

All the breath goes out of me and I'm swaying on my feet as I hear her telling the screws to make the necessary arrangements to let me out. Mayfield's smiling at me and I want to leap at him and kiss him.

'I'll meet you at the gate, Miss Walker,' he says, as the Governor picks up the paperwork and passes a couple of sheets to him. She opens the side door and they leave.

The screws take me to an office on the far side of the gate, making snidey remarks on the way, which I barely even hear because I'm so happy I could climb up the wall and dance along the battlements. They take my cuffs off and leave me with a bored-looking bird who rootles around in a cupboard until she eventually finds my clothes, shoes and shoulder bag. She puts me in a cubicle and I rip off the overall and get into my grey suit, scarf and shoes as quick as I can, before someone changes their mind and puts me back in solitary. When I'm done, I have to wait a bit until a pair of screws arrive and walk me to the gate, then there's another wait while the key holder's called and finally the gate swings open and I step out into a beautiful sunny day.

27

I'm feeling light as a feather as I walk towards Parkhurst Road. Mayfield's standing on the kerb. As I approach, he reaches out and shakes my hand.

'Congratulations,' he says.

'Thanks.'

'Would you like coffee?' he says, nodding towards a café, a short way along the street.

'Do you mind if we go somewhere a bit further away from here?'

'Of course,' he says, with a laugh. 'What about my office?'

'Sounds good.'

Mayfield hails a passing cab, gives him an address in the City and opens the door for me. He's discreet enough not to talk in the cabbie's hearing and when we get to his office building he tells a secretary to bring us coffee. As I follow him up the stairway I catch sight of myself in a mirror and see how awful I look. I ask for the ladies' room, and after I've washed my face and straightened my hair, I join him in his office.

'So what happened?' I ask.

'I'm afraid I have no idea at all. I was in the process of preparing a defence for you and I was just about to come and see you in Holloway this morning to discuss it, when the communication arrived from the Old Bailey saying the charges had been dropped. When I got to the prison, I found that the Governor had been informed moments before and I was able to get her agreement to release you immediately.'

'Is that the end of it?'

'Absolutely. The case has been effectively dismissed and under the double jeopardy rule you cannot be charged with the same crime twice.'

'You've no idea why they let it go?'

'None at all.'

The way he says it and the rather stern look on his face tells me that he thinks it's best to leave it at that.

'I should tell you that several of your colleagues on the film you were working on were very willing to appear as witnesses in your defence when it came to trial,' he says, standing up and moving to the door.

'That's good to know,' I say, drinking the last of his excellent coffee.

He opens the door and gives a slight bow.

'Thanks for your good work,' I say, shaking his hand.

'Goodbye Miss Walker.'

I go through reception and into the busy street. I stand on the pavement for a while and enjoy being back in the world, among people going places and the traffic bustling along. I look in my shoulder bag and I'm thankful to find my keys and a couple of quid still in there. I'm just about to flag down a cab when a familiar white Jaguar pulls up in front of me. The passenger door swings open and I get in.

'Welcome back,' says Bert Davis.

'How did you know I was here?' I say, closing the door.

'I came to Holloway to pick you up, then I saw you with the gent and followed the cab.'

'He was my brief.'

'Did he tell you anything?'

'No.'

'Makes sense.'

'What's there to tell?'

'I'll leave it to George.'

He pulls out into the City traffic and I sit back in the soft leather, breathe easy, and enjoy being chauffeured across London.

When we get to Lancaster Road, Jacky Parr lets us in, makes a big fuss of me and I can't avoid a kiss from his sandpaper lips. George is in his usual armchair in the living room.

'Good to see you Rina.'

Bert pours me a whisky, hands it to me and leaves. I sit down, take a drink and feel the tension in my muscles easing.

'So, what's the story?' I ask.

'It's all down to your good friend Lizzie Jenson.'

'What?'

'She started an escort business.'

'I know.'

'And I'm giving her a bit of insurance.'

'Protection.'

'If you want.'

I might have known that George would muscle in as

soon as there was money about.

'Go on,' I say.

'It's doing well, and then she tells me that her partner's pulling moody ones and going off with clients but won't tell her what's going on.'

'Gerald?'

'Right. So I put Ray on him and he watches him picking up a couple of old gents from a club in St James's, driving them to a boys' orphanage in Kent in the middle of the night, then bringing them back to London a couple of hours later.'

'Oh my God.'

'He gets a photo of them leaving the orphanage, using one of them night cameras, and Lizzie spots that one of the gents is Gerald's father-in-law.'

'Lord Hackett?'

'You know him?'

'I've met him.'

'It turns out Hackett's a bigwig in the Lord Chancellor's Department. A visit from Ray with the photograph, a bit of blarney about the bloke at the orphanage being ready to cough, His Lordship's wetting his knickers and you're out.'

'What about the witness, the woman who saw me chuck him over?'

'She never saw a thing. Brindle's lot got to her and bunged her to offer you up. I slipped her another couple of large to withdraw her statement.'

'How did you know about her?'

'I've got a DI at Islington nick.'

I've always had respect for George and his connections, but the way he's handled this is top drawer. It means I owe him, but I don't mind paying the price when the time comes. I finish my whisky and point at the bottle on the sideboard. George nods, and while I'm pouring myself another drink, I catch a whiff of fried bacon. Bert enters carrying a tray which he puts on my knee when I sit down.

'Thanks boys,' I say, and tuck into the best breakfast I've ever had.

When I've finished eating and Bert's topped up my drink and taken the tray away, George lights a fag and turns to me.

'The Teales have got to go,' he says.

'What have they been up to?' I ask, remembering Marlene's recent threats about what "her boys" would do to me when I got out.

'It's become known in Birmingham that Brindle was Dan Garner's son, thanks to some aunt of his who's put it about. Garner's making out he never knew, but now that he does and Brindle's gone, he needs to be seen to come after me and we know he's given the job to the Teales.'

'Why would he be after you and not me?'

'You're not the prize. Garner's ambition is to move into London, and if he can get me out of the way, he's got it made.'

'Where are the Teales?'

'They've bottled it and gone to Spain.'

'What?'

'With Mum inside they don't fancy their chances and done a runner.'

'So why not leave them there?'

'Doing them will mean we've swept them up, as well as Brindle, and get the right message to Garner.'

'Job done and I get my dad's loot?'

'Certainly,' says George, flicking his fag end into the fireplace. 'Ray will tell you how to find them in Spain and that. He's waiting for you in the Royal Oak.'

'Want a lift?' asks Bert.

'Why not?' I reply.

'Don't say I don't look after my firm, eh?' says George, standing up and looking at himself in the mirror.

'No one will hear it from me,' I say, as I follow Bert into the hall.

On the way to the Royal Oak I ask Bert if he's heard anything of Dawn but he says he hasn't. Talking about the Teales has made me wonder how she's doing. We get to the pub and I thank Bert for the lift and go in. It's quite crowded for a lunchtime, but I can see Ray sitting in the corner on the far side of the bar, reading an *Evening Standard*. I make my way over and join him at the table. He folds his paper. 'Result eh?'

'Thanks for what you did,' I say.

'I always like sticking one up the gentry.'

'Too bad some of them like sticking it where they shouldn't.'

'They're not alone. Do you want a drink?'

'I'm OK thanks.'

'Danny and Jack Teale, yeah?'

'George said they're in Spain.'

'That's right. They're in a house a few miles from a town called Denia.'

He hands me a piece of paper with a Spanish address on it.

'Maureen Teale bought it a while back and she's never even been there. Too busy putting the West End clothes shops out of business.'

'When did they get there?'

'Few days ago.'

'How do you know where they are?'

He looks away for a second. 'It's what I do.'

'OK,' I say.

'You fly to Valencia.'

'Right.'

'Denia's a couple of hours' drive. You can hire a motor at the airport.'

Suddenly the noise of the pub and the smell of beer and fags is getting to me and I feel an urgent need to get home and wash the prison stink off me.

'Thanks,' I say, as I stand up.

'Good luck.'

He takes a pull at his pint and opens his paper as I walk away.

I turn right out of the pub and walk past the El Rio towards Chepstow Road, where I know I can get a bus most of the way home. When I get to the bus stop a cab appears, so I flag him down and jump in. I tell him to stop at Harrow Road so I can buy some milk and a few things. When I get back in the cab, he's got the news on the radio and they're talking about Winston Churchill retiring from the House of Commons, what a great man he is, and how he won the war and that. The driver says it's true, but he couldn't have done it without the Americans and the Russians. I don't know much about all that, so I keep quiet.

I get out of the cab, give him a two bob bit and feel a sense of relief as I open the glass door to the building. As I'm crossing the foyer, Keith asks me if I've had a good holiday, which makes me think that Lizzie's given him and Dennis a reason for me to be away. I tell him I've had a lovely time, get into the lift, press the button and I'm wafted up to my floor.

I knock on Lizzie's door, but she's not there. I'm dying to see her and I'm hoping she'll be back later. I unlock the door to my flat, go in and pick up two letters off the mat. One has the Leavenden crest on it and the other just says Rina. I open it and recognise Lizzie's writing. She welcomes me home, says she's away and adds a phone number. I shut the door behind me, pick up the phone and dial it. After a few rings a woman answers. I ask to speak to Lizzie and she tells me to hang on.

'Hello,' says Lizzie.

'It's me.'

'Oh my darling girl. Where are you?'

'At home.'

'That's wonderful! When did you get out?'

'This morning. Can you come?'

'On my way.'

'I'll be in the bath.'

'Just where I want you.'

She puts the phone down and I open the Leavenden letter, see that it's from Georgie and go into the kitchen. I put the kettle on, sit at the table and read that she's in the middle of her A-level exams and she thinks they are going all right so far. If I know her, she'll be teaching the examiners something. She goes on to say that Miss Simpkins, the registrar, has confirmed that she'll be staying on for the autumn term to take the Cambridge entrance exam, and I'm so thrilled when I think she could be going to one of the best universities in the country. She says she's looking forward to coming home for the holidays in a couple of weeks and I just hope I can take care of this Spanish caper by then and be here for her.

I make myself a cup of coffee, go into Georgie's bedroom and write her a letter, telling her to keep up the good work and crack those A-levels. I say how happy I am about the Cambridge exam and that I'm looking forward to seeing her in a couple of weeks. I send love to her from Lizzie, seal the letter, stick a stamp on it and put it on the hall table. I take my coffee into the bathroom, put it on the shelf and turn on the bath taps. I slip out of my shoes, take off my grey suit and underwear, go into the kitchen, put the whole lot in a plastic bag and dump it in the bin.

I get into the bath and wash HMP Holloway off me. When I'm done, I get out, pull out the plug and watch the dirty water drain away, then I run a clean bath and pour in some of my nice Estée Lauder oil. Just as I'm turning off the taps, there's a knock at the door. I look through the spyhole, see Lizzie's lovely face and swing it open.

'You've caught me with my pants down,' I say.

'Good timing then,' she says, wrapping her arms round me.

As we kiss I feel the strength draining from me. We go into the bathroom, she slips quickly out of her clothes, with the skill she's acquired over a good few years, and we get into the warm water.

'Thank God you're out, my darling.'

'I can't believe it.'

'I couldn't bear to think of you in that horrible place.'

'I was so lucky.'

'Have you got the story?'

'George told me.'

'He was amazing.'

'How come you were involved with him?'

'You remember that woman who owns the Kazuko, who I told you was after a taste because I was using some of her girls in the agency?'

'The one in the gold dress?'

'That's her. Marie, she's called. When we start doing a lot of business, she sends a couple of gorillas round to the office who menace about a bit, smash a couple of pictures off the wall and tell us we'd better start paying or else. Gerald's white as a sheet while this goes on, and when they leave he says he hadn't bargained for this kind of stuff and he wants to wrap up the business.'

'But it was going well?'

'Much better than I'd ever expected. We were doing hundreds of notes a week.'

'And all legit. Brass plate.'

'Right. So I make him calm down and I go and see George. He tells me Marie's nothing and he'll straighten her and keep us dry, if I put him on a regular earner. We agree a price and I tell Gerald we're going to be protected and to shut up and get on with spreading the word among the posh chaps and he agrees.'

'How did you find out about Lord Hackett?'

'Gerald started going off at night, where before he'd hardly let me out of his sight, being all lovey dovey and let's get married as soon as the divorce comes through and all that. He wouldn't tell me where he'd been and he seemed like he was hiding something, so I told George and he got on his case. You probably know how it went from there.'

'I do.'

'I reckon Hackett was lucky he had enough clout to get you off a murder charge or George might well have had him done.'

'He hates a nonce.'

'He really does.'

I lie back in the water and stroke Lizzie's ankles. We relax like that without talking for a while until she pulls out the plug and the water starts to drain. We get out of the bath, pat each other dry with a big fluffy towel and get into bed.

• • •

A couple of hours later we're having a drink in the lounge and listening to Georgie Fame, before going out to dinner, and I ask Lizzie where she was when I phoned her earlier. She tells me she's been staying with her sister to get away from Gerald, who won't leave her alone. The agency's finished and she wants nothing to do with him after what he's been up to with his father-in-law. She's told him to sling his hook, but he won't stop phoning her and trying to get into the flat.

We decide to have dinner at Rules in Covent Garden, as it's well off Gerald's beat. I find the key to the car and we walk round to Hall Road. After a few attempts I get the Anglia to start and drive down Edgware Road, along Marylebone and past Seven Dials to Covent Garden, where I find a place to park in Maiden Lane. The doorman at Rules ushers us inside and the head waiter shows us to a corner table for two. Lizzie knows her wines and she studies the list, then orders a bottle of something that sounds French. I look at the lovely dishes on the menu and think of what the girls in Holloway will be getting slapped onto their tin plates tonight, then I order lobster and a fillet steak. The wine arrives, Lizzie tastes it and nods to the waiter. He pours, we clink glasses and I take a sip of a delicious red wine, share a smile with the woman I love and feel how incredibly lucky I've been.

After a beautiful candlelit dinner and another bottle of the French wine, we think about going to a club but decide on an early night and walk along Maiden Lane.

'Why don't we go away for a bit?' says Lizzie, as we get into the car.

'Funny you should say that.'

'Why?'

'I've got to go to Spain tomorrow.'

'How come?'

'It's work.'

'What are you doing?'

I wonder if I should spare her the details, for her safety, but then I remember that I told her about the whole business when she came to Holloway.

'George has got me going after the Teales.'

'Why?'

'They've gone with Dan Garner against him.'

'Brindle's old man?'

'That's him. Now it's known Brindle was his kid he needs to be seen to get satisfaction and he's put the Teales on it. They've bottled out and gone to Spain but George still wants them put away.'

'I don't think you should be doing it.'

'If I don't George won't give me my Dad's money and I owe him for getting me off a murder charge.'

'You've got to stop putting yourself in so much danger.'

'It shouldn't be too tricky.'

'You're hopeless, you are.'

'I'll be OK.'

'Well, I'm coming with you to make sure.'
'No you're not.'
'Yes I am. Now drive us home.'
I start the engine, and do as I'm told.

28

By ten o'clock the next morning Lizzie's gone off to buy us tickets to Valencia from the travel agent on Edgware Road and I'm wrapping my gun in underwear and putting it at the bottom of my suitcase, along with a blade and a wad of cash. Lizzie gets back and announces that we're leaving at one o'clock, on BEA Flight 619 from London Airport. She gives me my ticket and passport and goes to her flat to pack for the trip. Lizzie's been to Spain before, on business, and she says July is really hot, so I look through my wardrobe for something lightweight. I pick out a couple of silk dresses, a short cotton skirt and a couple of blouses, then throw my bathing suit in just in case, along with a pair of heels. I decide to travel in jeans and leather jacket and as I'm putting my boots on, Lizzie's knocking at the door.

The cab takes us through Knightsbridge to Hammersmith and along the A4 to the airport. I look at my ticket and tell the driver to take us to Building One. He drops us at the door and we put our cases on a trolley and head for the departures desks. BEA 619 is showing on the big screen as leaving on time and boarding at gate 18. We check in our cases and get our boarding passes from a tasty-looking girl in a tight-fitting uniform, with lustrous dark hair and great make-up.

'Maybe she'd like to come with us?' says Lizzie, as we walk to the gate.

'I think you might have to keep an eye on her, as well as me, with all those Spanish men.'

We're tempted to have a look at the duty free shops but decide to be good and go straight to the gate. We get there with a bit of time to spare, get coffee from the café and wait for the flight to be called. I look at Lizzie sitting opposite me, all fresh and lovely, and I hope I'm not making a big mistake letting her come with me. I tried to argue her out of it when we woke up this morning but she wouldn't have it.

The flight's called and we board the plane. I've got a window seat and Lizzie's next to me. She's flown quite a lot, visiting her various gentleman friends, and she's used to it, but I get nervous in an aeroplane, and when the engines rev up and make that big rumbling sound, I start to feel breathless and faint so I squeeze Lizzie's hand. The plane accelerates up the runway and I feel my stomach rising and my toes tingling, but once we're off the ground and climbing into the sky, I gradually calm down. I let go of Lizzie's hand, look out of the window and get a glimpse of England down below, before we fly into a cloud. The hostesses come along the aisle with drinks on a trolley and we buy two large whiskies and sit back and relax.

I'm just drifting off to sleep, after eating a sandwich and finishing my drink, when I notice a strange smell, as if something's on fire. I open my eyes and see smoke around me. I start to panic until I realise it's just the bloke in the seat in front lighting his pipe.

Lizzie's deep into her Mademoiselle magazine, so I take *Rebecca* out of my shoulder bag and read about further humiliation for our girl when she's taken to visit Maxim's grandma and the old bird starts wailing that she only wants to see Rebecca and how much she loved her. She's taken home, feeling upset, and then Maxim arrives, hears that the dashing Jack Favell's been there, gets grumpy and bans him from the house. The really good bit is when they decide to have a costume ball and Mrs Danvers persuades our girl to have a dress copied from a portrait of a lovely young woman that hangs in the stairwell. The evening of the ball arrives and once it's in full swing, she plucks up her courage and makes a grand entrance down the stairs, wearing the dress. Silence falls, everyone looks shocked and Maxim goes white with fury and tells her to go upstairs at once and change. She goes to her room in tears and the maid tells her that she's wearing the same dress as Rebecca wore at the ball a few days before she died. Eventually she goes back down in a simple dress and tries to make polite conversation, but she just feels as if everyone's talking about her. She goes to bed feeling awful and waits for Maxim to come and comfort her, but he never does.

The plane lands, I close the book and we go down the steps under the blazing sun, walk across the hot tarmac to the airport building and wait in a queue. There's a bloke in a shirt and tie sitting at a desk checking passports. Two men in dark green uniforms, wearing strange three-cornered hats made of black leather, that look like they're on sideways, are standing behind him and looking passengers up and down. Now and again one of the military types steps forward and takes a passport from the man at the desk, studies it for a bit, while the owner starts looking worried, then he hands it back to be stamped and waves the person through.

'Guardia Civil,' whispers Lizzie.

'What?'

'Police. You don't mess with them.'

When we get to the desk, my passport gets the extra inspection, as does my cleavage, before we're allowed through. We collect our suitcases and go past Customs to the main hall, where I find a newsagent's and buy a map. We head for a bank, I take the money out of my suitcase, hand over two hundred quid and get thirty thousand Spanish pesetas, which seems like a pretty good deal. There's a car hire desk at the far end of the hall. The girl speaks English and she tells us that they only hire out one car, a Seat 1400, which costs a thousand pesetas for a week. I show her my driving licence and passport, give her the money, scribble an illegible signature on the form and she gives me the key. I ask her how long it will take to drive to Denia and she tells me it should be about two hours.

We go to the car park and find the car, which is a solid looking four-seater that shouldn't be too conspicuous. I open the map and find Valencia Airport and then Denia and the route along the coast road looks fairly simple. My plan is to find a place for us to stay by the sea, not far from

Denia, so that I can leave Lizzie well away from the action, while I do the business. A place called Oliva looks likely and I pass the map to Lizzie, show her where it is and start the car.

The sun is low in the sky by the time we get to Oliva. It's an old town with a beautiful church and a convent, where Lizzie says she'll put me if I don't behave myself. Near to the beach we find a small hotel tucked away among some palm trees. I park the car in front and we take our cases out of the boot and walk under a tiled archway towards the white stone house, where an old lady in a faded blue overall is sweeping the steps. She smiles at us, greets us in Spanish and goes ahead of us to a reception desk in the hallway. With a combination of mime and Lizzie's few words of Spanish, we manage to book ourselves a double room, with a view of the sea. The lady takes us up to the room, which looks comfortable enough. It has twin beds, which is a slight disappointment, but Lizzie and I have long learnt just to push them together at bedtime, rather than risk outrage by asking for a double.

Once we've unpacked, we walk into Oliva and find a quiet bar. We have a few drinks and eat lovely snacky things, called tapas, from behind the bar. It's mostly seafood and olives and such, and I'm really enjoying it, until Lizzie tells me I'm eating an octopus. I take a moment to adjust to the idea and then go on wolfing it down. When we're done, we take a walk through the town and enjoy the warm breeze and the nice atmosphere, with

MALICE

music playing, people sitting outside their front doors and kids playing in the street.

We get back to the hotel, go up to our room and Lizzie says we should go for a swim before breakfast. The other times she's been here on business, she was only in Madrid and she's never been on the beach. I'd planned to get moving early, to find where the Teales' place is, but I reckon there's no harm in a swim before I start. We both squeeze into one of the beds, put our arms round each other and after a bit of a cuddle, we're asleep.

• • •

The heat is already building when I wake and see Lizzie over by the window, putting on her bikini. She pulls me out of bed and throws my costume at me. 'Come on sleepy head, let's go.'

I get into my rather boring costume, wishing I had a bikini like Lizzie, and we put on dressing gowns and go downstairs. The old lady is sweeping the steps again and she greets us as we pass her and cross the road towards the beach. There are only a few early swimmers about but I expect it will fill up later. We go along a wooden walkway onto the sands and Lizzie drops her towel and her dressing gown and runs towards the waves. I follow her and we dash into the water and strike out for the horizon. The sea is really warm and we swim out a good way and then back to the shallows where we splash about, ducking each other and wrestling like a couple of little kids. Suddenly we're hungry and we decide to go back and get breakfast.

As we walk up the beach, I see a black and white car near the hotel and two Guardia Civil standing on the walkway looking at us. When we get to our towels they come towards us. One of them takes a pair of handcuffs off his belt and slaps them on Lizzie's wrists, while the other one picks up her dressing gown and puts it round her shoulders. The one who cuffed her is barking Spanish at her and pointing at the hotel. Lizzie says something to him and they march her off along the walkway. I grab the towels and follow.

When we get to the hotel, the cop who cuffed her goes with her up to the room and I go after them. He takes the cuffs off her, leans on the wall and watches while she takes off her bikini and gets dressed. If he didn't have a gun on his belt I'd take him now, but I've no tools and his mate's waiting downstairs, so I sit quietly. He's still talking to her in Spanish when Lizzie looks at me and says she's being arrested for wearing a bikini. I tell her she must be joking but she says it's true. As soon as he's cuffed her again and taken her downstairs, I jump into my clothes, peel a bunch of pesetas off the wad, grab my passport from my suitcase, pick up the car key and get down just as the Guardia Civil car is pulling away.

The old lady is behind the desk, looking well flustered. I ask her where the Guardia Civil station is and she looks blank and then opens a door behind her and calls out a name. A boy of about eighteen wearing a white apron comes in and when I ask him the same thing, he tells me it's in Denia, near the port and names a street. I ask him how I can find it and he takes a map off the shelf behind him, opens it and shows me where it is and which way I'll come into Denia from the coast road. I thank him, put a five hundred peseta note on the desk and run to the car.

The road hugs the coast all the way to Denia and I'm careful not to drive too fast in case I get stopped. I get to the town in about twenty minutes and follow the map. I'm a few streets away from the police station and hoping it's the right one, when the traffic in front of me slows down to a crawl, I hear a brass band playing and a crowd of people are moving along the pavement on either side of me. The car in front stops and I look up ahead and see a carnival float with people in sailors' costumes and a man in a black sombrero and a white death mask playing the guitar. I smack my hands on the wheel in frustration, I want to jump out of the car and run the rest of the way but it would be stupid to lose the motor so I take a few deep breaths, grip the wheel and wait.

While I'm quietly fuming at this bit of bad timing, I happen to look round at the people on the pavement and get a shock when I spot a face I haven't seen in a long time. It's a young villain from the street I grew up in, called Sammy Neal, who I did a few blags with years ago, when he was going out with my best mate Clare. When he sees me looking at him, he disappears into the crowd and I know why. Sammy and Clare offered me up for murder, when the filth had them bang to rights on a big jewellery smash and grab that we'd done. We were only kids then and it's water under the bridge to me now, although I can see why he'd be scared of running into me. While I'm wondering what he can be doing in Denia, the traffic starts moving and we gather a bit of speed.

I leave the car outside the police station and walk in the main door. A cop sitting at a desk looks up and I ask him if he speaks English. He shakes his head and picks up the phone. He says something that includes a word that sounds like English, points to a bench and I sit down. A few minutes later a man in plain clothes appears.

'What can I help you for?' he says.

'My friend has just been arrested and I want to see her.'

'She is English?'

'Yes.'

'Name?'

'Elizabeth Jenson.'

'Come,' he says, and I follow him along a corridor and down some stairs. He takes me into an office where one of the cops who came to the beach is sitting at a desk writing. The plain clothes man says something to him, including Lizzie's name, and he looks up and recognises me. He sits back in his chair, folds his arms and looks steadily at me. I take the roll of pesetas out of my pocket and flick through a few notes. He looks at the money and smiles, nodding his head. I drop the money on the desk and he picks it up and counts it. When he's done, he shakes his head and holds his hand out for more. I reach into my back pocket and give him the pesetas I knew I'd need if this was going to work. He does a quick count of the extra money and passes it to the plain clothes man, who pockets it and goes out of the door. I know I stand a chance of being whisked off to a cell at any moment and I'm tensed up and ready to hurt anyone if they try. Minutes later the plain clothes walks back in with Lizzie. I take her hand and lead her out of the door and up the stairs, before anyone changes their mind, or arrests me for wearing jeans. The plain clothes man follows us and opens the main door.

'Thank God you found me,' says Lizzie, as soon as we're in the street.

'I just went for the nearest nick and got lucky.'

'Was it money?'

'Oh yeah.'

'How much?'

'About a hundred quid.'

'They work cheap then.'

'Just as well. Did they give you any trouble in the cell?'

'Not really.'

I know Lizzie can look after herself and I don't ask for details. I'm just glad she doesn't seem to have suffered. We get in the car and risk a quick cuddle.

'My saviour,' she whispers in my ear, before giving me a quick kiss.

'Breakfast?' I say.

'Lovely.'

I drive back the way I came and we can hear the carnival music wafting over from the direction of the sea. We find a little café on the edge of town, and I'm glad to discover that croissants have made their way across the Pyrenees. After we've stuffed ourselves and drunk several cups of coffee, we find a clothes shop, buy Lizzie a modest one-piece bathing suit and head back to the hotel.

29

I leave Lizzie on the beach, go back to the hotel, pick up my gun and blade, slip them into my belt and put on a long blouse to hide them. I look at the address Ray gave me and with the help of the lad from the kitchen I find the road where the Teale house is on the map. It's a couple of miles inland from Denia and the simplest way to get there is to drive into town and out again. The Seat bowls along the coast road and I open all the windows and enjoy the warm air on my skin and the view of the glistening blue sea.

When I get to Denia, the fiesta, as the boy at the hotel called it, is going strong and I can hear some really wild drumming that gets me tapping on the steering wheel as I drive near the sea front. I follow the map out of town and across rolling country, until I get to an area of white houses with swimming pools, on the slopes of a hill near a village called Pedreguer. The Teales' house is set apart from the others, with an eight foot wall round it and a solid wooden gate. I drive on up the winding road and stop on a bend, where I can look down on the house. It's a fair size, probably two or three bedrooms, with a terrace and a kidney-shaped swimming pool, with a small building beside it. There's no sign of anyone about and no cars. I reckon there's nothing I can do until dark, so I drive back to Denia and onto the coast road to Oliva and that golden beach.

There are a few cars parked outside the hotel when I get there and I'm wondering if more guests have arrived. I park the car and head for the beach to find Lizzie. There are plenty of people in the sea and lying on loungers, but I can't see her among them. I walk a good way along the beach, in case she's found a better spot, but there's still no sign of her. I walk back beside the lapping waves, trying not to panic, but she's not in the water. I take one more good look round the beach then run towards the hotel.

When I get to the road, the door of a parked car opens in front of me and Jack Teale gets out, holding a gun by his side. I throw myself at him, knock him on his back, rip the gun out of his hand and swipe the butt across his jaw.

'Where the fuck is she?'

As I pull back to hit him again, a hand's clamped across my mouth, the gun's whipped away, an arm goes round my waist and I'm picked up and thrown head first into the back of the car. As I struggle to turn round, Danny Teale gets in, settles his great bulk on my legs, pulls my gun and blade out of my belt and throws them on the front seat. He slams the door shut and holds a gun inches from my face.

'You all right J?' he calls.

There's a mumbling from outside the car and then Jack appears and gets into the driver's seat.

'Fucking bitch,' he says, with a hand on his jaw.

'Go, for Christ's sake!' says Danny.

Jack starts the car, puts his foot down and slews it round the corner and onto the main road. When we're up to speed and cruising towards Denia, Danny lifts his weight off my legs and I'm able to sit up. He keeps the gun on me and I see that a couple of his fingers are still taped up near the knuckles.

'Where is she?' I say.

'You'll see,' says Danny, showing a shiny new set of pearlers as he speaks.

As we drive on, I keep watching him, waiting for a chance to get the gun off him if he looks away, but he's got it two-handed and never takes his eyes off me.

We get to the house outside Pedreguer and Jack opens the gate, pulls the car in and opens my door. There's a moment when I could try something as I get out, with Jack beside me and Danny getting out of the other side of the car with the gun, but I have to know what they've done with Lizzie, so I don't make a move. They take me in the front door and through to the back of the house with the gun pressed into my back. Jack opens the door to the kitchen and Sammy Neal stands up. The slimy little weasel must have followed me, seen Lizzie and told the Teales where we were. I knew he'd done some work with them in the past and I'm kicking myself for not making the connection when I saw him in Denia. At the time, I remember thinking he was probably just another face who needed a bit of distance and was holed up in Spain.

'She still outside?' says Jack.

'I haven't moved her,' Sammy replies.

I hope my look tells him I'm ready to rip his head off as soon as I get the chance.

'Go on,' says Jack.

Sammy opens a door, goes out of the house and walks round the pool towards the building on the other side. I'm jabbed in the back with the gun and I follow him. He takes a key out of his pocket, but Jack tells him to wait and goes to a window. He has a look in, beckons to Danny to bring me over and I can see Lizzie sitting on a bed. She looks up, sees me and runs to the window looking so drawn and desperate that I want to put my fist through the glass, but I'm pulled away as soon as I've seen her, taken back into the house and sat down at the kitchen table. Danny sits opposite keeping the gun on me.

'Cup of coffee, Rina?' says Jack.

'Fuck off.'

'Now there's no need to be like that girl. We just need to discuss a bit of business, that's all.'

Jack sits down at the table. 'Two black coffees Sam.'

Sammy fills a kettle and opens a cupboard. Jack turns to me and puts an elbow on the table. 'Last time we met you knocked me out.'

'Shame I didn't finish the job.'

'Now there you go again with the disrespect. I could walk out of here now and blow your girlfriend's head off and you sit there giving me lip. What's the matter with you?'

'I had a bad upbringing.'

A smile flickers across his face and he looks across at Danny and then turns back to me. 'All right. Now listen.'

His eyes harden as he leans towards me. 'If you want to see that girl again you've got to do one thing.'

'What's that?'

'Kill George.'

I look at him, then at his brother, who could see me off just by tightening his finger on that trigger, and decide the jokes are over.

'Why me?' I ask.

'You're the best there is and you can get close.'

Sammy puts the coffee cups on the table. Jack picks one up. 'You go back, do the job, Lizzie's on the next plane home and so are we. Dan Garner's wiped the slate with you about Brindle, he takes over George's doings, and you're a top member of the biggest firm in the country.'

The only thing on my mind is how to get Lizzie away from these scumbags. I need to make them believe I'm going to do George, while I try and come up with a way of springing her. I turn away, as if I'm weighing it up, then I look at him and slowly nod my head. 'All right.'

'Good,' says Jack.

'One condition.'

'What?'

'She is not touched.'

'Three meals a day and use of the pool. There's even a TV in there.'

'Anyone goes near her and you know what I'll do.'

'Understood.'

He drains his coffee cup and puts it on the table. 'There's a flight at nine o'clock. If we get over to your hotel and pick up your passport, we should be in Valencia in time.'

We go to the car and I'm put in the front seat. Jack drives and Danny's in the back with the gun in his hand. When we get to the hotel they take me to the room and watch while I pack my things and pocket my passport and what's left of my pesetas. I gather up Lizzie's clothes and her passport, put them in her case and tell them to take it to her. As I'm leaving I notice *Rebecca* on the table between the beds so I pick it up and stuff it into Lizzie's case, to give her something to read. When we get downstairs, the old lady is behind the desk. She takes a look at Jack and Danny, standing each side of me like a couple of jailers, and seems mighty relieved when I ask for the bill.

Danny keeps the gun on me as we drive to Valencia, while Jack's silent at the wheel, with a grim look on his face. Maybe the consequences of what he's doing are hitting home, now that he thinks George is really going out. Marlene will have been the power behind this and with her in Holloway, her little boys are on their own and throwing their lot in with a man they don't know they can trust. Once Garner's used them he won't need them and he could well throw them away, but there's no going back for them now.

We get to the terminal, go to the BEA desk and Jack buys me a ticket for the nine o'clock flight to London. I check in, say goodbye to my suitcase, get a boarding pass and the man tells me to go to gate 12. Jack leads me to the glass wall of the terminal building and I get a view of a line of passengers boarding a plane.

'If we don't see you skipping up them steps in a bit,

your lady friend might not be so comfy tonight.'

'I'm doing it,' I say.

'And when you have, you call this number,' he says, handing me a piece of paper with a Spanish number on it. I fold it and put it in my pocket.

'Have a good flight,' says Jack.

I leave the two of them standing by the glass, go through passport control and on to the departure lounge. Ten minutes later the flight's called and I wait in line to show my boarding pass and then go along the tunnel, round a couple of corners and onto the tarmac. We're held for a moment while a baggage truck trundles past then we cross to the plane. As I go up the steps I look back and see the Teales watching me from the terminal building. The hostess welcomes me on board, looks at my pass and points vaguely down the cabin. I find I've got an aisle seat on the side of the plane facing the terminal. The other two seats are empty, so I lean over and look through the window, in time to see the Teales turn and make their way to the main doors of the terminal.

The plane fills up and people stow bags in the lockers and sit down. I stand up to let a woman and a little girl into the seats next to mine. The woman takes the window seat and I smile at the girl as she sits beside me. When everyone's on board the cabin door shuts with a bang, a steward starts making an announcement on the speakers and I start trembling and whimpering. The woman in the window seat looks at me and when I start blubbering, she puts her arm round the girl and pulls her close. I turn up the volume until I'm wailing and crying up a storm. Heads are turning and a stewardess is coming fast down the aisle. As she gets to me I stand up, shaking all over, 'I can't do this! I can't do it! It's going to crash!'

She takes me by the shoulders. 'Calm down please madam.'

'It's going to come down... It's going to...'

'Just come along with me now.'

She takes hold of my wrist and I keep raving as she turns, drags me to the front of the plane and pulls me into the galley. The steward has a quick look at me, knocks on the door to the flight deck and goes in. I keep the shaking and the waterworks going as the stewardess tries to hold me still and calm me, while her mate pours a glass of water. The door to the flight deck opens, the captain appears and I get on my knees in front of him and start wailing. 'Please, I can't do this, I must get off, you've got to let me off.' When I reach for the lapels of his jacket, the stewardesses pull me away from him and up on my feet and I hang my head and sob.

'This woman clearly can't fly. I'm calling the steps, ambulance and so forth. Keep her here until they come,' says the captain, turning and going back onto the flight deck.

I quieten down and the stewardess gives me some tissues, takes me to one of the crew seats beside the door, sits next to me and holds my hand. The other one brings me a glass of water and I sip it and give the odd snivel. The steward gets on the mic, apologises for the delay and explains that a passenger has unfortunately been taken ill and will be leaving the flight shortly to receive treatment. As he switches off the mic there's the sound of an engine outside, a phone beeps somewhere above my head, the steward answers it and speaks in Spanish. They tell me to get up and go back into the galley, while they swing open the door and lock the steps into place. A woman in a medical type of uniform comes up the steps, takes a look at me and exchanges a few words of Spanish with the steward. She takes my arm and I go down the steps with her, hoping I didn't upset the little girl who was sat next to me.

The ambulance car takes me to a room in the terminal. The nurse takes my blood pressure, looks into my eyes, taps my knees and elbows and speaks to the airport official standing by. He speaks English and he tells me that the nurse hasn't found anything wrong with me. I say that my dad was a fighter pilot who got shot down and killed in the war and that I've always been scared of flying. I thought I'd give it another try, but now I know that I really can't do it, I'll go home on the train. He says he understands and lets me go.

30

Before I leave the terminal, I go to the restaurant and sit at a table. When the waitress comes, I tell her I'm waiting for someone. As she walks away, I slip a table knife in my pocket and leave. When I get out of the terminal, I go round to the back of the building and make for a row of bins near the far corner. As I get near them I see a discarded table fan with a broken blade lying on the ground. I pick it up and use the knife to cut a length of single wire, about four inches long, out of the flex attached to it and put it in my pocket. I walk to the car park and check that there's no attendants about, then I head for a row of motorbikes in a bay at the far end and pick on a nice looking BMW 250. I check there's no one watching and sit astride it. I push back the cover of the ignition key socket, find the wires coming out of the back of it and follow them to the plastic connector under the fuel tank. I pull the connector open, stick each end of my bit of wire into the sockets and feel the bike switch on. I swing out the kick starter, bring my full weight down on it and the bike roars into life. I pull in the clutch, kick it into gear and head for the gate.

I find my way to the coast road and enjoy the warm wind whipping my hair back and caressing my body, while the moonlight glistens on the sea. The bike's got plenty of muscle but I keep it down to about sixty and a couple of hours later I'm entering Denia, and getting some looks from the lads out on the town. A boy on a moped comes alongside me, grinning and saying something I don't understand so I twist the throttle and leave him behind.

As I come out of Pedreguer, I'm wondering how I can find a tool of some kind. I get off the bike among the white houses at the bottom of the hill, where there are a few parked cars. I walk along past them, seeing if any boots or tailgates are open, in case there's a tyre iron I can lift, but they're all locked and it's not worth trying to force them as it could be noisy. I go further along the road until I see a house with no lights on, no car out front and a cover over the pool. It's got a big well stocked garden and a shed at the back of the house. I park the bike, shin up and over the wall and stay low behind it as I lope along to the shed. There's a dead latch lock on the door and a leaded window next to it. I break the pane nearest the lock, nip round the back of the shed and wait. When I don't hear anything, I come out, reach through the window, turn the lock handle and open the door. The first thing I see on the bench in front of me is a pair of secateurs. I put them in my back pocket and have a look at the rest of the tools. They're mostly too big to be any use, except for a small fork that's quite sharp on the points of the blades. I slide it in behind my belt, close the shed door as I leave and hop over the wall. I look up at the Teale's place above and reckon it's about half a mile away. I decide to leave the bike where it is and walk it.

The hill is quite steep and when I get to the house I wait a moment while my breathing slows down before I climb the wall and drop down into the garden. There are no lights on and the car is parked inside the gate. I creep slowly past the house and round the pool to the building where Lizzie was. The moon's on the wrong side for me to see anything through the window and there's not a sound, so she must be asleep if she's in there. I go to the door and have a look. There's a mortice lock that I could open in two minutes, if I had my picks, but all I've got is a pair of secateurs and a gardening fork. I take out the secateurs, open the blades, and gently push one of them between the door and the frame. The wood's quite soft and I'm thinking that I might just be able to prise the door open, when I hear a faint noise from inside.

I steal across to the window and stand back so that the moonlight catches my face. When Lizzie sees me, she clasps her hands and puts them to her lips. I kiss the glass, point towards the door and go back to it. I kneel down and push one blade of the secateurs in between the door and the frame. I lever it back and forth and gouge enough wood out until I can see the latch. I close the secateurs and push both blades in behind it. As I stand and put my weight against the handles, to force the door open, I hear a noise behind me. I turn and see two figures running round the one side of the pool and another coming the other way. I drop the secateurs, take the fork out of my belt and swing it at the head of the first one to reach me. He dodges sideways and as I launch a kick at him, I'm grabbed from behind and wrenched backwards. I get a blow to the head and black out.

• • •

I can hear a faint chattering sound and see a fuzzy blurred shape in front of me. I try to move but I can't. The shape slowly firms up until it's a light bulb and the chattering slows down, gets deeper and becomes a man's voice. I'm on the floor of the kitchen, my ankles are bound, my wrists are tied in front of me, there's a crushing pain in my head and Danny and Jack Teale are sitting at the table with a bottle between them.

'We'll never be able to go back if we waste them, you fucking idiot!' says Danny.

'So what d'you want to do, let them walk and wait to be knocked off? She's a fucking demon and I want to stay alive,' says Jack, picking up the bottle.

'I suppose you're right.'

'I wish Mum was here.'

'So do I.'

I look across and see Lizzie trussed up next to me. Her eyes are open and she turns her head and looks at me. Jack sees her moving. 'Hey brother, the ladies are with us.'

I roll onto my back and Jack gets up, picks up a gun off the table, stands at my feet looking down at me and pointing the gun. 'Couldn't stay away could you?'

'Just let her go and you can have me,' I say.

'Oh, that's it, yeah, so she can tell everyone we did it.'

When he looks round at his brother, I lift my legs and kick at his knees with everything I've got. He goes over, catches his head on the side of the table and grunts as he hits the floor. The gun lands beside me and I roll over and grab it. Danny gets up from the table as I'm trying to get a grip of the gun with my hands tied and he's on me and ripping it away before I can fire a shot. He stands over me pointing the gun at my head, takes a few deep breaths, shifts his weight from one foot to the other, then he pulls back the hammer and looks me in the eye.

'Go on then, for fuck's sake!' says Jack, from the floor.

I see Danny's finger tighten round the trigger, and I close my eyes and hope he does it clean. There's a bang, but I'm still here. I open my eyes and see a hole in the wall above me.

'You missed, you stupid fucking cunt!' says Jack, getting up on one elbow.

Danny turns away. 'I can't do it,' he says quietly.

'Oh for Christ's sake,' mumbles Jack, moaning with pain as he tries to hoist himself up off the floor.

'Not to a woman,' says Danny, putting the gun on the table.

'I've done my fucking back,' says Jack, crawling to a chair and levering himself onto it, gasping with pain. He grabs the bottle and takes a mighty swig. Danny takes it from him and does the same. Jack leans forward. 'You're a fucking wally, you know that? Can't off a bit of skirt?'

'Let's see you do it then.'

'I would if I could stand up.'

'Oh yeah?'

'Get the boy.'

'You think he can?'

'Just get him!'

Danny looks at Jack, picks up the gun from the table and goes to the door.

'Tell him to bring my piece,' says Jack.

Danny opens the door, shouts for Sammy and relays his brother's order.

I hear footsteps on the stairs and Sammy comes in, looking scared and sheepish, and offers the gun to Jack, who shakes his head. 'You're going to use it to plug these two.'

'No fucking way,' says Sammy, stepping back.

Danny moves behind him and presses the muzzle of his gun into the back of his head. 'If you don't boy, I will blow your fucking brains out!'

Sammy's rigid with fear as he's pushed slowly forward and round the table to stand in front of Lizzie and me. I try to engage his eyes as they flick between us but he won't connect.

'Do it boy, unless you want to die, right now,' says Danny, pressing the barrel into him and pulling back the hammer.

Sammy's sweating and breathing heavily as he slowly raises the gun. He brings his left hand up to steady his right and his finger closes round the trigger.

'Wait a minute Sammy,' I say.

He looks me in the eye, and for a moment I can see the boy I used to know, as he lowers the gun. Danny moves to the side of him and puts the gun barrel against his temple. 'Fucking do it!'

Sammy turns on him like lightening, slaps the gun

away, kicks him hard in the bollocks and Danny cries out and grabs his crotch as Sammy makes a dash for the back door. As he's unlocking it, Danny dives at him, turns him round, punches him on the jaw and Sammy hits the deck.

'Fucking finish it!' shouts Jack, from the table.

Danny picks up both guns, puts a chair in front of me, lifts Sammy onto it and slaps him back and forth across the face until he wakes.

'Let's try that again shall we? Unless you want to go out first,' he snarls, putting a gun in Sammy's hand and jabbing the barrel of the other one into his back.

The door crashes open behind me. Danny gets a bullet in the head, then two in the chest and hits the floor. Sammy drops the gun and bolts out of the back door as someone strides past me and shoots Jack twice as he struggles to stand up. When he slumps forward onto the table, the shooter turns, lowers the gun and Dawn is looking at me and smiling.

She takes a butcher's knife off the draining board, slices through my bonds and then frees Lizzie.

'Come on, quickly,' she says, going across the hall and out onto the patio.

I take a look at the dead brothers, check there's no pulse, then I take Lizzie's hand and we run after Dawn.

She's put a chair up against the garden wall and she's sitting astride the top of it. Lizzie steps onto the chair, Dawn hauls her up and over and then does the same for me. She drops down beside us, runs to a car a short way up the hill and gets into the driver's seat. I sit beside her and

Lizzie goes in the back. She slips the handbrake and the car rolls silently down the slope. There are lights coming on in the first house we pass and I look back and see a door opening. When we get towards the bottom of the hill, Dawn starts the engine and drives fast towards the main road to Denia.

'What the fuck's going on?' I ask.

'Let's just say I've been following your career,' says Dawn.

'You've what?'

'When Johnny Brindle was killed, I knew you must have done it so I did a bit of asking around while you were in Holloway. Right Liz?'

I look at Lizzie and I'm surprised when she nods.

'You knew about this?' I ask.

'She owes you her life and she wanted to watch your back, that's all.'

'And you told her I was going after them?'

'Kind of.'

'Well I'll be…'

'If it had gone off without any trouble you'd never have known I was here,' says Dawn.

'Where did you learn to shoot like that?' I ask.

'One of my brothers is a bit handy.'

I can't quite take in what I'm hearing. These two have got together to try and protect me and Dawn's risked her life to save me from getting shot.

'Well… thanks,' I say.

Dawn puts her hand on mine and I'm reminded of

doing the same thing with her, when I was driving her away from Brindle's aunt's house in Birmingham.

'When I saw the way you straightened the Teales and got me away from them, I wondered if I could be as strong as that,' she says.

'I think you've proved your point,' says Lizzie.

'And they killed my baby,' says Dawn.

We get to the outskirts of Denia and onto the coast road.

'Where are we going?' I ask.

'Barcelona airport,' says Dawn.

'Not Valencia?'

'I thought they might give you an Oscar if they saw you again.'

I laugh out loud. 'You knew about that?'

'Oh yeah.'

'What?' asks Lizzie.

'I had to do a bit of acting to get thrown off the plane earlier.'

'I was wondering how you got back.'

'You have got your passport?' asks Dawn.

'Yes,' I reply, checking it's still in my back pocket.

'I haven't got mine,' says Lizzie.

'It's in your suitcase, in the boot,' says Dawn, reaching under her seat and pulling out a bottle of whisky.

'To the woman who thinks of everything,' I say, unscrewing the cap.

31

We get to Barcelona airport at sunrise and buy tickets to
London. The next flight leaves at midday. The check-in
desk isn't open yet, so we have breakfast and sit in the
lounge. Dawn and Lizzie are soon asleep and I look at
them both opposite me and thank my lucky stars they're
still alive. When I think what Dawn's done for me and how
Lizzie helped her, I feel so moved and grateful that tears
start welling up and I have to get hold of myself. I take
a few deep breaths, go and get myself a coffee from the
café and sit opposite my two sleeping beauties. I suddenly
remember that I put *Rebecca* in Lizzie's suitcase, so I get it
out and find my place.

After the humiliation of the fancy dress ball, our girl
is having a row with Mrs Danvers, and the old cow is
telling her how perfect Rebecca was, what a waste of space
she is, and that Maxim will never love her. She takes her
to a window ledge and tells her she might as well jump
and our girl is so desperate that she almost does. Then
Rebecca's body is found in the sea and Maxim reveals that
it wasn't suicide at all, that he killed her because she was a
selfish bitch and when she wasn't being the perfect hostess
at Manderley she was in London, mixing with a dodgy
crowd and shagging everything that moved, including
Jack Favell. Maxim finally had it out with Rebecca in the
boathouse and when she told him she was pregnant with

Favell's baby, he shot her.

I'm just turning the page to find out what happened next, when the flight's called. I wake Dawn and Lizzie and we check in, go through passport control and along the walkway to the departure lounge, where we get chatted up by a couple of tweedy types who've been on a golfing holiday. When Lizzie tells them that she plays off scratch they look a bit miffed and move away. I ask her what she meant and she says she's no idea but a punter she used to have said it a lot.

We get on the plane, and almost as soon as we're in the air, the girls are asleep again. I'm back to my book and reading how the magistrate gives a verdict of suicide for Rebecca's death and Maxim's relieved he's got away with it, until Jack Favell says he knows Maxim killed her and tries to blackmail him. Favell tells the magistrate that he and Rebecca were lovers, that she was having his baby and that Maxim found out and topped her in a jealous rage. It's looking like Maxim's for it, which is a shame because him and our girl are now really close and in love again. Then Mrs Danvers finds Rebecca's diary and they see that she went to a doctor in London on the day she died. They all go and see the doctor, including the magistrate, and Maxim is convinced the doctor will confirm she was pregnant and he will be found guilty, but when they get there the doctor tells them that Rebecca was about to die of cancer and couldn't have children anyway.

Favell's shamed, Maxim's exonerated and he and our girl drive happily back to Manderley to start a new life together, only to find that the great house is on fire and burning to the ground.

I'm a bit shocked by the ending, but then I suppose Maxim's worth a few bob and they can just go back to Monte Carlo or somewhere and have a good time, so I suppose it's a happy ending.

I close the book just as the seatbelt sign comes on and people start stubbing out their fags and clicking their belts shut. I take Lizzie's hand and give it a squeeze to wake her. She sighs, turns towards me, snuggles up and gives me a long kiss. I'm loving it and hoping it'll go on forever, but then she opens her eyes, remembers where we are and sits back in her seat. One of the golfers is watching us from across the aisle. Lizzie gives him a wave and he turns away, looking a bit queasy.

The plane lands and we go through passport control, pick up Lizzie's case off the carousel, go through customs and come out into the main hall. Dawn and I change our pesetas for pounds, shillings and pence and we make for the exit. When we get to the cab rank I ask Dawn where she's going. She hesitates as if she's not sure and I ask her if she wants to come and stay with me. She thinks for a minute, then she thanks me and says she wants to go to her own place in Highgate. The three of us share a cab to Maida Vale and when we get there, Dawn and I swap phone numbers, have a tearful farewell and Lizzie and I wave her off from the pavement.

'What a girl, eh?' says Lizzie.

'I'll say. I still can't believe it.'

We go in through the glass door, say hello to Keith and take the lift. We stop at Lizzie's door, arrange to go out later to a club to shake some of the Spanish dust off.

She says she'll pick me up about eight and I go into mine. There's no mail on the mat so I pick up the phone and dial Bert's number. I'm just about to hang up when he answers.

'It's done,' I say.

'Both?'

'Yeah.'

'That's quick.'

'I want paying.'

'I'll call you back.'

I put the phone down, go into Georgie's room and put *Rebecca* back on the bookshelf. I look at all the books she's got and I think about her coming home to this flat in a week and how difficult it's been to keep her away from all the slippery stuff that I'm involved in. I'm glad that she's growing away from her background and getting well educated and mixing with a different type of person, but at the same time she's the only family I've got and I don't want to lose her. As soon as I've got my dad's money, I'm going to find a place well away from it all, that she can call home and where we can get settled.

The phone rings and I go into the hall. It's Bert Davis.

'Outside yours in half an hour and bring your passport.'

'Why?'

'Just bring it.'

The line goes dead. I have a quick bath and wash my

hair, put on a black Dior trouser suit and some make-up. Not that I need to impress Bert Davis, but I just feel like getting smart again. The phone rings and it's Keith telling me the car's there. I go down, get in the car and we drive down Edgware Road.

'Aren't we going to George's?' I ask.

'No.'

'Where then?'

'To the money.'

'OK.'

He drives along Marylebone Road, turns right at Kings Cross into Grays Inn Road and stops outside Lloyds Bank. I follow him inside and he tells me to wait by the door while he talks to a man in a pinstripe suit, sitting behind a desk. Bert calls me over and while he fills in a form, the man asks me for identification. I show him my passport and he writes the details down and clips them to the form that Bert's now completed, puts them in a drawer and gives Bert a key. He gets up from the desk and we follow him across the banking hall, down some stairs and through an armoured door, into a room with safety deposit boxes lining the walls. He tells us to press the button when we've finished and closes the door behind him. Bert takes out a key, opens a box on the second tier, pulls out a canvas holdall and unzips it. 'Two hundred large, less the two we bunged your witness and what you've had in expenses.'

'Fair enough.'

He lifts the bag out and gives it to me. I open it up, have a look at more money than I've ever seen in my life

and say a silent thank you to my dad. Bert locks the box
and presses the bell. I zip up the bag and the man in the
pinstripe opens the door and escorts us up the stairs. When
we get to the door, I tell Bert I don't want a lift home and
he leaves. I go to the desk where the man in the pinstripe
sits and tell him I want to open a safety deposit box. He
looks at the bag by my feet, asks for my passport again and
brings out the paperwork. Once it's done, he gives me a
code that I have to quote when I want the key and takes
me back down to the strong room. I open the bag, take out
a bundle of fivers, put them in my pocket, then I stow the
bag in my box and lock the door.

I pick up a cab on Grays Inn Road and get him to
drop me at Savills estate agents, by Marble Arch. I go in
and have a look at some of the big houses in the country
section, pick out a few likely ones quite near London and
get the brochures from one of the assistants. I put them
under my arm and get another cab home.

I take the brochures into the lounge, pour myself a
whisky and sit on the sofa. I'm leafing through them when
there's a knock on the door. I go and open it to Lizzie. She
asks me if I want to go and have a meal before the club. I
say I do and ask her to come and have a drink first. We go
into the lounge and I pour her a whisky.

'What are these?' she asks, looking at the brochures.

I tell her about my fears of losing Georgie and how I
want to be able to offer her a good home and a better life.
She looks at a couple of brochures and drops them back
on the coffee table.

'And what are you going to do with yourself in a nice Cotswold village?'

'I'll be with Georgie.'

'No you won't.'

'What do you mean?'

'She's growing up and making a life for herself. She'll be away at university and going on trips in the holidays, and when she's got her degree she'll be working in London, or somewhere else, maybe abroad, and you'll hardly ever see her.'

'Of course I will.'

'Now and again maybe. What are you going to do in the meantime? Join the Women's Institute? Invite the county set round for drinks? Join the local hunt?'

'I could do the garden.'

'Don't make me laugh. You can't keep a pot plant alive for five minutes.'

What she's saying is making sense. Georgie will live her own life, as she should do. She won't need me like she has until now and I can see that I've got to accept that.

'You've kept Georgie safe and given her the chances to make something of herself and she's taken them. You need to stand back and let her go her own way now.'

I make a pile of the brochures and put them on the floor.

'You're a London girl born and bred and you'd go mad living out there,' she says.

'You're right.'

'And I'm fucked if I'm schlepping out to Hertfordshire

every time I want a cuddle.'

I laugh and dump the brochures in the waste paper basket.

'So let's go out and have a good time!' she says, as she jumps up, downs her drink, takes my hand and whisks me out of the door.

Lizzie takes me to a new club called Annabel's that opened a few days ago, underneath the Clermont Club in Berkeley Square. By the time we've eaten a delicious meal, had a few brandies and danced ourselves dizzy, among a great crowd of London's finest, I'm more than convinced that I don't want to live in the country.

• • •

I'm walking past the Kings Road Cinema a few months later, on my way to Bazaar for some new threads, when I notice a familiar face on a poster. I take a closer look and see that it's Kim Daley. The film's called "The Hard Way". Kim's standing in a dark London street, turning to look back at the camera, and I realise that it's the one that I was in with her. I look at the showing times and see that the matinee starts in ten minutes, so I buy a ticket and go in. After the newsreel and the Pearl and Dean adverts, the film starts and it all comes back to me as the story unfolds. Kim's really great in it and by the end I'm really rooting for her and egging her on to toast Challoner. The actor playing him is a really evil bastard and I can sense the relief among the audience when she kills him and feeds him to the pigs.

On the way out, I look at the reviews on the wall in the foyer and read that the film's a big success. It's been nominated for some awards, including one for Kim and I'm really pleased for her.

The girl doing my part looked a lot like me, but I didn't think much of her acting.

The End

Hugh Fraser is best known for playing Captain Hastings in Agatha Christie's '*Poirot*' and the Duke of Wellington in '*Sharpe*'. His films include *Patriot Games*, *101 Dalmatians*, *The Draughtsman's Contract* and Clint Eastwood's *Firefox*. In the theatre he has appeared in *Teeth'n'Smiles* at the Royal Court and Wyndhams and in several roles with the Royal Shakespeare Company.

He has also narrated many of Agatha Christie's novels as audio books.

You can follow Hugh on Twitter @realhughfraser

HARM

Book 1 in the Rina Walker series

ISBN: 978-1-910692-73-8 • £8.99

Acapulco 1974: Rina Walker is on assignment.
Just another quick, clean kill. She wakes to discover her
employer's severed head on her bedside table, and a man
with an AK-47 coming through the door of her hotel room.
She needs all her skills to neutralise her attacker and
escape. After a car chase, she is captured by a Mexican
drug boss who exploits her radiant beauty and ruthless
expertise to eliminate an inconvenient member of the
government. Notting Hill 1956: Fifteen-year-old Rina
is scavenging and stealing to support her siblings and
her alcoholic mother. When a local gangster attacks her
younger sister, Rina wreaks violent revenge and murders
him. Innocence betrayed, Rina faces the brutality of the
post-war London underworld - a world that teaches her
the skills she needs to kill...

THREAT
Book 2 in the Rina Walker series

ISBN: 978-1-911129-75-2 • £8.99

London 1961. In the dying days of the Macmillan
government, George Preston is in control of crime in
West London and Rina Walker is his favoured contract
killer. When Rina is hired by Soho vice king Tony Farina to
investigate the disappearance of girls from his clubs she
discovers that they are being supplied to a member of the
English aristocracy for the gratification of his macabre
sexual tastes. Rina's pursuit of the missing girls and
her efforts to save the innocent from slaughter become
increasingly perilous as she grapples with interwoven
layers of corruption and betrayal and makes her way,
via the louche nightclubs of Berlin, towards a final
confrontation with depravity.